The Newgate Jig

A Victorial Crime

Ann Featherstone

W F HOWES LTD

This large print edition published in 2011 by
W F Howes Ltd
Unit 4, Rearsby Business Park, Gaddesby Lane,
Rearsby, Leicester LE7 4YH

1 3 5 7 9 10 8 6 4 2

First published in the United Kingdom in 2010
by John Murray (Publishers)

A CIP catalogue record for this book is available
from the British Library

ISBN 978 1 40746 888 4

Typeset by Palimpsest Book Production Limited,
Falkirk, Stirlingshire
Printed and bound in Great Britain
by MPG Books Ltd, Bodmin, Cornwall

For Holly,
the best of friends

PROLOGUE: GOING TO SEE
A MAN HANGED

There is nothing more dreadful, surely, than seeing one's own father hung.

All the horrors of this world, the wars and famines, plagues and pestilences, cannot compare with the sight of one's father upon the scaffold and the rope around his neck. It arouses the most extraordinary sensations – of awe, at the enormity of the event, and despair at one's utter helplessness in the face of it. One might be forgiven, at the very moment the hangman pulls the bolt, for going quite mad, tearing at one's hair and crying through the streets. Oh, yes indeed, quite mad.

Thus muses aloud, to no one in particular, an elegant gentleman, glass in hand (though the hour is still early), comfortably established in the upstairs open window of a tavern. There is much to see, such variety of humanity in the gathering crowd below: the blind beggar and his attempts to escape the thieving attentions of a bully, the brightly gowned young woman and her companion debating whether to purchase a 'Last

Confession' from a street-seller, and a thin, pale-faced boy, perhaps nine or ten years old, whose clothes were once good ones (a serviceable jacket and trousers, a shirt and neckerchief), but which are now worn and shabby, in animated conversation with an older man. Leaning out of the window, the elegant gentleman can catch it all if he so desires, for the boy's voice rises and falls like birdsong above the din.

'You should come away now, Barney, before it begins. This is no place for you,' the man is saying with warmth, taking the boy's arm and turning him about. 'Look. That crowd which is coming and going and looking as though it has daily business in any shop or counting house, is here for only one reason. That crowd intends to be amused, and you should not be part of it.'

'I'm not amused,' says Barney defensively, shaking himself free. *'I've* not come to laugh.'

'But you'll be standing cheek and shoulder with those who have,' returns the other, 'with the followers of the Drop, and those who take pleasure in the misery of their fellows.'

At this, the boy winces and works his mouth around as if he is about to retaliate, and rubs his red eyes vigorously with his two fists until the tears, which are threatening to spring forth in a flood, retreat.

'I know all about them,' he says, finally, 'and Pa did too.'

'Yes, and that is why he is here, and why you

would do well *not* to be! Your father was foolish. He should have known better.'

'Someone told lies about him!' cries Barney. 'Pa said it was all lies.'

'Aye, maybe it was, but it has still marched him to the gallows!'

Once again, the boy is moved to reply, and again rubs his eyes until dirt and tears are smeared across his cheeks.

'Pa has a friend who will not betray him. A clever fellow.' He swallows hard. 'Pa said he wrote a letter and gave it to him and he would send it to the Queen and the Lord Mayor of London.'

Like he is repeating a prayer so often uttered that the words have become only sounds, his voice trails away.

'He has it,' says the other, quietly. 'He has the letter. But go now, while you can.'

Barney shakes his head, turns about and joins the army of humanity as it tramps on, whilst the older man debates whether to follow him, watches him out of sight and then, hunching his shoulders against the cold, posts himself through the next tavern door.

Although the hour is still early, the crowd is growing by the minute around the platform, which crouches dark and square and ready against the grey stone of Newgate. All is grey. Especially the sky which, like a sodden rag, wrings out of itself a dirty mist, soaking the crowds which flood towards the prison walls. Wrapped tight against the early morning cold, they are still cheerful, calling to each other across the foggy streets and pressing into the square. Since before the murky dawn, the taverns and hotels, butchers' shops and coffee houses have already had their full quota of paying spectators: every window and doorway that offers a view of the square is occupied. Now, anxious not to miss a moment's pleasure, they have climbed trees and posts and walls. A slight young man, with a shock of orange hair like a human pipe-cleaner, has shinned up a drainpipe onto the roof of a private house and, despite the best efforts of the owner to get him down, is perched with his back against the chimney-stack, perished with cold but determined not to miss a trick.

Barney sees all of this. And nothing. Allowing himself to be swept along by the crowd, he plunges into the mass of bodies, determined to get close to the front. Square shoulders rise up in front of him like a bastion, however, and though he wriggles and squirms through a forest of legs, and endures hard cuffs and elbows and kicks, he has eventually to be content with being wedged between a tall man in city-black (perhaps an undertaker's assistant) and a chimney-sweep, also in dusky attire, just on his way to work. Thankfully, neither is inclined to conversation and both are so studiously determined to keep their places that, in so doing, they allow Barney to keep his. And they are in stark contrast to the wild carnival crowd pressing around him, hallooing and cheering and so merry that the pie man and the gingerbread-seller hardly need to call out their 'Here's all 'ot!' or 'Nuts and dolls, my maids!'

But this is no country fair, and even Toby Rackstraw, up from the country to try the humours of the city, could not mistake the roars of *this* crowd for good-natured festivity. No, this is something quite other. Here is a congregation gathered to worship not some whey-faced saint, but the noose and the gallows, and as the human tide fills the square and laps the streets around, there rises from it a murmur of voices like a catechism, telling the moments as the hour hands of neighbouring church clocks move on.

There is activity around the scaffold. Policemen push back the crowd and patrol the perimeter, keeping their eyes peeled for pickpockets and ignoring the taunts of the boys who, five deep, form the first line of spectators. The rumble of carriages (for the gates of the prison are close by) signal the arrival of officials, and the crowd lurches forward to catch a glimpse. A ripple of information – 'It's the sheriff!' 'It's the judge!' 'Not the clergyman, for he will have been attending him for the past hour!' – is passed from one to another.

Past seven o'clock now, the bells ringing out the moments and cheering the spirits of the crowd which, despite the heavy rain, is still in a holiday mood and surges to and fro, ripples of laughter rising and falling. The boy is sensible of the mighty

5

crush behind him and glances anxiously over his shoulder, but his stalwart companions (who have been silent for almost two hours, the chimney-sweep chewing slowly upon a piece of bacon fat and only once taking a long draught from a stone bottle in his bag) stand firm.

At last, the clock strikes eight, and the boy's unblinking gaze is trained upon the door.

Such a little door.

When it opens, such a change comes over the holiday crowd! Jocularity trembles, good humour shrinks, and there rises an ugly murmur of satisfaction as the platform fills, until the last, much-anticipated figure appears, when a terrible silence falls. He is small and slight and, staggering slightly, is supported by one of his attendants to whom he turns and thanks, only realizing at the last moment that the gentleman who steadies him so gently, and looks for all the world like a linen-draper, will shortly assist him into the next world. With a hand under his elbow, the linen-draper directs him to the great chain dripping black from the beam and, from that singular position, the loneliest place in all the world, the man turns to face the crowd. He does not see any single faces, but his gaze ranges across the expectant mass all turned and fixed upon him. With a gasp, the boy raises himself up on his toes and sets his face, like a beacon, towards the figure, as if trying to arrest his look. But the man is stubborn and will not see him, and the boy mutters something beneath his breath, at which the undertaker's assistant glances sharply and seems inclined to speak.

'I will serve him out!' Barney whispers, and then with increasing noise and urgency, as the tears spring to his eyes, 'I will serve him out! I will serve him out! I will serve him out!'

The linen-draper is poised with the hood, the clergyman is done for the day. Even the rain has stopped. Suddenly the man on the scaffold hears the boy's cry rising above the humming silence, turns his head madly back and forth, searching the crowd, and even trying to stumble forward, though the linen-draper prevents him. The boy continues to call, and the chimney-sweep and the undertaker's assistant, though a little discomfited, say nothing. But someone must. The congregation is hungry for the spectacle, and from deep within the throng a voice roars, 'Get on with it!', and another, 'Murderer!', and finally, 'Stretch his neck!' In an instant, that general appeal is taken up, whilst on the scaffold the man unpicks the crowd, frowning in his effort to find one face in ten thousand until, like a moment of revelation, it is there. The man's ashen face tightens and the boy, desperate with misery, still cries, 'I will serve him out! I will serve him out!'

Sturdy leather straps have been produced, the linen-draper securing the man as quickly as a knot in a reel of cotton.

The man struggles.

'No, Barney, no! Let it be,' he cries, his face

broken by grief and fear, and if anyone cared to listen, they would have heard him cry, 'My son! Barney! My son!'

But this crowd does not hear. And besides, this crowd needs to have its parties attired in black or white, needs to be partisan, so that, finding it does not know who, or even what, to support, it begins instead to bay, at which the linen-draper, with one swift action, pulls the hood over the man's head and in two steps reaches the post and draws the bolts. The crowd roars with one voice, but the boy, as if he is trying to ensure that *his* voice is the last sound the man hears, soars above theirs, over and over.

'Pa! Pa! Pa!'

Really, it is remarkable how quickly the streets empty and everything returns to normal almost immediately the rope ceases twitching. Crowds simply melt away down the dripping streets. With a clatter of slates, the slight young man releases his grip upon the chimney pot, slithers down the roof and the drainpipe, winds his muffler about his neck with all the nonchalance of a circus acrobat, and joins the departing throng. Now windows are closed, doors fastened against the wicked weather, and the line of carriages (for the wealthy love nothing better than 'a good hanging') disappears into the mist, which has dropped again like transformation scenery. And alone on that stage is the boy. His companions, having

8

enquired after his well-being (for they are decent enough men and will tell their wives how they stood next to the boy ''oose father was 'ung this morning' and how he cried out) and pressed a sixpence each into his cold hands, have gone to their work. He is rooted to the stones, oblivious to the biting wind which tugs at his short coat and paints his nose and hands the same scarlet colour as his eyes. His tears have dried into pale veins upon his cheeks, his lips are dry and chapped. But still he stands.

The scaffold, growing blacker with the pouring rain, still bears evidence of its unseen guest, for the chain moves slowly back and forth, shuddering imperceptibly with the weight of the man suspended just out of sight. There is no activity about the square now, just a handful of constables still patrolling the perimeter, ensuring that the incumbent hangs undisturbed for his statutory hour, and keeping an eye upon the boy whose solitary vigil they have all remarked upon and, being kindly men, have debated amongst themselves whether to summon Mr Corns from the miserable recesses of the Homeless Institute and beg him to remove the boy before he freezes to death.

Moments divide moments. The boy is as conscious of the space of time between the spits of rain as he is of eternity, and unconcerned with both. He shifts a foot, slowly and stiffly, for the first time in an hour and as he moves, so does another, quite

9

the opposite in size and bearing. From the shelter of a doorway at the other side of the square emerges a veritable grampus of a man, cheeks as pink as a pair of pippins, and wearing a smile, despite the bitterness of the wind and rain. Pulling his long, pale Benjamin about him and turning up its collar, he tacks, like a boat in a choppy sea, across the cobbles towards the boy, weaving right and left until, at last, he comes alongside the lad and grasps his shoulder in a pudgy hand.

Barney turns, looks, but there is not a flicker of recognition in his face. Conversely, the fat man is all knowledge, all familiarity.

'So sorry – ah – your loss.' His voice is surprisingly high, like a child's, and when he smiles, he reveals teeth which are so small, so insignificant, as to hardly have broken through the gums. A smear of whiteness only.

It is a surprising face, but Barney barely registers it. Only when the man, still firmly grasping his shoulder, puts his mouth to the boy's ear and whispers for some moments does he respond, and then it is as if he has received an electric shock, for he jumps out of the man's grip and backs away. Producing a shilling, pinched between his fat fingers, the grampus advances upon the boy and, in a sudden lurch, makes to grab his arm. But the boy is quicker, and staggers out of his reach, putting two yards between himself and the grampus before he stops and then, with a little cry, turns and runs.

CHAPTER 1

BOB CHAPMAN AND
HIS SAGACIOUS CANINES

If you passed me in the street, I would lay ten to one you wouldn't know me, though I might have appeared before you hundreds of times. My face would be, like that of the Queen's footman, one often seen but barely remarked upon. You might, if you had more leisure to give my features a regular eyeballing, say, 'Hello, here's a face I have seen before!' or 'There's a fellow I seem to know!' and never come to a firm conclusion.

But spy me in the very same street with my two dogs at my heels, and you would sing a different tune. And with a full chorus. You would certainly recognize us then, and feel emboldened to greet us with, 'Hello, here are Brutus and Nero, and their man, Bob Chapman,' and believe yourself to be on terms of such familiarity with my companions as to scratch them behind the ear and demand they roll on their backs or oblige you with a paw. You might even notice me and want to shake *my* paw! But if you thought I ever felt put out or resentful of my four-legged companions when all and sundry stop to greet them and ignore me, you

11

would be quite on the distaff side, for they are the finest pair of chums a man could wish for, and if I live to be a hundred, I will never discover their like again. Of course, they are hard-working fellows and earn their keep thrice over every week, and they are as dear to me as if they were my own children. Brutus, you should know, stands as high as my knee, an English Retriever, golden in colour, with the mildest eyes and the most gentle and amiable disposition. I am certain he would rather sleep than breathe! But put him to his work, on the stage or in the circus ring, and he will stay at it until the deserts flood. His speciality is to pick up an egg in his mouth – it is a trick people like to see – and place it, without a crack or break, in a basket of others. Kittens and day-old chicks he carries as if he were their mother, and little children may ride upon his back.

But Nero now, he is as black as a Moor's head, a Newfoundland breed (but not pure-bred), and as valuable for his looks as he is for his tricks. I have been offered fifty pounds for him more than once, but will I part with him? Not I. And if you have seen him at his work, opening gate latches and ringing bells and carrying lanterns onto the stage, you will know why. Not only is he handsome, but clever also. The quickest dog for learning tricks I have ever known. Give him but a little encouragement, a morsel of liver no bigger than your thumbnail, and he will have a new trick in his head inside a week. And so proud is he of his cleverness, that he will make sure never to forget it! Nero is a good companion too, steady and sure, and careful of Brutus, who he minds as if he was a brother.

Yes, I am indeed a fortunate man to have two such noble and affectionate creatures as my companions, and I think this every morning as we walk from our lodgings to Garraway's establishment, where we eat our breakfast. For you should know that I am not an adventurous man. I like a life that is calm and well ordered. Excitement is a trouble to me. I do not relish change, and like to see the same faces about me and walk the same streets and look into the same shop windows and see the same goods for sale. Some might think me dull, but I have my own reasons for preferring a simple, regular life and, though I work in the exhibition business (which might appear to go against this preference, being all the time before the public), it is still my nature to be quiet and ordered. Nevertheless, quietness will not put food upon the table. Nor will a wet nose and shining coat secure a bed, and although we have been together, Brutus, Nero and I, for these last five years, we have not always been as comfortable as we are now and have had some troubles which caused me distress. Indeed, even now, when rent day rounds the corner, I am driven to consult my pocket-book and savings and do some arithmetic, and make out those sums over and over again. Only the other day, Mr Abrahams commented upon my studiousness, with a blowing of his cheeks and a thorough tidying of his nose. I am much obliged to him and not a little in awe, for he is an astute gentleman and my employer, the owner of the East London Aquarium and Museum, with many years of exhibiting to his credit. So when he gave me a second look and said, 'Now then, Bob!' I immediately felt anxiety rising in my breast.

'I know what you are about to ask me, as if I could read your mind,' said he. 'And, if I could, I would give you the answer you want to hear.' Then he shook his head and looked mournful. 'But you know the exhibition business as I do. Fair weather one week, foul the next. If the needle points to wet and windy on a Saturday, I can do no more than let you go, otherwise I would be a fool to myself and unworthy of my customers' high esteem.'

I am pleased to say that, up to now, that needle has been steady on 'Fair', but such is the strange temperament of patrons of the exhibition business, that I can appreciate his caution. For what will attract and amuse them one week, and have every human being within ten miles clamouring at the Aquarium door, might the next be sneered at as a regular non-goer. I have seen it happen countless times. Why, only last year, Madame Leonie, the lion-faced lady, could do no wrong for six weeks, and felt confident enough to be looking out for better rooms and hiring a dressmaker when,

14

one morning, I found her packing up her bags and wiping a tear from her hairy cheek. Without warning, her show was empty, the public were suddenly against her, and there was ugly talk abroad of smashing up her stand and slashing her paintings. I am glad to report that, when last heard of, she was doing well in a Cardiff waxwork show, but at the time it was upsetting, and even Mr Abrahams, with all his wisdom, could not explain it. 'Ah, you see, Bob,' he said, as sad as a mourner, 'how fickle is our business! Here we are, comfortable one day and the next – pphff!! We are all at the mercy of the people.'

I didn't like to contemplate this gloomy prospect, though, for we were very happy at the Aquarium, and I had started to call it my 'place of work'. It was not simply that it was a regular and cosy shop, and that I made enough coin to put a little by. No, it was that I had become as fond of it as any place I had ever known, and also the people in it. Certainly, the Aquarium was one on its own. An eighth wonder of the world. And not a fish to be seen! Everyone remarked upon it, 'from rogues to royalty', according to Mr Abrahams. The building in which the Aquarium was situated was, I understand, a great warehouse in the past. That would account for the four floors, attic and cellar, all connected by staircases (some very grand) and landings decorated with coloured-glass windows (like a church), and statues, fancy ironwork, and so on.

On every floor were wide rooms divided up into many smaller ones (though the partitions are only flimsy wood and lath), and those too were sometimes divided again so that, to a stranger, it was a regular labyrinth of cubbyholes and nooks. But not, of course, to those who worked there, and what an odd collection of marvels and misfits (another showman's phrase from Mr Abrahams) we were! Our company changed by the week. One week we had posturers and tumblers, the next wizards and human oddities. There were permanent employees like Conn, who oversaw the menagerie on the top floor, and Pikemartin who sat in his box to issue tickets and did the rounds of dusting off the waxwork figures and opening up and closing the shutters. But they were unusual. Mostly, our company came and went and that was sad, for a friend might be made and lost in a week. I hoped for better things to come, of course – 'prospects' as Madame Leonie called them – but I was content, for the present, to turn up every morning and do my shows in the second-floor front salon (Mr Abrahams had some odd affectations), and take my chink at the week's end. It was not a hard life – I had known much worse – and it was made pleasurable by the little habits I had invented, which a man is inclined to do when he is left to his own cognizance, and with no wife to order his days.

Of a morning, I liked to take my breakfast at Garraway's, just around the corner from the great

Pavilion Theatre, and a bare ten-minute walk from the Aquarium. It was not a fine eating establishment, nor even a good one, the coffee being liable to grittiness and the bread likewise, but the plates were large and well filled, and if the serving girl was frowsy-headed and the waiter wheezed like an old kettle, well, they were obliging enough. Every morning, at a quarter to nine, you would find me at my table in Garraway's front parlour, the dogs at my feet, enjoying my bread and coffee and, on high days, a chop or a slice of bacon. The fire was warm, the view from the window (of the busy street) distracting, the newspapers plentiful, and it was quiet enough to allow a man to compose himself for the labours of the day. It was there that I first encountered Fortinbras Horatio Trimmer, author of dramatic pieces for the Pavilion Theatre, and tales of a riproaring character for *Barnard's Cornucopia*, a weekly journal of literature, published every Saturday, price 2d. Messrs Picton Barnard of Silver-street were his most demanding employers and when I first set eyes upon Trim (as he allows his friends to call him), he was hard at work for them, frowning and scribbling at a table in the parlour corner, with only a single cup at his elbow, and a slice of bread (no butter), upon a plate before him. It was Brutus, that friendly fellow, who, as they say, broke the ice for, unprompted, he sidled over and laid his golden head upon Trim's knee. It was a touching sight and though I might have

17

summoned him back to my side, I did not, but watched my faithful pal out of the corner of my eye. A hand absently fondling those silky ears was all the encouragement old Brutus needed to shuffle closer and then to lie at Trim's feet, as if they were pals together and had just strolled through the door.

To be so singled out for affection touches most people, and indeed it would be a granite-hearted man who was not moved by the simple gesture of an innocent creature, so Brutus remained, and Trim returned to his scribbling, accomplished with a very stubby pencil and many sighs. For his part, Brutus was content to snore the hours away, stretched out upon his new friend's feet, and would have remained there all day, had not Nero roused himself, stretched and turned his wise old head to me with what I call his 'enquiring look'. Of course, he was right – we always leave for the Aquarium at half-past nine, and Brutus was ready, though I cannot tell how he knows the time. Trimmer too was roused, and he scratched his head with the end of his pencil and with his other hand rubbed Brutus' head, which was once again resting upon his knee. I summoned the dogs to me, saluted him (he didn't reply, but gazed vaguely in my direction), and we left for our work.

And that was our first encounter, Trimmer and I, though we regularly shared Garraway's breakfast parlour, and Brutus, needing no introduction now, looked for him every morning. Trimmer was not always there, and I soon realized that his breakfast very much depended upon the condition of his purse. Sometimes I didn't see him for weeks, when I supposed he was on what theatricals call a 'starve'. If he appeared and ordered only a single cup of coffee and a slice of bread, then chink was scarce. But when he breakfasted regally upon coffee and bread and bacon, and invited me and my canine pals to join him, then it was certain that he had sold a story or found a manager interested in his latest dramatic piece.

'Please, Chapman – Bob – come and join me! Here, you—' to the hovering waiter, 'set another place for my friend.'

There would appear a snowy white cloth, and Trimmer, beaming and bountiful, made regular belly-cheer of Garraway's humble fare. Neither were Brutus and Nero ignored, for bread and bacon were brought for them, as well as any scraps the cook might have put by for the cats'-meat-man, until I quite feared for their condition. Satiated, we would enjoy a pipe, and it was in these confidential moments that Trim spoke of his work for Barnard's and the business of the dramatic writer, which seemed to necessitate the continuous burning of sixpenny candles until the sun rose. Messrs Barnard were voracious in their appetite for his stories, he said, and would take one a week, if he could only turn them out! But he had his dramatic work as well, and it was a keen balancing act he must perform. There were starves and feasts in the pen-driver's world, just as there was in the exhibition business, and he could not rest from either.

One morning, we were enjoying a modest repast (the needle was still hovering above 'wet and windy' for us both), and Trim was musing, as ever, over his prospects. He had just finished another dramatic piece, *Elenore the Female Pirate; or the Gold of the Mountain King*, for Mr Carrier, the manager of the Pavilion, as well as a story, *The Vulture's Bride; or the Adventures of Fanny Campbell, the Terror of the High Seas*, for Barnard's Penny Series.

He smiled. 'I know what you're thinking, Bob. Far too many female pirates! But, you know, they're very much 'the thing', and I'm eager to have 'the thing' at my pen's end. I don't care much whether it's a thundering melodrama at the Pavilion or a bloody romance in the hands of old man Barnard. I've had some little success in both camps, you know. Gentlemen high-waymen, for example. My pocket novel, *The Black Highwayman; or Roderick, the Knight of the Road*, has been constantly in print with Messrs Barnard for the last half year. And Lovegrove did sterling work in *Jack Blackwood the Gentleman Robber* at the Pav.'

I tried not to smile, for my friend was desperately proud of his success in the penny novel line, and aspired to great things on the stage. It was only a matter of time, he often told me, before

Mr Phelps of Drury-lane noticed him, and the great publishing houses of Chapman and Hall or Murray of Albemarle-street were sure to recognize his talent, which he sincerely believed was quite the equal of Messrs Thackeray and Dickens. As for the stories of pirates and the highwaymen, they were simply journeyman tasks, whilst he waited for the jewel of his inspiration and a hearty dose of luck to arrive. Then he produced two packets from his coat and laid them reverently upon the table.

'Here, Bob, is *The Vulture's Bride*, a roistering tale of romance on the Spanish Main, which I shall deliver to the copyist before I attend the Pavilion Theatre where, at ten o'clock, we read the new Christmas piece, *Elenore the Female Pirate*. *En assemble*, of course. I think old Carrier will be pleased with it. Pirates and savages are certainly a change from Harlequins and all that old-fashioned baggage!'

I was not convinced. Call me a sentimental sort, but I like a pantomime at Christmas, no matter how old the jests or tawdry the tinsel. That is the essence of pantomime, in my book. A jolly jaunt with familiar friends, Harlequin and Columbine and Pantaloon. And if poor old Clown has been forced to change his clothes and masquerade as a Policeman, I can bite my tongue and still give him three cheers, as long as he is predictable and merry. But do away with him altogether? Even worse, do away with the Harlequinade and the

21

Transformation Scene, where the skill of the scenic painter is shown in rippling water and toad-stools becoming fairies? Never! Do away with this, and there will be more than me offended! Half of London will be on their feet, roaring, and the other half keeping their sixpences in their pockets and staying away from the theatre.

But Trim will have none of it.

'Oh, come now, Bob!' he said, seeing my down-cast face. 'We must embrace change. Even in the theatre. The Pavilion will survive Christmas without a dusty, old-fashioned pantomime!'

I was still not convinced. Folks around here are keen on old-fashioned things, dusty or not. But it was a hopeless cause, for Trim was already wiping his mouth and wrapping his muffler three times about his neck to keep out the cold and damp which had descended, like a stage cloth, about the city. And he was as cheerful as a dog with two tails.

'I have a full day's work ahead of me, Bob,' he cried, 'and at its close, a month's rent and break-fasts. If not more!' and he strode out of Garraway's like a man just knighted! It was a pleasure to see him thus, for my friend Trimmer was given (he won't mind me saying) to periods of gloom and despondency, when the blue devils sit on his shoulder and he is fearsomely dejected. I think it is the artist in him, for I have noted in other men, the great Mr Dickens among them, and Mr Thackeray also, a world-weary disposition when I linger over their photographic portraits, displayed in the shop windows.

But this morning, Brutus, Nero and I did not stop at the stationers on our way to the Aquarium. And it was not our day to take the quickest route around the back rows, nor a picturesque ramble along thriving streets of shops and new houses with their glimpses of cottage gardens. Today, our morning walk took us to a nearby expanse of waste-land which had been growing for some months and which seemed to change at every visit, for there was much hurry to complete a new railway line, part of which went under the ground in just this region and emerged, like a mole, miles away. Only a week ago, houses stood above the great cavern which had been dug out, and now, like a basher's grin, there was nothing but jagged gaps and piles of smoking rubble. A new vista, like a panorama, had opened up, showing the backs of buildings: dirty windows with missing panes and doors which had not seen a lick of paint, nor the soft end of a duster, in all their lives, displayed now for anyone to gawp at. Beyond them, an entire church spire rose up, where before there was just a weathercock, and everywhere seemed wider and bigger. At my feet, among the clayey puddles and mounds of earth, I had come across coins and pieces of ancient pot lying on the ground for anyone to find, and I had once again taken up my old pastime of antique-hunting, while my canine pals wandered at will with their noses to the ground.

But this morning was mizzley, and not the weather for digging. A bitter wind laced with rain was at our back, and then flew in our faces like a scold's fury as we rounded the corner of Hob-lane, with the attic roof of the Aquarium just in view, and even Brutus and Nero looked enquiringly at me as we bent into the blast. On the other side of the deep chasm, a line of tidy, old houses, home to families on every floor (and in the cellar and attic too), was leaning further southward, like a deck of cards, and, by evening, might be boarded up or simply have tumbled into a heap of dust. For, in these days of improvement, many buildings simply fell down unaided, slipping into piles of bricks or collapsing into the great holes which suddenly appeared beneath them, their occupants killed, and even innocent passers-by. These houses, however, though their roof tiles had slid away and rags of curtains fluttered in the glassless windows, were at least shored up with timbers which stretched like bones out of joint into the soggy ground.

On the fencing made from more old timbers (to prevent, I supposed, the houses falling in the other direction, into the diggings) the bill-poster had been active. A pageant of colourful announcements of sales and circuses, balloon ascents, gaff theatres and even the Aquarium, marched in close order in great black, inky letters on yellow, red and blue backgrounds. How strange to see them, fluttering and bright, across the terrible dark gulf

24

carved out of the mire and mud. Before us lay the chasm, very deep, and at its bottom the dismal blackness of the railway cutting and a tunnel being built, one of many burrowing through the city. It was my horror. And my fascination. I was drawn to the very edge of it, to look down into its depths, to smell that stink of old earth and rottenness, and sometimes felt that an unseen force was pulling me towards it and I was powerless to resist, and it was only the hooting of the labourers that brought me to my senses.

But what labourers they were! For this hard work attracted a species of 'cazzelty' (in the common tongue) like no other, one accustomed to the darkness and toil, and whose natural state was to be covered in dirt and clay. One news-paper writer claimed that these railway workings had produced 'a new species of men', 'troglodytes' he called them, and an artist in Mr Lemon's *Punch* showed them in a comical picture with shovels and picks for arms. And, in spite of my horror, I was fascinated, and have stood and watched them digging and clawing in the soil, hauling upon ropes and hoists to lower timbers and bricks and drawing up cart-loads of spoil, whilst roaring and cursing like savages. But in these foul places, where the filth and stench of the earth take the place of God's good air, men, I think, become more like beasts, and are reduced to the very baseness of their natures.

Even in the regions above, there was no escaping

them. Those cazzelties who could not afford lodgings simply claimed an empty house or set up make-shift camps, and here and there on the wasteland, thin strings of smoke from fires and from the canvas mushrooms of their rough tents rose into the murk. It seemed to me the most wretched of existences, yet these men brought their families with them, and I have seen grubby, bright-eyed children splashing in the muddy pools whilst their mothers crouched over blackened pots, all of them as filthy as if they had just crept out of the mire below. Of course, tales about them quickly sprang up, though not so pleasant even as your Bluebeards or Spring-heeled Jacks. Stories were rife of thievings and barbarous assaults (the usual crimes done by the poor and ignorant), but also of attacks upon women and child-stealing, which we all know are the crimes favoured by foreigners, and gypsies especially. Not a hundred paces away, a woman and two small children were watching me, so I gave them a wide berth, straying closer to the chasm's edge, close enough indeed to have that stink of wet earth and ancient corruption rise up to greet me from the gloom like an old friend, and to feel myself, as ever, drawn to those fearsome regions.

Suddenly, there was a rush, a roar and the world turned over, with me in its arms. Someone, no more than a bundle of rags, I at first thought, and in a great hurry, glanced my shoulder, sending me careering to the ground, where I landed heavily in a pool of clayey water. I lay there, momentarily stunned, as cheers and laughter rose up from the cazzelties below, although whether at my dousing or in encouragement or warning to the boy, it was impossible to say. What is certain is that the plunging figure *was* a boy, and he *was* running and sliding along the top of the rough embankment as though every devil in hell was at his heels. He was in a desperate, a frantic hurry, perilously close to the rough edge of the chasm, and entirely careless of his own safety. But why he was running, or from who or what, was a mystery. When the cry of 'Who chases?' rose up from the cazzelties, I expected at every moment to see a burly constable or chimney-master in pursuit of him. But there was no one. The sky had grown dark with clouds and rain, the air thick and murky, almost a fog now, and all I could see were a handful of idlers peering over the fence on the opposite side of the cutting. Not a cry, nor a 'Stop, thief!', just the muffling dankness of the winter morning. And certainly no one in pursuit of the fleeing boy. But pursued he believed he was, for I watched him from my puddle, slipping and sliding and constantly looking over his shoulder, running blind again, teetering upon the brink and almost losing his footing and threatening to descend, head over tip, into that oblivion, only to recover himself at the last moment and press on.

I did not see it happen, and could only suppose that the boy did stumble and lose his footing and slipped over the edge of the cutting. But if he grasped at the muddy banks, at the loose boulders and soil, even the straggling bushes and grasses, he did so silently, and then plunged out of sight, for he made not a murmur. Of course, I struggled to my knees and crawled through the sticky mire to find him, but when I reached the edge of the chasm, on all fours, with the mud soaking into my clothes, expecting to see him clinging to the bankside, he was nowhere to be seen. And below was that terrible descent of clay and rock and darkness.

Brutus and Nero lent their keen noses to the pursuit and trailed back and forth along the edge and, had I let them, doubtless they would have found a way down the steep bank, but I held them back. It is no secret that I cannot abide close places, and the black hole of the tunnel, viewed even from this distance, gripped me with terror, and so with my heart thumping, I stood for some minutes, with the rain pelting down, looking into that underworld, noting the flicker, here and there, of lanterns as the cazzelties laboured on, burrowing into the ancient London soil. The boy must have gone somewhere! I looked around me at the wild expanse of wretched earth, and across the chasm at the houses and their unblinking windows. And I waited, with the gale howling in my face, for the boy to clamber up the chasm face, or to shout for help from the bottom.

But I waited in vain. After five, ten, fifteen

minutes, when there was not a sign of him, and the only sound the echo of spade and pick, I turned my back upon the cutting and bent into the wind.

CHAPTER 2

MY FRIEND TRIMMER

I did not expect to see or hear about the boy again. Why should I? Certainly, he had given me the trouble of mending my torn breeches and sponging away the foul clay which stuck to them, and if I did, when we next traversed the wasteland, contemplate the cutting and wonder if he had slid to the bottom of that terrible gulf and his body was lying there under a heap of bricks, I was not inclined to enquire further. In fact, if I had the inclination to worry, it was about myself and my dogs and our future, for my every moment of leisure these days was spent in sending out cards and letters to likely places (halls and pleasures gardens and the like), and scanning the columns of the *Era*, just to keep track of my competitors. There is one man, Mr John Matthews, who I regard as a keen rival, and he is often favourably reported, with his excellent hound, 'Devilshoof'. Matthews is a busy man, also, and has more strings to his fiddle than I, being also an exhibition swordsman. What work he does not get with the dog in the circus or theatre, he can make up for with his sabre on a military show. He is a clever man, and no mistake. I wish I had his many skills.

Keeping body and soul together in these uncertain times and trying to put a little by, that was my constant worry. I was forever inventing new tricks for Brutus and Nero, little novelties which were easy to learn, but would amuse and keep spectators returning and asking for Chapman's Sagacious Canines. It was a wearying time. My boys were quick scholars and diligent at their work and right as ninepence after only an hour in the back-yard, but I was more often worn out after a day's performing and ready for a cup of tea and a few pages of a rollicking story before I answered the sweet siren-call of my mattress.

One evening, not many weeks after the business with the boy, Mrs Gifford, our housekeeper at the Aquarium, caught me as I was homeward-bound and waved a letter at me. I had just finished my last show, had quickly rounded up my dogs and was on the stairs, already contemplating supper in my own room with a nice little fire, when I heard her footsteps behind me, and her 'Mr Chapman! A moment, please!' I generally avoid her if I can, and would certainly rather stare at a blank wall than meet her eye. But a glance at the folded note she held out made me as close as snatch it from her. 'To Chapman, Aquarium, URGENT!!! By Hand. URGENT!!!' quickly announced to me that its author was Trim, and within was the simple instruction, 'Meet Cheshire Cheese. 11 sharp.

Urgent. T.' It was unusual for Trim to issue such a summons in such a way, but I was not about to reveal that to Mrs Gifford. I held it close to my chest, read it once, twice, three times, before I folded it carefully and put it in my pocket. I needn't have bothered being so careful.

'I hope I wasn't the bearer of bad news, Mr Chapman,' said Mrs Gifford, clinging to my back like a shadow as I hurried down the stairs. I would have wagered a week's chink then that she had already looked at the note, and when she forgot herself and said, 'The Cheshire Cheese is not a respectable tavern, you know. And tonight there is an auction in the yard, so it will be crowded,' of course no further proof was needed. (She had, as Trim once remarked, the gall of the French.) She continued, 'You should take care, Mr Chapman. It's a place that attracts the light-fingered sort, so don't you go losing your handkerchief or those handsome dogs of yours.'

Gifford was standing on the next to bottom step of the big staircase at the Aquarium, with a bunch of keys in her hand, and wearing that high-nosed look as though there was a bad smell, and I was the cause of it. My dogs, waiting on either side of me, were as still as headstones, though Nero gave a low growl, little more than a rumble in his throat. But it didn't tell. She wasn't moved at all, though her mouth drew itself into a thin line. 'You want to watch that dog, Mr Chapman,' said she. 'It might turn nasty, and you wouldn't want the police taking it away and putting it down. What would you do then?'

We hurried out of the door and, though I never looked back, I could swear that she watched us until we turned the corner, and we did not stop, not even to smell the freshly baked pies at Mrs Quilter's shop. Only when we heard the roar of voices and a rosy glow lit up the street, did we slacken our pace, for it announced the nearness of the Cheshire Cheese. And Mrs Gifford was at least correct in her prediction of the auction. In the Cheese's great yard (regular host to marionette and theatre shows) was raised a gaily lit canvas booth, inside which was a platform and seats, crowded to the rafters with people eager to be parted from their pennies and shillings in exchange for 'handsome parcels of beef (unfit for dogs) and 'handsome clocks and watches' (unfit for time-keeping), which Harris the Hawker, as he was popularly known, and his cohort of street-wise assistants were selling 'from the plank'.

The Cheese was low in all respects. It stood at the corner of a low street in a low neighbourhood. Many of its ceilings were so low that they required a man to stoop all the way to his seat or risk bruising his head on the beams, which were old and knotty, just like the assortment of benches and tables which might have been dragged from both dining rooms and barracks, so ill-matched were they. It was very old, I believe, and Drinkwater, the landlord, liked to boast about

Shakespeare and Julius Caesar having sat in its best room and carved their initials on his oak settle, and took pride in showing them to visitors, who felt obliged to be impressed. But the Cheshire Cheese itself, though low, is not a bad place, and when we meet, Trimmer, Will Lovegrove and I, we take ourselves to a corner of the remotest room in the house and there enjoy our supper of bread and cheese and a glass of the best. I am not a drinking man, but I enjoy the company of my friends and so I am willing to put up with the little discomforts of heat and fug. And Brutus and Nero, of course, were happy in any place as long as they found kind, affectionate friends! They were eager to find Trimmer and Will Lovegrove, then, and it was not difficult to do, for they sat in our usual corner with a jar each and one ready for me, and the plate of bread and cheese on the table before them. Only it stood uneaten, the cheese sweating in the heat and the doorsteps of bread drying to stone. And my two friends like statues themselves, in attitudes of silent anxiety, were only slightly relieved when Brutus and Nero, tails a-wagging with joy, demanded their customary attention. Will Lovegrove clapped my shoulder and shook my hand.

'Ah! Bob Chapman. A good evening to you – and to Brutus and Nero, of course! Come and join us, and see if you can relieve poor Trim here of his worries. If you are unable to, I very much fear that they will consume him completely and that, alas, we will be forced to carry him home in pieces, so broken is he by his fretting! Haroo!'

Will Lovegrove, leading actor at the Pavilion, sometimes found it difficult to leave his dramatic roles in the theatre. He was a fine William Brave-heart and John Masterman, a roguish Captain Freestaff and Mynheer Deepson, and did Trim much good service in the representation of his highwaymen and pirates. Jack Blackwood, a heroic gentleman of the road, was cheered on – and off – the stage for months, and as tall, handsome Ruggantino, the Spanish Pirate, had many young women lingering at the theatre door and their men threatening to fight him! But Will was a good soul, as brave as those heroes he represented, and with such a fine figure he had no need of PFCs (padded false calves, which are shoved down the legs of their stockings by less shapely actors) and wore his own dark hair long and curling about his shoulders. Will Lovegrove was probably the most handsome man I had ever seen and certainly. Trim and I, being just everyday lookers, had reason to be envious when Lovegrove turned the head of every pretty young woman in the street.

But Trim, anxiously twisting his gloves about and not wanting to look either of us in the eye, was above and beyond his usual state of agitation. Will frowned and nudged him encouragingly, and said in that rich, sailor-hero voice he reserved for serious occasions, 'Now then, old fellow. Buck up and hoist yer topsail! Tell Bob here about your dreadful shipwreck.'

Trimmer smiled weakly and laid his hands upon the table. 'It is simple enough and you already know the first instalment, Chapman. I left Garraway's this morning with a full stomach, a light heart and a manuscript copy of *Elenore the Female Pirate, a Christmas Extravaganza* in one pocket and *The Vulture's Bride; or the Adventures of Fanny Campbell, the Terror of the High Seas, A Novel,* in the other. I arrive at the Pavilion Theatre with *Elenore* in a muddy and despicable condition, and *The Vulture's Bride* in the hands of a stranger.' He paused, for dramatic effect. 'I've been robbed. Distressing enough, of course, but that's not all.' Trim wound the ends of his muffler around his fingers. 'If it were just a robbery, I should not mind. The fact that it *was* my only finished copy of *The Vulture's Bride*, and it'll be the devil's own job to re-write it from working scraps, is bad, but it can be done.' He reflected. 'No, it's not just the robbery. Rather the manner of it. And what went with it.'

And then followed a description of his route, what and who he saw on the way, and finally his strange encounter with a street boy – 'Skulking in the shadows!' – just on the corner of Dunfermline-street, where the pavement was narrowest and the shadow of the London and South Metropolitan railway bridge was deepest. 'I suppose I wasn't looking where I was going, and tripped over this

36

boy. I hit the ground rather hard and dropped the manuscript, and it scattered everywhere. Whilst I was trying to recover it, the boy hooked the novel from my pocket and made off at a lick.'

Will was frowning and tracing pot stains on the table. 'An unusual robbery, I'll give you that.'

'The boy was sitting on the ground,' continued Trim, 'with his back to the wall, like some Chinese statue. And just out of sight, round the corner. No doubt waiting for me.'

Will nodded thoughtfully. 'If you say so, old fellow. Was he alone?'

'I didn't see anyone else,' said Trim, 'but there might have been someone hiding. There are plenty of rows and courts around there.'

Will considered.

'Just a passing thought, old fellow, but don't you think it's rather out of the way for a *boy* to rob you like that? On his own? Pick your pockets in a market, yes. Trip you up on a dark street at midnight, certainly. But even then, with someone else larger and taller to hold you down, or kick you, or beat you with a club, before robbing you. And it doesn't sound like a garrotting either. From your description, it sounds more like an accident.'

Trim's eyes widened in indignation. 'Well! Clearly, I've had a narrow escape! By rights, I should be weltering in the road! Or have had my throat pressed by a nasty man till I'm insensible.'

'All I am saying—'

'No need, Will,' said Trim, trying, I think, to

keep his irritation under a sack. 'As a matter of fact, I have already formed my own opinion. I think this is a simple matter of professional jealousy. A conspiracy to steal my new story even before Barnard's have seen it and pass it off under a different name. I can think of two or three likely candidates in the penny novel business even now.' He shook his head. 'Jealousy is one thing, but theft!'

I was not convinced, and don't think Will was either.

'You may be right,' he said, patiently, 'but it seems a lot of trouble to go to just for a packet of paper, even if it is your very excellent story. After all, how would this boy know you had it on you? You are sure nothing else is missing? Not your purse? Your handkerchief?'

'No. Only the manuscript.'

'And the boy,' continued Will, thoughtfully. 'What was he like? Short? Tall? Red-haired?'

But Trim couldn't remember, though he swore he would know him again if he saw him for but a second. 'He was small. Dirty, of course. But aren't they all? He wore a scabby short coat and boots out at the toes. A red handkerchief around his neck, showman style. Remains of a hat – what do they call them? A flat poke, I think. Maybe a tooth or two missing. I don't really know. I didn't get a very good look at him.'

Will laughed. 'But you took in everything at a glance! Woe betide us all! Witnesses?'

'None,' Trim said quickly. 'Not one. No one around at all. Unless – but I can't see how he had anything to do with the business – there was a strange-looking creature who delivered a page into my hands.'

The clock ticked, the fire crackled and sputtered, Brutus and Nero snored lustily. We were warm and snug for now, but opening up a mystery, had we but known it, which would affect all our lives.

We waited and, after a moment's thought, Trim explained.

'He gave me a page from the drama, *Elenore the Female Pirate*. I'd dropped the whole lot, as I told you, and there was paper scattered everywhere. I thought I'd collected them all, but one escaped, I suppose, and he rescued it and gave it back to me. A strange-looking creature. Perhaps I should try and find him.'

'In what way strange?'

Trim wriggled in his seat. 'Well, to begin with, he was enormously large,' he said, 'like a pudding about to burst, and with a head as round and smooth as a cannon ball. And he was strangely dressed. All pale. He might have been an actor. You fellows can be extravagant in your costumes.'

Will seemed not at all put out, though he was affecting a rather large collar and a scarf which was also oversize. And, of course, his hair was long and curling about his neck. In an actorly fashion.

'Was he foreign, perhaps?'

'No, not foreign, but not regular either. He had an odd way of talking, rather overdone.'

Lovegrove stared at our friend and ran a hand through those glossy locks with such careless elegance that I could have been envious. 'My dear fellow, his size and his bald pate, and what might be an actor's lisp to boot – this stranger must stand out like an honest man in parliament! We will make enquiries. He seems a prime candidate.'

Trim shook his head and gazed at us, by turn, with an anxious expression.

'No, no. You are very kind. Good friends both. But I fear,' he said with a dramatic emphasis that Lovegrove could never have taught him, 'I very much fear that I shall never see him, nor the boy, nor *The Vulture's Bridge* again.'

He was, of course, completely wrong.

CHAPTER 3

THE PAVILION THEATRE

My dogs and I are comfortably seated at the side of the stage of the Pavilion Theatre. Mr Carrier has requested our attendance in connection with some occasional work in the forthcoming Christmas extravaganza written by that talented dramatic author, F. H. Trimmer, *Elenore the Female Pirate; or the Gold of the Mountain King.* We are as pleased as a dog with two tails – Brutus and Nero in partic.! – and not just because it puts some extra shillings our way for the penny bank. No, it's the novelty of a theatre show, for we haven't had so much as a sniff of greasepaint for almost a year – since we were usurped at the Bower Saloon by our friend Mr Matthews and 'Devilshoof' – and, according to Trim, it is a buster, and will reach the pages of the *Era* and the notice of other managers. All in all, a *good thing.* So we are happily waiting upon the manager and our friend Will Lovegrove, who has yet to arrive, but who I am certain we have to thank for this opportunity.

Mr Carrier has certainly taken a risk on Trim's Christmas piece and has dispensed with the

Harlequin theme altogether, and Will says he is the only London manager to do so. 'Traditional' and 'time-honoured' are bywords for the pantomime, and woe betide the man who will contemplate an alternative. We are used to *Harlequin King Rumbledetum and the Fair Princess Who-Will-Have-Her-Own-Way*; or the Bright Secrets of the Dark Lake and a Misty Plot to Boot. We expect a foggy story, topical songs and jests, gorgeous costumes, a brilliant spectacle with banners and flags of all nations, a fairy ballet, effects to take one's breath away, and a transformation scene to dazzle.

Pantomimes are all the same, every year. No matter what.

Until this year.

Yes, Mr Carrier is taking a risk.

'Mr Hennessey at the Oriental,' he confided to the company only last week, 'is rumoured to have secured the services of Van Ambrose, the great equestrian and animal trainer. I have heard that his act two finale will present a magnificent procession of camels, horses and elephants. Then, at the Duke's Theatre, I understand Mr Goldhawk is building an entire Chinese pagoda, complete with turtle doves for his transformation scene.'

'But,' said Mr Pocock, his faithful secretary, 'Mr Willard plays safe with *Ali Baba*, though his forty thieves are all, to a man, female and rather lumpy.'

There was a titter from the ladies and something ruder from our low comedian.

42

'No laughing matter, ladies and gentlemen,' Mr Pocock gloomily continued, 'particularly since he has secured the services of Mr Lawrence, the firework manufacturer and pyrotechnist. We know, from our own experience, that mighty explosions and clouds of smoke will be the order of the day.'

A back-hander, according to Will, since old Lawrence nearly burned down the Pav one year in an accidental burst of blue fire when the drop-scene went up in smoke.

'Of course,' continued Mr Carrier, 'thanks to Mr Lombard, we are not short of wonders at the Pavilion – the ship-in-full-sail in act three will be a 'stunner', I am sure.'

If the quantity of wood and paint, the healthy dollop of paper and paste, and the shortness of Mr Lombard's temper were anything to judge by, it will be a marvel to behold. There will be sails and rigging too, said the Boss, beaming like a Chinaman, and all in working order so that 'a talented chorus' (Mr Carrier does not name names) might shin up the ropes and ladders and perform an 'aerial ballet' at least ten feet above the stage.

Mr Lombard, the Pavilion's stage artist, was as busy as a hen with one chick, and worried not only about the construction of the ship-in-full-sail, and the desert island with waving palm trees, but also the more pressing business of scenery for the new drama on the stage next week – *The Path of Pride; or the Housebreakers of London* – in which

43

he was required to suggest, with terrific realism, a prison cell, London streets east and west, and the rooftop of an aristocratic residence in Larkhill-square.

'All of this to be built and painted. *When*? I am asking of you.'

He shot this in my direction and I, like a fool, looked around me, expecting to see Mr Carrier or Mr Pocock ready with a sharp answer, but there was no one except the shadow of Mr Mint, the doorkeeper, and a collection of Mr Lombard's assistants, bustling here and there.

'"There are set scenes which might be dragged out from the store and refreshed,' says the Boss. *When*?? I am asking of you. 'There are only two which must be got up from scratch," says he. *When*? I am asking, a third time.'

This was a new experience for me. At the Aquarium, we are often as solitary and quiet as a nun's parlour for hours, but in the theatre, it seems, everyone talks. Constantly. Mr Lombard, who looked more like a grocer in his long apron and with his pipe clamped between his teeth, interrogated everyone and the thin air beside, and now and again fired off an angry enquiry at me and my boys, who were sitting ducks at the side of the stage. I do not think he expected a reply. Mr Lombard had been early upon the Pavilion stage, with gas lit and curtains drawn, for he wanted two drop-scenes painted, and another underway, before the daily irritation and interruption of performers commences.

'Thorns in my side,' he grumbled.

But today, even those precious hours of industry were denied him, for noises off signal the arrival of, not only the regular company, but a small and growing battalion of girls and their mamas, eager to try for the children's ballet. They were not due until after twelve and had a good two hours or so to wait, but eager mothers and weary-eyed children were already in the queue at the theatre door. Through them, like a trail of conscripts, trooped the company, rubbing sleep from their eyes and complaining about the inconvenience of such an early hour to professionals who have not long been in their beds. One of these stragglers, remarkably bright-eyed and cheery, was Lovegrove who, though we talked – and Will drank – in the Cheshire Cheese until very late, looked for all the world as if he had had a full eight hours in a feather bed. Tall and elegant, with that easy, shambling walk, as though his boots were half a size too large, he passed the time of day with Mr Mint, tipped his hat and murmured something inaudible to a gaggle of ballet girls who gasped and giggled behind their hands, and, grinning at me, drew up alongside Brutus and Nero, who vigorously wagged their affection for him. Even Mr Lombard, whose opinion of 'professionals' is as low as a Methody's, nodded his head and muttered, 'Mornin', Mr Lovegrove,' as though he meant it.

'Bob,' said Will, still scratching Brutus's ear, 'I'd be obliged if you could spare a moment to come

45

with me and take a breath of briny air. Just a step or so out of the theatre door onto the fo'csle, don't you know?'

We ambled back there, and he stood at my shoulder on the step, but held me back from going outside.

'No, wait a moment, my old shipmate,' said he, 'and before you dirty your shoe leather, just cast your peepers across to starboard, there, and see what you can see in the shadow of Cheeseman's noble establishment. See if you can espy a boy, hunkered against the wall.'

I did as I was told, and peered through the buzzing crowd of mothers and children, where I did indeed descry a small figure, hunched upon the ground. There was only one, and he looked to me like any other street boy – thin and dirty, with his boot-toes out, and wearing such a ragged collection of clothes that it was impossible to see where his shirt began and his jacket finished.

'Now,' he said, 'another test for you. Look across the road. There, standing at Strang's table.'

I strained my eyes, for although it was mid-morning, the light was grey with fog and the sun would not break through the gloom today. Yet I could see a man at the table outside Mr Strang's bookshop. Given his immense size and remarkable costume – a Benjamin made of some light-coloured cloth, with tall hat to match – he was hardly flying low! Apparently deep in contemplation of a volume, he would turn into the light now and again, the better to read it. And the better to look around and about him also, I thought, for I noticed his head was constantly bobbing up and down.

'I wonder,' Will was saying in a low voice, 'if this unlikely pair might be the two who tripped our friend Trimmer and stole his penny novel? The boy and the grampus he described to us. At the very least, it's an extraordinary coincidence to have two specimens who so very nearly fit the bill here in the street together, don't you think?' He scratched his head. 'I wonder if they were intending to rob Trim of something particular, and failed, and so they've come back to try him again again . . . I don't know though. It's rather out of the way. Perhaps we should just call the constable and have him put it right.'

But Mr Lombard's bell sounded and saved us the bother, and we were summoned to the stage.

(I wonder if that was our first mistake, and whether, had we simply sent around the corner for a bluebottle, everything that followed would – well, perhaps might – have taken a different course. But hindsight is a wonderful invention, as someone wisely said.)

On the gloomy stage, the Pavilion company was assembled, and by the time Pilcher, the gasman, had turned up the light just enough to make reading possible, Trim was the only interested party notable by his absence. After ten minutes, even Mr Carrier was glancing at the theatre door and his pocket-watch, and finally he signalled to Mr Pocock to hand out the pieces. At first, everyone bent their head silently over their pages, and then were heard a few grumbles, mainly concerning 'business removed', for actors are uncommonly precious about their 'lines' (as they call them), and count them up religiously, regarding themselves hard done by if they lose, rather than gain, even a handful.

'To commence,' said Mr Carrier, in his business-like manner. 'In brief. Act one, scene one, no alterations. Scene two, strike Mr Wherewithal's speech. Scene three . . .'

And so it continued, with Mr Pocock furiously scribbling at his little table a summary of what Mr Carrier had added and cut from Trim's original.

'Act two, scene thirteen—'

'Very brief,' chipped in Tom Daley, the clown, 'nothing to it!' and everyone laughed, for he was correct. When it was held up, act two, scene thirteen was a blank page!

'Quite right. This is where we require the services of our dramatic author,' said Mr Carrier, drily, looking towards the theatre door again. 'Given that our closest rival, Mr Hennessey at the Oriental—' – here the company cried 'Boo!' and 'Yah!' and noisily made fun, but Mr Carrier held up his hand – 'I beg your serious attention, ladies and gentlemen. This is no matter for jest. I learned only this morning that, in addition to his act two finale, Mr Hennessey's pantomime will also present a stud of trained zebras, racing dogs and monkeys in a mock Derby.' He looked around the circle. 'This is a tight business. We cannot afford to be upped by our nearest competitor. Which is why I have asked Mr Chapman to attend upon us today.'

He took me by surprise! But I jumped to my feet and brought Brutus and Nero to heel and we stood to attention, while Mr Carrier waved us onto the stage. If there were some sniggers and remarks made behind hands, there were also ripples of clapping and a 'Well done, Bob!', which came from Lovegrove's direction.

'Mr Chapman and his Sagacious Canines are well known to visitors at the East London Aquarium,' said Mr Carrier, 'and I have no doubt that those same visitors will be eager to see him and his clever dogs on the Pavilion stage. I sent round to Mr Trimmer last night and asked him to work up two or three scenes in which these excellent dogs might be seen to good advantage.' He looked again at the theatre door and then at his watch. 'I can only suppose that their devising took rather longer than I, a mere theatrical manager, could have anticipated.'

As dry a man as ever I've met, Mr Carrier. And if further proof were needed that he knew his business, he had two theatres to wrinkle his brow: the great Pavilion and also the smaller Royal Clarence on the other side of the river. He could often be seen dashing between the two in his little dog cart, holding onto his hat and talking nineteen to the dozen to the driver, who was, of course, his secretary, Mr Pocock.

'I hain't workin' wiv no dawgs, sir,' piped up Phil Connelly, the low comedian of the company. 'I 'ave been nipped more times than I 'ave 'ad 'ot dinners. Dawgs don't favour me.'

'These dogs don't nip or do anything detrimental, Phil,' said Will Lovegrove lazily. He was rocking on the back legs of his chair and winding his scarf about his neck. 'They are thoroughly reliable.'

'All dogs nip,' returned Phil morosely. 'You can 'ave my part for a green'orn, Gov, but I ain't workin' wiv no dawgs.'

This brought me up, and Brutus and Nero also, and for a moment I thought our little number might be reduced to nought, all on account of Phil Connelly and his prejudices. But Mr Carrier was having none of it.

'The dogs are well-trained, Phil, and well-behaved. I have seen them myself, performing at the Aquarium.' (I had no idea the Gov had seen my show, and certainly I had never clocked him.) 'I can assure you all that no one is in any danger from these two excellent creatures –'

'Brutus and Nero,' put in Will Lovegrove.

'And indeed they will enhance the show. Besides,' and this was the crucial point, 'I have already put Mr Trimmer to the trouble of writing two or three new scenes.'

That was that, and as if to underline it, there was a clatter and a cry and Mr Trimmer appeared from the darkness of the auditorium, very much out of breath and brandishing a sheaf of papers!

'Most sorry, Mr Carrier! Apologies to one and all! Ladies and gentlemen! Very sorry, I am sure. I have been working half the night on the new scenes, including the special "dog scenes" you requested, Mr Carrier. Here they are,' and he leaped upon the stage and, dropping the manuscript once, scrabbling through it half a dozen times, he extracted a small bundle of paper, Trim thrust it into Mr Carrier's hands, and then looked beamingly, if a little strained, around the company.

'*Elenore the Female Pirate*, ladies and gentlemen, with a children's ballet and two sagacious dogs. I have given them ample opportunity, Bob – er, Mr Chapman – to demonstrate their mighty powers.' Unwrapping his muffler, he turned to me for the first time and nodded to Brutus and Nero who, I think, were listening with great interest. 'In the first act, they will swim to the pirate boat, run up the pirate flag and show their allegiance to the pirate captain by guarding the helpless heroine and snarling at her when she tries to escape; in the second act, they are discovered sneaking through the jungle and felling the hero, thus assisting the pirate villain in his evil plots; and in the third act, they are poisoned by bad meat and so come to a deservedly bad end!'

The muffler still in his hands, Trim looked

eagerly around the company with a smile of satisfaction upon his face, but it was not reciprocated. Certainly not by me, and not by anyone else. Even the bad-tempered Phil Connelly wore a frown.

'You are jesting surely, Trimmer,' cried Will, a frown wrinkling his brow. 'These handsome dogs, Brutus and Nero, snarling and sneaking? Assisting a villain? Poisoned? They could not do it, could they, Bob? Even if you trained them every day for a year. Not these dogs! They are British dogs, through and through. Proud, honourable, dependable, decent dogs, incapable of a mean action.'

The company hummed in appreciation.

'Oh really!' said Trim, laughing. 'Don't be such a clown, Lovegrove! It is but the plot of the drama, and casts no adverse reflection upon the character of the dogs! Indeed, it supposes that they must be well-trained and good canine actors if they are to perform against their natural inclinations and assume villainous roles.'

But this argument fell flat, and a tide of noisy protests from the company rose to meet it! It was not my row, however, and, feeling uncomfortable, the dogs and I tiptoed quietly outside to breathe calmer air. For I dislike arguments, and shouting distresses me very much: I must have heard a barrelful of discord as a child, and even now my stomach tightens and my eyes water when I hear angry voices.

So, with my pipe and a biscuit or two for my canine pals, I stood in the theatre doorway and contemplated the black and greasy wall opposite. The crowd of chattering children and their mamas had grown, of course, but they gave me a wide enough berth when I lit up, and I puffed quietly until a voice at my shoulder said, 'Are they still there, Bob? The boy and the grampus?'

Will took me by surprise and I jumped. I had not given them a fly's thought. But clearly he had.

'I wonder if they're waiting for a second go at old Trim. Picking their moment, when he's hurrying off somewhere with his head in the clouds.'

He frowned and peered through the crowd whilst scratching Nero's ear.

'By the Lord Harry, here's a plan. Would you lend me your noble boys as supporters to go and round up the grampus and, if he's unwilling, fetch a constable to assist? Then we'll haul these two prodigies of nature before poor Trim and see if he isn't the unwitting hero of a terrible awful gagarino!'

Will eyed the boy – 'Keep your peelers on that young shaver, Bob!' – called Brutus and Nero to his heels (sometimes I think they love him more than me) and hurried through the crowd without another word.

I didn't protest, and I had not looked at the boy, nor given him a second thought. And so to spy again this undersized creature, curled like a grub against the grimy wall with his toes, like buds, sticking out of his boots, gave me a little shock. I

53

saw now that his legs were barely covered by his
trousers and those had more holes in them than
trouser, and it was the same for the coat upon his
back which was more tatters than cloth and
considerably out at the elbow. His head was bare,
his hair trossy and his face – I couldn't see it at
first, so deeply buried was it in a pair of grubby
hands. But as I drew closer and two weary eyes
peered up at me, ah then, I knew who he was,
instantly. And it didn't seem at all strange that he
should be the boy who had sent me flying into
the mud before he flew into the darkness of the
railway cutting.

We stared at each other for some moments, then
he reached inside his shirt and drew out a packet,
tied up with string and held it out. It seemed to
me he did so with some little effort, as though it
hurt him to move.

'I know you. You're the dog-man from the
Aquarium. I've seen you walking with
Mr Trimmer. In the street. You could give this to
him. He dropped it and I picked it up. And when
I went back, he was talking' – he bit his lip and
rubbed his eyes hard – 'he was talking to the Nasty
Man, so I legged it sharpish. And if the Nasty Man
asks, you can tell him from me, I 'aven't got
nothing! He can kill me first!'

He spoke quietly, with long waits in between, as
if he was not in the habit of speaking and the
sound of his own voice took him by surprise. He
looked about him as well, his red eyes constantly

54

on the peel, though he gave Trim's packet, now lying in my hands, not a second glance. Then he got up and without another word, but keeping a steadying hand upon the wall, walked away. And that was that.

I watched him to the road and could not help but feel a stab of sympathy for him. Hadn't I been just as he was now? And how much would I have appreciated a kindness from a stranger! I thought he might at least take a sixpence from me (he looked as though it could not do him any harm) so I caught him up. But when I put my hand upon his shoulder, he jumped as if he had been scalded and cried out, 'No you don't, you devil!' and there was such a look of agony and horror upon his face that I was blown back also. He bolted across the road, dodging a cart and a pie man and, without looking back this time, plunged into one of the narrow alleyways between a baker's and Strang's bookshop.

Lovegrove, just returning, saw where he went, called after him and followed him a little way, but he was long gone.

And the fat man was also disappeared. The table outside Strang's was empty of customers, and the grampus was nowhere to be seen.

Will scratched his head.

'Where did he go, the fat man? Boy legged it, grampus melted away. Curious strange that, Bob, for if we go by Trim's account, they are a pair, in snacks together, the man and his number two.'

I produced the packet and we both inspected the contents.

'Dash my wig! *The Vulture's Bride*! And the boy gave you this? Well, I'll be a monkey's uncle – and Trimmer a happy man! But what a strange business, Bob! "The first time I've ever known a tail-buzzer return the nicks!" as dear old One-Eyed Jemmy Lightfinger would say!'

Will was eager to return the packet to its rightful owner and hurried back inside, while I, still with the boy and his strange associate in my mind's eye, ambled with Brutus and Nero up and down the street a little way. It is a busy place, bursting with small shops and stalls, eating places and food-sellers, and shifting crowds always, day and night. Quite typical of a theatre street, in fact. There are many small taverns, some hardly more than a single room, and others, like The Bell and Leper, which is closest to the Pavilion, are rambling buildings with a grand yard, concert room and dark little passages which wind around and about, and through which pass only the unwary or the thief (and occasionally both). The Bell and Leper had been open for business since early morning, and its dark passage was occupied now by little knots of people, mainly ladybirds and their customers and, hovering in the background, just out of sight, their bullies. This passage, or one like it, I thought, was where the boy had probably burrowed, but I had no desire to explore further and risk my purse and my throat. Nothing to be gained by that at all, even though a pretty ladybird was giving me the glad-eye, and inviting me over to be robbed and beaten.

I turned, intending to go back to the theatre. And there he was. On the steps of the Pavilion, with its white marble front and fine portico, he was leaning against one of the pillars, like a regular stroller I thought, and looking directly at me.

The grampus.

The fat man.

He was, just as Trim had described him, full faced and with a head as round and bald as a bladder of lard. He looked, for all the world, like a baby, but old in years, if such a thing can be imagined. And this sensation was increased by what might have been an amiable smile, except that it revealed teeth that were much too small for his mouth. A ghostly smudge of white on very pink gums.

He bowed and saluted with his hat.

'A fine morning, sir,' said he, gesturing to the sky. 'Though misty now, I think it will improve.' His voice took me by surprise. It was high, like a little child's. 'But – ah! – days in London, sir! What joy! What sweetness! These young ones' – and he gestured with a flourish to a group of four or five little girls playing on the steps – 'how they thrive, sir! Bloom and ripen! Their rosy lips! Their rosy cheeks! Red as a well-scratched slit!'

From beneath pale lashes, his eyes flickered, but whether he was gauging my reaction to his

57

obscenity, or looking at the children, I could not tell.

'One hopes, of course, that they are well-behaved. That their mothers chastise them often. With a stick, perhaps. Or a strap. To make them *good* children.'

This was the very man, I thought, described by Trim. There could not be two in all of London. There could not be two coats like his. Tailored to his massive form, allowing him easy movement, and beneath it, a light-coloured waistcoat, pale-yellow satin, I would say, and exquisitely brocaded. An old-fashioned crimson bow dropped beneath his bull chin. Down the steps he came, appearing to tiptoe, elegantly, lightly, for such a giant and, with his tiny eyes upon mine, extended an ungloved hand. Pale, fat fingers, like sausages in tight skins, and on each one were many rings, all smothered by a surfeit of flesh. The hand which grasped mine was warm and moist, and from him came a very pleasant aroma of good soap.

'You are a theatrical man I see, sir?' he said without preamble. 'Ah, what a profession! All the world is surely a stage, sir. And all the men and women merely players, as the great man said.' He was performing, surely. 'But just men and women, sir? What of the children? What of them, sir? With their soft limbs and willing temperaments. Ready to do our bidding, sir, or be whipped into obedience if they don't.' He put a finger to his mouth as if to suppress the giggle which, like a child's, high and uncontrolled, erupted from him. He rolled and guffawed and held his stomach, and produced a huge scarlet handkerchief and wiped his eyes and lips. And then he began again.

Repulsion is a strong word. It rarely springs to my lips, for I am a man who will generally tolerate the oddities of his fellows. But it defined this man, with his pink and fleshy face, his tight rotundity, his pleasant odour of warm pampering. Only good manners forced me to nod and smile whilst I tried to pull away, though he, still smiling (and how very small his teeth were!), held my fingertips firmly in his.

'My dear sir. I detain you. My chattering. Unforgivable. And your clever friends. Yes.'

Did he reach down and give Brutus's soft ear a tug? I think so, for my boy flinched and turned his brown eyes, questioningly, upon me.

'Do you have the packet about you, sir? I observed that the boy handed it to you before I could claim it. A very naughty boy. Taking things which don't belong to him.'

His face had grown pink now, and his eyes were narrowed into mere slits.

'Stealing's stealing, my little mother used to say, and whipped me soundly until my little cheeks were red and I was sent to bed. A bad boy.' He paused and tugged at Brutus's ear and wiped his face again with the scarlet handkerchief. But instead of replacing it in his pocket, he began knotting it. One, two, three, and so on, evenly along, and with a swiftness that was mesmerizing.

'So, sir, the boy, the packet. Containing the pictures, don't you know. Belonging to – another party – who is impatient for their return. Don't be stubborn, sir. *You* know, and *I* know you have it. Isn't that so, Brutus?'

My boy knows his name and looked up at the man with mild and trusting eyes.

'A noble animal, sir, and a noble name,' he said. '*I* have a name, Mr Chapman. They call me the Nasty Man. Ha. Perhaps it is familiar to you? In my green and tender youth I had a certain – reputation.'

Suddenly, the handkerchief, with its knots, was around Brutus's neck. My boy struggled and I put out my hand to stop the business, but the man caught it and slipped his fingers between mine, crushing them hard against the heavy rings, and drawing me into his breathing space.

'Don't signal to your other hound, or this one is dead. A skill once acquired, sir. One never loses it, does one? Believe me, I will rub out this creature with one hand before you can blink.'

He drew me closer.

'The Nasty Man, Mr Chapman. Definition? The apple-picker, sir. The pipe-player, sir. The g'rotter, sir,' and he gave a tug on the handkerchief, at which Brutus struggled wildly. 'I am more familiar with the human gullet, but I don't draw a line at a buffer's. I want the packet, sir, the one the boy gave you.' He was no longer smiling.

Brutus was choking and writhing and I struggled in the Nasty Man's grasp. At length, pursing his lips, he released us, and I grabbed both dogs and pulled them away. Brutus, panting and wide-eyed, fixed himself to my leg, whilst Nero growled low. I rubbed my throbbing fingers, which were already bruised and beginning to swell.

'Now, you are perfectly sensible as to our arrangements, my dear sir? And the consequences? You would not wish to lose your position, sir. Not given these difficult times and the favour with which you are generally regarded. It would be an evil day, sir, if a wicked tale were put about. One which besmirched your good reputation.'

It was as if he were a different man! His voice, the manner in which he spoke, the words which fell from his mouth in a stream, without pause. Not vile and dirty, but as though they were slicked with butter! He inclined his head, nodded, raised his eyebrows. We might have been a couple of acquaintances, passing the time of day.

He wanted the packet and its contents. He had followed the boy, seen him give it to me. *Ergo*, I must know him. He tried to snatch the boy, but he got away again. He was tired of the business. He didn't need to repeat himself, did he? There would be undesirable consequences for me if I persisted in my stubbornness. He would find me again. He was sure I understood.

61

Then, as though we had finished our conversation with pleasantries and he had pleaded an appointment with a clergyman, he smoothed his coat, adjusted his rings, saluted me and said, with a smile that revealed again that smudge of teeth and pink gums, 'Brutus. Nero. Sir. A pleasure. A pleasure indeed.'

He moved slowly along the street with an easy step, as though he owned it. Not simply because he was so large that people had to step aside to let him pass. Nor that he smiled and nodded with beguiling amiability. But it was the authority with which he did everything, from the tipping of his hat, to the flashing of his rings, even to the wearing of his coat, which waved about his ankles but never once drifted into a puddle or glanced a cabbage leaf. With two fingers, he delicately pinched up his skirts so that they were not dirtied, not a thread of them. Any other man might be reckoned a regular Margery and called after in the street. But not this man.

Never this man.

CHAPTER 4

A MORNING WALK –
STRONG'S GARDENS

I spent a restless night, which is uncommon for me. My boys, too, were unsettled. And I knew why, for the Nasty Man was like a smell which lingers in your nose and will not be got rid of, no matter how much lavender and lime you splash about. Sleep would not come, and worries had begun to take up residence in its place, so we got up with the milkchurn, and set out for Strong's Gardens.

I recognize the onset of melancholy – a condition I have lived with for many years – and I know that if I treat it early, I can put it away. And as my boys and I stepped it out briskly in the chill air and worked up a glow – for it is easy to walk these early streets, with no crowds and little noise – I began to feel easier with the world. We made good time, and needed to, for this was no leisurely meander. Before we returned to the Aquarium, we must reach a bridge, wide enough for two carts, and with steps at each end for those on foot, where the water is clean and, in the shallows, clear enough to see fish. There are grassy banks on either side on which ducks roost, and there are those trees which dip their leaves and branches into the water. Beyond the bridge, hardly a sparrow's hop, is Strong's Gardens and, as we legged it out, I pictured it getting closer and closer. I always take heart as the houses become villas and then cottages, and there are fewer warehouses and more blacksmiths, for these are signs that the countryside, with its clean air and green fields, grows ever closer. We quickened our steps when, round the last bend in the road, the bridge came into view. Then Brutus and Nero scurried down the bank and plunged into the river, scattering ducks and sending up waves. They are not great swimmers, for they are not accustomed to water, but they do enjoy, I think, the cold water on their bellies and feet, and in the warmer weather they stand on the sandy bottom drinking in great gulps and watching the ducks float by. For my part, I am happy to wait for my boys to quench their thirst and I take pleasure in their enjoyment, and in the anticipation of our goal.

Today, although the sky was grey and the air chilly, we were still cheered to see the little bridge and the trees and the river, and Brutus and Nero enjoyed the water, though it was cold and they risked only a dip rather than a plunge. I sat on the step by the bridge and paused to watch the carts go past. Mostly, it is the early greens that go rattling over the cobbles, when the dozy carters (some of whom have travelled through the night) begin to rouse themselves and boys' heads appear among the watercress and cabbages. They are so very much *of* the country, and by no means can they be mistaken for a city carter. It is not simply their manner which is generally slower and gentler, but something more. Sometimes they do bring the country with them into the city streets. In summer, for instance, many carters have a sprig of buttercups behind their ear, or in their hat a rose or a twist of ivy plucked from the hedgerow. In the winter months, I sometimes notice a blade of grass caught in the horse's harness, and then I think of the farm they might have come from and the clean simplicity of that life. Perhaps, turning out of its yard, waiting for his master to close a gate or call to his boy, the patient carthorse tugged at a tuft of grass and enjoyed its freshness, his last taste of the countryside before the city. And, because of his eagerness, a blade or two is caught in his harness and travels with him, through the night, along the lanes, a gentle reminder that there is home and a comfortable stable after his hard day's labour. As a child, I lived for a while among fields and hills, and it was perhaps the happiest time of my life and why I take pleasure now in earth and sky rather than bricks and buildings. The city is all I have known for many years, but I have sweet memories of yellow fields of corn and the smell of the rain upon dry earth, and those remembrances will calm my terror of the shadows and sweeten dark melancholy.

We had our destination in view now, and following the carts over the bridge and along the road a way, we came to a little fence and a sign that said 'Strong's Gardens. Finest Quality Vegetables. Suppliers to Royalty'. I unlatched the gate and we went in. This was the spot, and it gives me such pleasure to come here that, sometimes, I have waited by the bridge just to make the pleasure of arriving last a little longer! Today though, my boys were ahead of me, bounding down the path, on either side of which are fields of cabbages, all as neat and tidy as a widow's pocket. At the end of the path is a small house (once a lodge, I think, for this area belonged to a lord and there was a great house, long since destroyed) and, in the doorway, Mr Titus Strong. He is built like one of his horses – broad-shouldered, a strong head and a clear eye – and, like them, good-natured. The best of men. He is perhaps sixty years of age (it is difficult to be certain for, to me, he has always looked the same), but he it was who gave me friendship and a kindly word when I was in great need, and who I visit whenever I can.

We went into the kitchen and I sat at the scrubbed table and watched him cut bread and bacon and fill a cup with strong tea. He pushed the plate towards me and bade me 'Eat well and God be wi' ye, Bob' (for he is a religious man of the Methodist persuasion and struggles to keep it to himself) whilst he fetched scraps and water for

Brutus and Nero. Then he settled himself opposite me and filled his own cup and talked about the Gardens and the crops, what cabbages will fetch and how he had bought strawberry plants 'to try out and see if they will do anything' this year. After I'd supped, he picked up his hat and stick and we went out into the chill air. The gardens were misty and damp, and the cabbages rose like so many heads from the ground. We took this path and that, winding in and out, and my friend pointed to 'that plot, Bob, by the big plum tree, where I shall try artichokes this year and see if they will do anything'. That is his philosophy: to 'see if it will do anything'. Never forcing a crop, but tending the soil and the seeds and making the beds just so with spade and muck, and then simply watching and waiting. For if he has a quality which rises above all others, it is that of patience.

'And now, Bob, you know what I want to hear. Have you seen her, my Lucy?'

Brutus and Nero lingered at either side of him and when he touched their heads, ever so lightly, they wagged their tails in appreciation. He smiled down at them.

'These are your children, Bob. You care for them, keep them safe. You would give your right arm to protect them.'

I thought of the Nasty Man and his wicked handkerchief.

'I hoped you had come with news of *my* child. But I see you haven't.'

He struggled to control his grief, and coughed loudly, turning away so that I shouldn't see his tears. But his wife, Grace, had, coming through the gate with a basket of eggs. She was tall, very tall, and with features which, though never beautiful, were striking. A man might look twice at her, though if they stared, she was not above giving them a terrific tongue-lashing.

'Her past,' Titus Strong once said to me, 'is still her present. She was a circus child and as wild as a feral cat when I found her and brought her to God. But though He has multiplied her affection and tenderness, He has not yet seen fit to curb her tongue.'

'Bob,' she said to me with a smile, and then took her husband's hand in hers. 'Now then, my dear, what's all this? Lucy again?' She turned to me. 'I tell him: Lucy will be found when she wants to be found, and not before. You must let her be, and not pester Bob to go out looking for her.'

When I first worked in the city, feeling that I should oblige my old friend, I went out and searched for Lucy Strong, who had run away from home to follow an actor. This fellow had, of course, ruined her and deserted her almost immediately, and she was ashamed to return to her parents. That was the tale Strong told himself, and who was I to dispute it? I diligently tracked the streets in search of her. Knowing that her lover was an actor, I visited the back door of every theatre, high and low, and scoured the taverns and publics which actors visited, but it was like seeking a pearl in a hailstorm. Had she changed her name? Or joined the profession? That was possible, but made her no easier to find. Eventually, though it pained me to see her father's desperate conviction that Lucy would be found, I was ever more convinced that she was lost, sunk so low that she felt her shame was intolerable. And I think Mrs Strong was of the same opinion, though she would not break her husband's heart by saying so. But I have seen her shake her head and bite her lip as he spoke of his hope of finding Lucy.

In the chill of that winter morning, in the midst of cabbages and kale, I realized I had much to be grateful for: my good friends, Will and Trim, Mr Abrahams, a kind employer, and Mr Carrier too, perhaps. A clean room in a tidy neighbour-hood and a life which, strangely, suited me. Bar the unpleasantness of the past few days, it was mostly peaceful, and if I could keep this calm and ordered way of being, it was a life I could be happy with. My needs are few, I live simply enough so I can afford to put a little money by. I save a penny here, sixpence there. Sometimes a shilling. And not for my old age! A year ago, in this very kitchen with his wife frying bacon in a pan on the fire, Titus Strong put a proposition to me.

'Now then, Bob, we know each other pretty well now. How many years is it since you came here, broken-down and weary?'

A long time ago, I thought. Ten years? Who

knows? Time flies apace. But once there was a pale young fellow, with no money and no heart. And along came Titus Strong, with an arm swelled up like a balloon (it had turned septic), and a shilling in his pocket for a man to drive a cartful of cabbages to a city market and back. He gave me that shilling and a hearty dinner and, when I returned, a bed for the night in the tool-shed. The following morning, he gave me another sixpence and a slice of bread and bacon, and reminded me that honesty towards my fellow man would bring its own reward. And to be sure and visit him if I ever strayed that way again. Which I did and have done ever since.

'He talked about you all the next day and for weeks after,' said Mrs Strong. 'He said, as soon as he saw you, he knew you wouldn't make off with his cart and horse and a load of cabbages. Mind you, his judgement is not always up to Solomon's,' she continued. 'There have been them who have led him a right dance. What about the lad who robbed you of every spade and shovel, hoe and trowel, you owned?'

Strong laughed. 'Aye, and the wheelbarrow to carry them away with!'

The fire crackled and the bacon spat in the pan. We sat for a long time, until Mrs Strong clicked her tongue impatiently.

'Well, Mr Strong? Are you going to keep Bob waiting here till the final trumpet? What about your proposition?'

Titus Strong frowned.

'I was putting together the right words in my head, Grace, my dear, before my tongue uttered them.' He paused and stared at me long and hard. 'Well, Bob, we know each other pretty well. After all these years, I've come to think of you like a son – and you've always shown an interest in the gardens – and I'm not as young as I was – and – well, I'd like you to consider – whether it wouldn't be half a bad idea – if you were to come into the business – in a small way to start with. Your own cart? And some customers to take care of? Think about it, eh?'

'Something to consider, for the future, Bob,' put in Mrs S.

'Indeed,' said Strong. 'No decisions necessary today, lad. Give it a thought, that's all. And I will pray on it to the Lord and listen to Him. We'll talk about it again.'

That was a year ago. Now, warm and comfortable back in the kitchen, I noticed Titus Strong's Bible on a little table by his chair, snug up to the fire, where the kettle was rumbling away.

'Bob,' he said, 'you remember that matter I mentioned to you? About you coming into the business? Well, the Lord has put it in my mind again this week.' He patted the Bible. 'He tells me it's time we made some plans.'

Mrs Strong smiled. 'To speak plainly, Bob—'

'Nay, Grace,' said her husband, sharply. 'This is my tale. My moment in the sun.'

'Look sharp, then,' she retorted, good-humouredly. 'Bob hasn't got all the time in the world like some market-gardeners!'

'Well then,' said my friend. 'Bob. We have talked about you coming into the business. We've agreed that you should start with your own bit of trade. Get yourself some regular custom in the city, a regular run to the market, and out to his Lordship in the season.' (This was Lord Bedford, or some such titled gentleman, whose table Titus Strong supplied.) 'I want to take my ease a little more.'

Mrs Strong was listening carefully, that elegant face still and serious.

'So I have decided, Bob, that come the spring, you shall, if you want it, have an interest in this place. Now, you'll need a horse and cart, and I cannot give you that. I have only the one and I still need it myself, for I have my customers and my local trade. But, if you can raise the money and buy a good cart, not wormy and falling asunder, and a horse that will not need the services of the knacker-man within six months, then you and I can sit at this table and, as they say, "agree terms".'

Mrs S shifted in her seat. 'He has talked about it to me, Bob, and I am in agreement.'

She had a beautiful smile, which she turned upon him and, for a moment, I envied my old friend. Grace Strong was perhaps twenty years younger than her husband. Even more. And yet there was such love and affection between them, they might have been a young couple in the honey-days of their marriage. He took her hand and kissed it.

'Now, Bob,' he said, 'will you give my proposal your best attention? And give me an answer the next time you call? And I hope that will be before Christmas?'

I drank tea and ate a slice of Mrs Strong's plum cake, and warmed my toes on the fender. Brutus and Nero, with much sighing and snoring, lay at our feet, stretched out in front of the range, toasting their bellies and only raising their heads to enjoy a scratch, and I thought, this could be my life, one of industry and ease, work and comfort. It had much to recommend it, and with only a little effort on my part, by the new year, it could be within my grasp.

We set out for the Aquarium with a light step and a warm heart.

CHAPTER 5

FISH-LANE – PILGRIM AND
THE OTHER – TIPNEY'S GAFF

We made good time – I have worked out a route through the back streets which avoids the congestion of the main thoroughfares. Besides, I had a lot to consider. With the extra work at the Pavilion, I could save more, but I would have to work harder at the Aquarium to make up for the hours lost. Mr Abrahams, I was sure, would be accommodating, but I could not be all the time away from my stand, otherwise he would give it to someone else. Or I'd be forced to share it. All of this was ravelling through my head whilst we walked, but I was glad to have something heartening to dwell upon.

Our route took us along Fish-lane, a strange, crowded street of dark, little shops selling stale cakes and flat ginger beer alongside candles and coal, and a few establishments which considered themselves a cut above the rest. Freeth's, a theatrical bonnet-maker's, was the first one we came to. And a little further along, Hadzinger who dealt in boots. And Miss Bailey, a mantle-maker and hairdresser. Then a wine shop and a barber's and a tiny tailor's shop – all without a name, wanting to keep themselves quiet, as it were. Then Pilgrim's bookshop, which was thin and tall, with a bulging window. The glass was thick, like bullseyes, so that trying to see the books and engravings behind it was like looking through a bottle bottom, where everything was out of shape and woolly about the edges. Outside, flapping in the wind, were art journals and old serials pegged on sticks, and little trays of books on a table covered with sacking to keep out the damp. Pilgrim was an old friend (we met long ago in a place we never speak of) and he told me that he inherited the shop from a distant cousin and, though he was not at all bookish, resolved to keep the business because of family 'obligations'. It was wedged between a rusty-looking hardware shop on one side and the blank windows of a shop which changed owners as often as dogs barked in this neighbourhood. Long ago, this neighbouring shop had been a dairy, with a single miserable-looking cow stalled in the rear. Then it became an undertaker's, a fruiterer's and last, and most recently, a haberdasher's. Even that had failed, and now it was closed, though never unoccupied, for the yard was always crowded, and these days it was impossible to leave anything out, for whether it was the crown jewels or a feather duster, it would be stolen in a blink. Pilgrim had been concerned about this empty place for some weeks and not just because of the rats, which had increased fifty-fold. The neighbourhood was losing its character by the week, he said darkly.

75

He was peering from his doorway as we hurried down Fish-lane, a curious sight in his tasselled smoking hat, embroidered with fabulous birds, and a knitted comforter complementing his fir-green working coat and fingerless gloves. And, of course, there was no creeping past for, as if he had been expecting us, he nodded us into the shop, bolted the door and drew the blind.

'Now then, Bob. Nero. Brutus.'

Now then indeed, I thought, stepping around the piles of books and papers, the teetering towers of three-deckers and two-parters, and charting a course through the shop in Pilgrim's wake. He had already disappeared into the gloom, where the flame of a solitary candle was the only beacon for us lone sailors. Shelves and stacks lined the walls, tables were buried under volumes which had not been opened let alone read for many a year, and in the darkest depths of the shop, a veritable cavern of books which, had they been piled by Sir Christopher Wren himself and cemented by his own dust and cobwebs, could not have been better built. Pilgrim's bower was a masterly example of books laid in good English bond, and it fitted around him like his own skin. He was already in there pouring tea into two cups (I was glad I couldn't see their condition, for my friend was a stranger to the scullery) and nodded me to a fifteen-volume history of the Macedonians (arranged vertically), on which I perched.

Pilgrim's oddness didn't present itself simply in

his curious shop and odd appearance. The towers of books and mouldering pamphlets, those oddments of velvet and chinoiserie, the hats, the regal Benjamins and sub-species britches, were only for display. When he spoke, you would realize that there was more to Pilgrim than just an eccentric dresser. You would realize that he was, in fact, two men in one body, and that these two men were sometimes opposites. One mild, the other wild. One reasonable, the other argumentative. One careful in speech, the other given to cursing. Today they lived quite amicably together, taking it in turns to speak, but tomorrow they might erupt and disagree.

'Now then, Bob,' said gentle Pilgrim, 'here is a thing. Them creatures next door.'

('Ah, they. Who are they?' said wild Pilgrim.)

'Bob Chapman knows them.'

('Does he? How is that?')

'Same trade. They are Irish, Scotchmen, a Frenchy, a Polick. Men and women. Young 'uns too.'

('How should Bob Chapman know them?')

'Strollers, you fool. Have you no brain? Mummers. Theatricals. Grubbers.'

('Grubbers?')

'The lowest. Gaff-actors.'

('Ah, there you have it, Bob Chapman. A nest of gaff-actors and all the kindling-thieves this side of Newgate pouring in of an evening.')

We drank our tea in silence, and I wondered

what was coming and how I might make an exit, for I was thinking of the time and being at my place when Pikemartin opened the Aquarium doors. And, for once, I was not thinking of the Nasty Man or the boy or any of that business.

The candle perched on a book in Pilgrim's bower was only a tuppenny one and threatened all the time to plunge us into darkness or burn through and keel over, when we would all go up like a fireship, part and parcel. I shifted on the history of Macedonia and my two boys, squeezed as tight as three shillings in a Jew's purse underneath a table of stacked music, started to peel themselves out. Pilgrim cocked an ear.

'Hear that?'

('I do. What of it?')

'Banging day and night. They are setting up.'

('Call in the peelers.')

'Not on your life! What? And have my throat cut in my bed and all my assets, inherited with obligations, cleared out and sold on a barrow? What kind of a fool do you take me for?'

('Bob Chapman is silent on the matter.')

I was brushing the cobwebs from my good trousers and trying not to cause an avalanche of books. But perhaps I didn't need to be so careful, for the thunderous activity from the empty shop next door was already creating little tremors in the mountainous regions of print and paper, and ominous clouds of dust were gathering in the dark and lofty canopy above.

'Bob Chapman has his own business to attend to,' Pilgrim replied to himself and followed us to the door, and then onto the street, where he cast a suspicious eye at his neighbours.

There was activity next door, that could not be denied, and a deal of it, though whether it was demolition or destruction was difficult to say. Half the boarding of the front windows had been taken down to let in light, and I could see the black hump of the old shop counter, half-buried under rubble and timber. One of the toilers, a burly individual with a broken conk and a hostile disposition, appeared.

'Clear off!' growled he, and he brandished half a brick and a lump hammer to add weight to his point. 'Private property. No, 'awkers, beggars or religious!'

'We are none of those,' piped up Pilgrim, 'but occupy next door.'

('Until we are forced otherwise.')

'Clear off back there then,' he growled, closing one eye, 'and mind *that* business, not this one.'

'You see the problem, Bob Chapman?'

Well, I saw boxes and barrels among the bricks and rubble, and a pack of dogs, muzzled and tied up, with red eyes and scarred noses, and some shifty-looking coves, trying not to be seen out the back. I saw also that it was time for us to depart, since the church bell was chiming and, more to the point, the Growler was still meditating upon whether to clock us with the hammer or the half brick.

'Come back and see whether we are still in our skins, Bob Chapman, or if the savages have turned us into purses!'

('He will. He is a good friend, is Bob Chapman. And his handsome associates.')

The Growler looked at me, and then at my boys, and curled a lip to go with the one eye.

'Yourn? Handsome! Do they scrap?'

We hurried away with the laughter of the Growler and the assurances of Pilgrim rattling our ears, and with some relief reached the quiet and stillness of the Aquarium.

It was not time yet to fling open its great doors. The hallway was dark; noises from upstairs signalled that Alf Pikemartin was opening up the shutters in the salons and sweeping the floors, so we hiked up the grand staircase, past the execution chamber and the display of hangman Calcraft's rope and bag, and the Happy Family – cats, mice and birds, all stuffed and nicely mounted in their box – to the second floor. My canine friends, of course, required no bidding, and went ahead of me to their work. Each morning we follow the same order, Brutus and Nero going up to our salon – a name which dignifies what is really a small space, partitioned off, in a much larger room – where Brutus will open the large door (one of his tricks) and Nero will lead the way down the central aisle to our platform, which has been closed off by a screen for the evening and which I remove to the back wall every morning. We retire behind this screen between exhibitions and keep our few 'properties' there, and a little stove. In front of it there is a small platform, approached by four steps, which sets us up just high enough for the spectators at the back to see our show. It is a simple affair.

After our early start and the business with Pilgrim, I was looking forward to dropping anchor behind the screen and enjoying a hot, sweet brew (in a clean cup) and perhaps forty winks, but – here was a strange thing – climbing the last few steps, I found Brutus and Nero not disappeared into our salon, but waiting on the landing, where the cabinet of waxen eyes was displayed. (Every morning I wished that Mr Abrahams would put them somewhere else, for it was unnerving to have them staring out so naturally from that dim corner.) The door to our salon was open, and Nero was growling his low warning grumble, while Brutus stood quite still, sniffing the air. It was quiet on the landing, only a fly buzzed in the dusty window, but it was as clear to me as it was to my dogs that something was amiss. If it had been dark or getting towards evening, I would have fetched Pikemartin and together we would have investigated. (Once before, we were obliged to seek out an intruder, an escaped convict, who we discovered hiding behind a sarcophagus and who, in his struggle to retain his liberty, gave Pikemartin a sore head with a blow from an ancient cooking pot.) But it was scarcely eleven o'clock in the morning, the public were not admitted, and I could not believe that footpads and desperate criminals were abroad so early. So I followed Nero into the large room, with Brutus at my side and an assegai in my hand for protection.

There was light enough to see the cases of insects, the display of shields and swords from a Welsh castle, the grand termites' nest and part of the trunk of a giant tree discovered in the New World and brought back by a relative of Mr Darwin. I touched Nero's back and he went about his business, and with his nose to the floor, sniffed and snuffled in every corner and then stopped and looked back at me with a puzzled expression. It was as if he was saying, 'I don't understand, Bob. I could have sworn someone was here.'

Certainly there was no one about, for we peered behind every cabinet and inspected every jar and pot, and threw open the shutters wide, the better to inspect the darker corners. But no, there were only spiders and dust and that feeling, hanging in the air, that someone *had* been there who was not long gone. If we had straightaway gone out onto the back landing, I think we might have spied someone on the stairs, and certainly we heard footsteps upstairs in the menagerie, but there are always strange noises coming from up there.

I have my own ways and like everything ship-shape. I like order and to be able to lay my hands upon something, knowing exactly where it is, so my refuge behind the screen, though it is small, is also very neat. I have hooks for my coat and costume; a shelf for my tea box and pot, and for my boys' water dish and their biscuit-tin; another shelf of books, for I enjoy reading in the brief lulls between performances; and there are boxes containing properties for our show. One for balls, one for eggs (property eggs, not real), another for ribbons and ropes, and one for the letters that Brutus takes out and opens. All carefully arranged, with their lids tight on. Except that this morning, they weren't, and I didn't discover it until I was almost ready to begin the first exhibition. I went to the box which contained the balls and discovered that someone had been here, had opened the lid and not replaced it properly. The boxes were disordered also. Those which contained the lantern and the cannon ball were always at the bottom, but now were on the top. My little tea box had been emptied and roughly refilled, for there were tea leaves strewn upon the table, and even the rug on which Brutus and Nero lie had been taken up and shaken about. Someone had been there and gone quickly through my few belongings, looking for – well, I could not imagine – and made a hasty attempt to disguise it. I was more upset than I could explain, and though my few things were easily restored and there was nothing of any value among them, I felt out of sorts and hardly inclined to continue.

But a sizeable crowd had assembled, and were

even now gathered around the platform and chattering, as they do, about the 'remarkable dogs' and their cleverness and bravery. So I took off my outdoor coat and put on my costume and set about my business. My dogs, knowing *their* business, were already in position, wagging their tails to show their keenness, and so we gave the story of *Mungo Park*, in which Nero assists in the liberation of the African (myself) by slipping off my chains and his own, and unbarring a wicket gate (stage scenery, of course, but still accurate in every respect). Then a comfortable-looking woman on the front row piped up, 'Give us the one about the dog with the poorly foot!' and there were approving murmurs of 'Yes, that's a clever trick!' And then a clerkish gent put his hand into his pocket crying, 'A shilling for you, Chapman, if your dog howls on cue and with feeling!' How could I refuse! A shilling towards the cart and horse and balmy days in Strong's Gardens! So we gave, with all our skill, *The Lion of the Desert*, in which Brutus imitated the story of Androcles and the lion, and limped as though he had a thorn in his foot, howled as though it pained him, and then growled when he first offered it to me to examine. Then he licked my hand in gratitude as I removed the thorn, which appeared to have been deep in his paw but which was, in fact, secreted in my hand. Our sponsor was very pleased, and roared, 'Bravo, Brutus! Bravo, Chapman!' and tossed a shilling into the plate. Finally, we gave a selection

84

of tricks: Brutus opened a box and removed a letter, carried a lantern, with a candle in it, and placed it on the ground without tipping it over or causing the light to go out. Then Nero took an egg out of a pail of water without breaking it, rang a bell by pulling on a rope, and both dogs nosed a light cannon ball across the platform and stopped it with their paws.

It was a good exhibition, full of variety, and I was pleased that Brutus and Nero showed their skills, and the people who paid their pennies to come and see us were so appreciative. We gave half a dozen exhibitions like this, and I hardly stopped to breathe, as they say, which helped me more easily to put aside the unpleasantness of earlier events. But when the evening dropped down and the room was quiet, I fell to thinking about it and felt heavy again with that melancholy that comes over me when I am upset. No wonder that my hand shook as I scraped the stray tea leaves from the table and straightened my pot and cups. My little collection of books were all awry, pulled off the shelf and shoved roughly back, and the picture of the Queen, which was propped on the top, had slipped behind and only her crown was showing. It quite sent me off my hinges and I made haste to go home to be rid of the world and back in my own little room, safe and sound.

Upstairs it was all quiet, but for the gentle rumble of Bella, the lioness: Conn was shutting up the menagerie for the night. In one of his rare moments of conversation, he once told me that the animals know when the Aquarium has closed.

'They fall silent,' he said in his own strange tongue, half-Irish, half-darkie (for he was of a mulatto strain). 'The apes stop swinging from the bars and sit in their corners. Birds stop calling. Bella, she lies down and sings herself a lullaby.'

Bella was the great golden lioness that Mr Abrahams had bought from a travelling menagerie, along with her keeper, Conn.

'Old Bella, that fine, fierce girl, she knows well enough about everything that goes on. She keeps her teeth back though.'

Conn was as affectionate in speech about Bella as I was about my dogs, but there the similarity ended, for I could pet and play with Brutus and Nero, but Conn could only stand and stare at the bars of the cage.

'She had me once, Bob,' he confided, when I had taken a packet of medicinal powders up to him for Bella's skin, 'and she will bide her time until she can finish me. Look into them old eyes, will you, and tell me if they are not full of love and blood-lust.'

Indeed, I could not say! Riddles dropped easily from Conn's lips and when his voice faded to a whisper, it was difficult to know whether he was in all seriousness or in drink, for he did have a weakness in that area. When he was overcome, he would stagger up to the menagerie to sleep in an empty cage, and later would terrify Nightman (a nameless dwarf employed to mind the menagerie through the night hours), who never quite got used to Conn's habits. One gloomy afternoon I discovered Conn crouched upon the second landing, nursing a bottle and clutching by the tail a petrified lizard from one of the cabinets. He caught it, he said, when it was trying to steal away. And as he drained the bottle, he said more. About his life on the road. The travelling menagerie. The woman he had loved and lost. And Bella, the lioness, raised by him from a cub, who one day turned upon him and tore the flesh from his back and arm.

'Here,' he whispered, tearing at his back, 'is where she laid her claws upon me and caressed my spine! And here is where her mouth kissed my shoulder and arm till I thought I should die from the pain.'

He talked of his nights of agony, of the pain endured as doctors struggled to stem the blood and sew up the flesh – 'with thread so fine you couldn't see it' – and the fever and delirium which sent him nearly mad.

'They tied me to my bed, Bob, and I howled like a dog, and wanted to die. Who would not want to die, in my place, with a back torn to shreds and an arm useless. I begged Holy Jesus to take me, but He wouldn't. And as I screamed and howled, Bella roared back to me. Talked to me. Beast to beast. 'Next time,' she cried, 'next time it shall be the rapture for you.' And that,' he said, laying a hand upon my arm, 'is death.'

Then the drink overcame him and he slumped under the Roman table, with his head upon the petrified lizard. I laid his coat over his shoulder and dragged a rug across him to hide him from the visitors, for he was much troubled and I couldn't help but pity him. In his drunken rages, he would pull off his shirt to reveal the terrible wounds which the lioness had inflicted upon him – 'Look at my back, Chapman!' he would cry. 'Get a cloth and stop the blood before I bleed to death!' But when I examined his back and shoulder, there were no gouges of flesh and skin, no torn muscle and ragged sinew, no raw wounds, still open and bleeding, as he often claimed. Just the hard, white stripes of childhood beatings, like the grain in wood, deep and ridged. Scars of the belt and the lash applied often and long to his young skin and paining him still, so much so that he had to invent a story to account for them. Bella, the lioness. The nearest thing to a family Conn had ever had.

But whether she had mauled him or not, Bella was the most vocal of the creatures in the menagerie, and she could be heard all over the Aquarium. From a terrifying roar, which made my two boys stop in their tracks, to the gentle rumbling lullaby which I could hear now. Unlike Conn, I couldn't tell what she was saying but, having already had an unwelcome visitor to my stand, I wondered if something might be amiss. So it was out of concern for the animals and Conn, and the disquiet over that earlier intruder, that I mounted the gloomy back stairs to the menagerie, what Mr Abrahams called the 'service stairs', the route by which Conn brought up straw and animal food, and used by all of us if we wanted to avoid general scrutiny. The stairs were plain and bare, narrow and dimly lit, not intended to be seen at all, and had the advantage of leading to all parts of the building.

I opened the door and was greeted by the warm smell of animals and straw and the sound of them moving in their cages. Brutus and Nero sat, obediently, in the open doorway, their noses high, sniffing the unfamiliar scents, whilst I cautiously stepped in. Conn had turned down the lights and left, and all was dim and shadowy. It ran the whole length of the building, a great, high room with long windows and a skylight. Full of cages. When it was first opened, there had been fish up here, in an aquarium, the biggest in all London, according to Mr Abrahams.

'But,' said he, 'the weight of a tank full of water, you know, Bob, caused the floorboards to sag, so it had to go. I sold it to a man from Manchester. In twenty parts, each one labelled separately. And the fish in buckets. I hope they survived the journey.'

He had looked sadly around the long room.

'I liked to come up here and watch the fish. My Mimi liked it too. We would sit together in the dark, and watch them. Peaceful, she used to say, like another world under the water. And she was right. It was popular, Bob. We had the only aquarium in the whole of the city that contained not only seasnakes, but a speaking fish too. In a separate tank, of course, and his own keeper. Pongo was the first talking fish since Jacko was exhibited in the Strand thirty years ago.'

He had pointed to a flash above the door.

'That's him. Pongo. A clever creature.'

It was still there, a painted board. 'See Pongo. The talking fish. He will count!! He will sing!!!'

But now, instead of a great glass tank in the middle of the floor, cages ranged as far as the eye could see, and the animals within, lizards and apes, pigs and snakes, as well as Bella, the lion, were crowded together like the inhabitants of a strange ark. A snuffling creature from Africa in a cage alongside a badger from Wales. Birds with feathers the colours of a rainbow fluttering in a cage next to one in which lay a sleeping fox. I peered into the tank of snakes where, in the corner, they were coiled and heaped, one upon another, and in the cage above it, a rabbit, grey and white, with ears that trailed upon the ground, its eyes bright and its nose twitching. Cage upon cage, they were crowded together, offending my sense of order and design, but that was not the worst of it for me. It pained me more acutely to see wild animals so confined, and so I rarely came up here. Brutus and Nero were similarly uneasy and would follow me into the room only if commanded, preferring to sit in the doorway as they did now. It was clear, as I walked along the range of cages where eyes blinked at me out of the gloom and Bella grumbled away, that there was no one here. No intruder, and surely nowhere for them to hide.

But passing Bella's cage, I realized that it was Nero and not the lioness who was growling, a low rumble in his throat, and barely audible except, perhaps, to me. I went quickly along the length of the cages to the door where he was now on his feet, growling still and looking hard at the flight of stairs up to the attics where, standing at the top, framed by the open door, was Mrs Gifford.

'Chapman. Why are you still here? And what are you doing, creeping about like a burglar? You're fortunate I haven't called the constable and had you run in.'

I wanted no truck with this woman and started down the stairs, but she was not about to let me go and hurried after me.

'Just you wait there, Chapman. Don't you budge an inch!'

I waited, though it pained me to obey her and she caught me up, standing three or four steps above me and staring me out.

'If you have interfered with anything in there, Mr Abrahams shall know about it,' she said. 'You've no business in there, Chapman. Your place is on the second floor.'

She continued finding fault, reminding me of my place, complaining about my dogs, the untidiness of my workplace, and yet all the time was looking beyond me, over my shoulder, never meeting my eye, until – was it my imagination? – I heard the soft thud of the front door closing, when she released me with a peremptory 'Good night'.

I felt as though she had kept me there on purpose, and when I reached the hall, I stood for a moment, as it were, in another's breath. There was an unfamiliar scent upon the air and when I looked up, Mrs Gifford was still there, leaning over the banister.

CHAPTER 6

THE PAVILION THEATRE – EM PIKEMARTIN

I am a busy man these days, for I have prospects in view, to which end I have been scouring the 'For Sale' columns and found a number of market carts which will fit my bill (and pocket, eventually), and horses too. I have made calculations and worked into them the cost of feed and stabling and general upkeep – things which I think Mr Strong would be pleased I had considered. I feel as though I am almost a man of business!

But I must earn and save the money to do it, so I had my work at the Aquarium, giving six shows a day, and more on Friday and Saturday nights. And I was attending rehearsals at the Pavilion Theatre, where Mr Carrier had Brutus, Nero and myself in the cast of the Christmas extravaganza of *Elenore the Female Pirate*, to open (and Mr Carrier will not give way on this tradition) on Boxing Day. So I was constantly running between the Aquarium and the Pavilion, with my dogs at my heels. People who knew me in the neighbourhood (for it was small and close) started to notice, and called after me, 'Hoi, Chapman! Dragged again!' and 'Run, don't walk!' after Mr Scarsdale's humorous song 'Walk, don't run, Sonny Jim'. And when Mr Carrier got to hear about it, he suggested that, because I was well known now for trotting around the district with Brutus and Nero at my heels, I should make our entrance in *Elenore* in this fashion – on the trot, as it were!

Chapman's Sagacious Canines already had a name, of course, but a little extra attention in the exhibition business never goes amiss and helps to keep up numbers at my Aquarium show. Indeed, I believe one had already helped the other, and would increase in that way once *Elenore the Female Pirate* was running nightly at the Pavilion, for Mr Abrahams said more than once that he hoped Mr Carrier's enterprise was a success and had no doubt it would be a plusser for my business at the Aq.

My friend Trim had also been brought round, and with a little persuasion had agreed to include noble rather than villainous dogs in his extravaganza, though I think it took our good friend Will Lovegrove an entire evening of flattery and attention to the bottle to achieve this. Now he is a man whose hand I am happy to shake every time I see him! And I am glad to say that I saw him more often these days, and not just of a night in a fuggy room at the Cheshire Cheese, for he took to joining Trim and me at Garraway's for breakfast before rehearsals. Happy days indeed!

However, I could not forget the unpleasantness of the Nasty Man, and I wondered too about the boy, and why he returned Trim's precious package when he might simply have tossed it upon a dust-heap. And at night, when I was alone in my room, I thought about that generous action and how it had put me in the Nasty Man's eye, and I sometimes wished the boy had not been so kind and had consigned Trim's scribblings to the fire. But that was an uncharitable thought.

One morning, we were strolling to the Pavilion, Trimmer, Lovegrove and I, after a hearty breakfast at Garraway's (courtesy of Trim, who had just sold another blood-curdler to Messrs Barnard, but told us he had promises – 'More like agreements and memoranda, no less!' – from houses of even greater note). The extravaganza was almost complete, but only after many frustrating weeks of amendments and additions, and so many extra scenes appearing – and disappearing – every day, that I was completely mystified! Only last week, Mr Carrier announced that he had secured the services of Mons. Gouffe, the man-monkey, for whom poor Trim was obliged to invent what he called 'casual business' at a moment's notice. (Of course, we have not yet seen Mons. Gouffe, though a quantity of black ink has been used in 'puffing him' from here to Hackney.) Poor Trim was at his wits' end and swore that he would never again attempt an extravaganza and, indeed, would rather compose any number of *Little Jack Horners* or *Old Mother Hubbards* than invent another 'new and original' Christmas entertainment.

But that is the world of the stage. For my part, I attended the Pavilion when summoned; I put my boys carefully through their new pieces and even added a few novelties; I took my instructions carefully, and looked forward (with that hope and anticipation which so many theatricals embrace) to the multiplication of good fortune. 'How we apples swim, quoth the horse turd!', as Moses Dann, the Boneless Man, was fond of saying. A vulgar expression, but it always made me smile, especially when Dann whispered it in that wheezy, thin voice and clattered his teeth and put his bony hand upon his bony hip. But he was right. How very unexpected and delightful was my little success!

This morning, Mr Carrier called us up for a 'final reading' of *Elenore* and we were assembled on the Pavilion stage early, heads down and bowling along for, despite Trim's claims that it was a 'serious piece of dramatic writing', there was not so much dialogue, and Mr Carrier, who was 'reading in the business' and describing everything that happened, had much the largest part. There were but four pages or so to go before the Transformation Scene (which, much to Trim's disgust, Mr Carrier has insisted upon) and he was steadily steering the pirate crew to whoops of triumph as they captured the slave boat, claimed the treasure, released the captives, and the hero, Redland Strongarm, the handsome pirate (ably and heroically read by Will), was reunited with Susan Goodchild (Miss Bella

Jacques), the virtuous daughter of Dairyman Goodchild, but also cunningly disguised as the female pirate, Elenore.

'Ho,' cried Susan, 'I am discovered. Shall I surrender or stand and fight? What shall I do? Where shall I fly? All around me is terror and distraction!'

'Destruction,' murmured Trim, who is possessive of his words.

'Ho, how I wish my dear James was here! Then I would share with him my dreadful secret! I would reveal the awful truth! He loves me, Susan Goodchild, sweet and chaste. But will he still love me when he learns that I am Elenora, Pirate Queen of the High Seas and Mistress of the Hisp . . . Hisp . . .'

'*Hispaniola*,' put in Trim. 'And you are Elenore, *not* Elenora.'

Miss Jacques (pronounced 'Jay-cwees') bristled under his corrections, and sucked in her cheeks so that her breath whistled through the gaps in her teeth. She was a fair actress, but a poor reader. To see her fixed upon her cue book, her fingers pressing hard upon each word as if to force it off the page, was agony for all concerned. Usually she had Mrs Crockett at her elbow, a grey and mouldering lady who, according to Mr Lombard, had in her day been the toast of the Lane and the Wells, but now toasted herself nightly in cheap gin, and suffered the indignity of being a Boswell to Miss Jacques' unworthy Johnson. So Mrs Crockett it was who softly murmured the words into her ear and helped her con the lines, and suffered, for her pains, the many indignities Miss Jacques heaped upon her. But Mrs Crockett was indisposed today, and our leading lady was forced to shift for herself. She ignored the author and turned her complaints upon the manager.

'I must protest, Mr Carrier, about the quality of the copying.'

At which Mr Pocock's head shot up from his little table: he is the copyist (amongst his many other duties).

'It is always the same,' she thundered on, her voice rising with every syllable, 'perfectly h'awful! How I am supposed to read this wonderful drama proper is beyond myself!'

She smiled brilliantly at Trim.

I was thankful that Miss Jacques turned her nose up at me entirely, and did not even notice my dogs. For to be within her eye's orbit was to risk being battered about by one of her dramatic storms, and when she sat like a duchess, with a mantle around her shoulders and a ridiculous feather bobbing in her hat, glaring at everyone – except Trim, of course – she was difficult to sail around. Only Mr Carrier had the skill to chart that particular course.

'I will have Mr Pocock attend to it, Bella,' he returned, mildly, whilst the man in question continued to fix her with a very hostile gaze. 'Let us please continue to the end of the scene – and the end of the drama. And then we might all take care of our other business.'

There were murmurs of agreement, for the dinner-time bell was ringing at the Bell and Leper, in harmony with the collective belly rumbles upon the stage. Miss Jacques settled herself, and out came the gloved forefinger to find its place upon the page.

'Ho, James! My love! My sweet James! Would he not clasp me in his strong arms! Would he not fight them pirates!'

'Ah, Susan! My pirate sweetheart! He *is* here!' cried Will, giving the words his very best heroic emphasis. Redland Strongarm is, as everyone knows, none other than James Moreland, the lover of Susan, sent to sea by an evil uncle when he was but fourteen years old, captured by pirates, only to become a good and honourable pirate chief – were there such a profession! – and running his blacksmith's forge in the off-season.

'It cannot be!' cried Susan.

'Yes! Yes!' Will returned. 'Close your eyes, Susan, and trust the beating of your heart as it answers mine!'

Miss Jacques did just that, causing a ripple of laughter around the company. Everyone knew that she had her heart set upon Will Lovegrove, and it was a matter of some amusement that she would insist upon rehearsing, more than once, their passionate embraces. The laughter broke the order, and Mr Carrier seized the opportunity to quickly bring the reading to an end. He had few comments (none of them written down), but they were all to the mark.

'Ladies and gentlemen of the company – my customary remark at this point in the year. You will be, of course, by next rehearsal, as my provincial colleagues express it so prosaically, DLP: Dead Letter Perfect. Now to the leads. Pay more attention to your articulation, Mr Lovegrove, and try not to over-reach yourself. Miss Jacques – more charm, less archness, if you please. We are the virtuous heroine, not the comedy chambermaid. Mr Pettifer – I pay you to be comic, Mr Pettifer, not bucolic.' And so on.

The cast were not at all put out (except Miss Jacques, who bit her lip and tapped her foot) and allowed themselves a smile. They were to reassemble, concluded Mr Carrier, and work upon the ballets with Mons. Villechamps, and there would be costume fittings for the principals. 'Attend, if you please, at 2 o'clock.'

And then he turned to me. Brutus, Nero and I had sat patiently by the side of the stage, listening, I have to confess, with great interest to Trim's dramatic work. I had been party to the ebbs and flows of his dramatic temperament as the piece was revised and rewritten, and felt that I knew it thoroughly already. But hearing it performed, as it were, in its entirety for the first time and, even more, hearing Mr Carrier say, 'And here there will be business for Brutus and Nero' and 'At this point, Mr Chapman's dogs will bound upon the stage and seize the villain by the throat,' made it suddenly leap into life.

'Now, Mr Chapman,' he said, 'you will have, by the end of the day, a finished copy of your cues from Mr Pocock, and we will this afternoon finalize the detail of your pieces. If there is anything you require, anything at all, see Mr Pocock. I am sure you and your fine animals will be a great success. Good day to you, sir.'

And he shook my hand, and greeted both my lads with a pat upon the head and hurried away, pulling on his gloves and signalling to Mr Lombard. I felt as important a fellow as any upon that stage! Mr Pocock, busily scribbling at his little table, was copying *my* cues. Mr Pettifer was admiring *my* dogs and looking them over as if he was a judge at a show. And Will Lovegrove, who is *my* friend and received many admiring glances from the company, strode over and clapped *me* upon the shoulder saying, 'There you are, Bob. Didn't I tell you! Now, let's find ourselves a decent pie-shop for our dinners!' and steered me towards the stage steps down into the auditorium, with Brutus and Nero in train. What larks, indeed!

I had never seen the stage of the great Pavilion theatre 'undressed', as it were. Like most folks, I was used to seeing it set with scenery and occupied by actors, but to stand in the great central aisle and see the massive stage in a shambles, with properties for the evening performance covered over with cloths and with a London street scene half-suspended from the gridiron, and hear not the dramatic tones of actors' voices, but a chorus of clatters, thuds and hallooing, was strange. The half-dropped scene flew, as if by necromancy, into the rafters and was replaced by another (showing a blue sea and sky and a golden sandy shore) which rushed down from the heights of the flies and stopped, with inches to spare, above the stage floor. Palm trees made of lath and plaster appeared, and sandy-coloured hillocks, and from behind them appeared Mr Lombard, the scenery manager, with his hat clamped tight to his head, barking orders left and right. An asthmatic wheeze announced Mr Parry, the rehearsal musician, with his fiddle and a roll of music, and poor, over-worked Mr Pocock was forced to relinquish his table, chair and corner of the stage and shift to the front row of the auditorium.

'Bob, my old friend,' said Will, gently, 'I have been calling you these last five minutes! I fear you are bewitched by the stage, so I will consign you to its magic, and your noble Romans shall accompany me whilst I fetch us two mutton pies and a large jug.'

I could not argue with him, for I was indeed entranced by the noise and activity, and besides, this was something of a holiday for me. I had even put up a sign in the Aquarium – 'Chapman's Sagacious Canines – gone to the Pavilion Theatre' – just as General Tom Thumb did when he visited the Queen at Windsor! – though I was cautious to add in small letters at the bottom, 'Back later.' And after the anxieties of the last few days, I persuaded myself that I deserved a brief ticket-of-leave, so I shifted a seat cover and settled down to watch as if I had paid my sixpence and bought my ticket.

The stage hands, having cleared away the chairs under Mr Lombard's watchful eye, were set to their tasks – one reattaching a palm leaf to its trunk, another adding a dab of paint here and there to a boulder. A man with a face bound up with a large piece of dirty flannel, was crouching over the floats, collecting the dust and straw which caused so much trouble to Mr Pilcher when the gas was lit. Another swept and watered the floor and brushed the curtains. Everywhere I looked someone was hammering, painting, moving a property bush or hillock, all to the tune of Mr Parry, who was sawing away on his fiddle and practising his churchyard cough. Then, from the wings, appeared Mons. Villechamps, the dancing master, who clapped twice and summoned the children's ballet and their mothers, hundreds, it seemed, like a swarm of buzzing insects, all come from far and wide for examination and selection. With a whistle, Mr Lombard called off his men and they left with much muttering and shaking of heads. Now Mr Parry shifted himself to within eyeshot of Mons. Villechamps and the trials began.

The children were tried, some in twos and

threes, some singly. The good Monsieur was an exacting man and went about everything with a great deal of energy, racing across the stage, even standing in the aisle of the auditorium, and talking to himself in a Frenchy-English sort of way, putting his head first on this side and then the other. 'Theese leetle one? *Peutêtre.*' And then some Frenchy nonsense followed when he seemed to persuade himself and then nodded. '*Oui.* Yes. *Bon.* She ees good, this leetle one.' The 'leetle one' was a mite of perhaps four or five years with a round, a very round, pink face and golden curls like curd, tied up with a broad blue ribbon. She had no particular talent, but looked well, and her mama was mightily pleased and unable to suppress a grim smile when Monsieur said, 'You – *maman* – come and see me at the *finis.* We will discuss, *oui?*'

And so it continued. Monsieur liked to arrange his diminutive charges across the stage to ensure that there were no rank weeds amongst the daisies and violets. Some little ones were pointed at and summarily dismissed, with a 'You, *cheveux justes, oui,* number three. You must go. Too *grosse,* not 'andsome.'

Whereupon the child – small, thin, dark-eyed – looked around her, counted, gazed at Monsieur, saw him staring at her, realized that she was found wanting and, with head hanging low and tears already pricking her eyes, scurried away to the stage side and her mama's skirts, with ten dozen pairs of eyes watching her. Her mother, a narrow-lipped, hard-faced woman, with a baby bound to her breast, and another clinging to her side, was inclined to argue with the Monsieur, but she had no more chance of bettering him than a cat in hell without claws. Her Billingsgate was no match for his Frenchy-squashing, which was given fast and loud with many 'pah's and 'foh's and good dollop of 'yagh's for emphasis.

'She eees no gooood,' spat he. 'She eeees like *elephant*. So—' He stomped about the stage with his knees bent and his legs apart, his long arms dangling by his side. It was amusing, but nothing like the little creature who, though it had danced without any skill or grace, certainly did not lumber so grotesquely. And I thought it cruel to so shame the child who had tried her best, but was no coryphée. She wept as he mimicked her pathetic efforts, and the chorus of mothers and children sniggered, out of relief, I suppose, that he had not lit upon them. Finally, the mother gave up her protest, grabbed the child by her wrist and marched her away.

'*Alors*,' said the Monsieur, straightening his coat and smoothing his goatee, 'now we are rid of de *animale de zoo*, we can commence. *Les papillons, les oiseaux tropicaux, les insectes*, if you pleeese.'

Some fairies, butterflies, tropical birds and insects were very small indeed, and as the examination progressed, they became weary, and crept onto their mothers' laps and fell asleep for it was a long and tiring business.

'Cheeldren,' Monsieur began with the new cohort, 'I would la-ike you to show me your most bee-u-ti-fool pirouettte. Not like ze *elephant* – so.' He aped a lumbering circle of heavy steps. 'But la-ike de *papillons*. Now, and now, and now, and now, and now,' and drumming time with his cane whilst the mites staggered and spun like dizzy insects to the rollicking tune of Mr Parry's fiddle. At first, of course, it was a game, but soon little legs became tired and little arms cold, and there was no end to Monsieur's demands – 'be a leetle flow-er', 'make a leetle curtsey'. They were weary and fretful and it was only the iron will of their mothers (accompanied by fierce threats) which kept them there.

Two wet noses at my hand and an odour of gravy in my nostrils signalled the return of Brutus, Nero and Will, the latter bearing two mutton pies ('Handmade by Mrs Lovett, Bob!') and a stone jar of ale. He settled in beside me, putting his long legs up on the back of the seat in front and munching vigorously on the warm pie.

'So, my good friend, the joys of the stage, eh!' he said, between bites. 'Once you are stung by *apis histrionicus*, you are itching for life.' The theatre was dark, but I could hear in his voice the seriousness of his expression. 'Be careful, Bob. In the theatre, as in life, things are not always as they seem. We are magicians, illusion is our trade and for a few hours each night this little wooden platform, these foolish actors become whatever we – and you – desire them to be. But when Pilcher turns down the gas and Lombard rings down the curtain, this is no longer a sunny island and we are no longer pirates and heroes. It is just a put-together world, Bob, and not ever what it seems to be.'

What, I wondered, had brought about this seriousness? But he said no more on the subject and turned his attention to the poor children and how they appeared 'half starved and tired to the bone', and how their mothers attended more to the shillings than to their welfare. I have a fellow feeling with Will, for like me he is given to dark moods as well as gay ones. I put it down to his profession: a man cannot be so pressed and agonised each night by the heroes he represents without some effect upon his spirit. So we ate our pies in silence after that, and the spell was broken.

Once the stage emptied of children and began filling up again with the company, Mr Carrier reappeared. Miss Fleete, the keeper of the costume store, had been summoned, with her assistant, to measure the whole cast of principals for their dresses and to discuss with him (for he liked to be consulted about everything) their design and colour.

'Ladies and gentlemen,' he began, addressing the chattering company, 'let me beg your indulgence for but half an hour whilst our excellent Miss F works her necromancy upon our wardrobe for which, as you know, the Pavilion Theatre is deservedly well known. This year will be her crowning success.' He cast a critical eye over the company and then looked about him. 'Where is Mr Chapman? And his excellent canines? Has he left?'

Will took me by the arm and propelled me towards the stage!

'Here he is, sir,' as we climbed the steps. 'Shipshape and Bristol fashion – or soon to be when the divine Miss F has worked her wonders.'

(For the second time today, I am included in the company!)

All eyes turned as Miss Fleete approached, small and hunchbacked, with a short right leg and, because of her distortion, permanently bowing. But crooked or no, she was the mistress of her craft and created the finest, most extravagant dresses and costumes from the most unpromising materials. She had no measuring tape nor pins as she made the rounds of our company, but could eye up a leg or waist or sleeve and, quick as a Barnaby, would call, 'Mr Corben, 32 with a little,' or 'Miss Vickers, a nippy 18 but allow for activity,' to her assistant who stood quietly at her side with a pencil and notebook. That assistant is Emily Pikemartin, the daughter of Alf Pikemartin, our Aquarium doorkeeper.

I think I am in love with Em. To see her hurrying along the street or stopping to look in a shop window, to hear her light step upon the stairs and smell the faint fragrance of linen and cotton which surrounds her, gives me joy immeasurable. And I am fortunate that I see her often, for she helps her father in the Aquarium of an evening when she has finished her day's work with Miss Fleete, and though her eyes must be sore with the close work she has been doing and her shoulders stiff with sitting all day, I have never heard her complain. She always has time for Brutus and Nero, sitting upon the stairs with a golden and black devotee on either side, talking sweetly and quietly whilst they listen and, now and again, lick her hand or put their head upon her lap. I would it were me! I would gladly kneel at her feet and listen to her soft voice and kiss her hand and never want for anything in the world ever again. But I have seen the looks she gives Will Lovegrove, secretly, from downcast eyes, and if he chances to look in her direction, she blushes very prettily and pretends to examine the hem of her dress. And he does glance often at her, and quite often it is more than a glance. When he comes to the Aquarium, he follows her about like a puppy whilst she is sweeping the floor or dusting the waxworks, and recently I have seen them walking and talking together. Of course, I tell myself that Em *would* love me, if she had not already fixed her heart upon Will.

Having greeted Will (who, of course, bowed and took her hand and kissed it) and said, 'Ah, Mr Lovegrove, a fine leg, chest – well, manly – let us hazard, shall we Emily?', Miss Fleete is in a little fluster, and must smooth her dress and adjust her hairpins before she could finally make anything of me. 'Ah yes, Mr Chapman,' she said, 'shoulders 40, a short sleeve, a belt I think, Emily, if we can find one.' Emily and Will catch each other's eye and I saw, not for the first time, a rare expression upon my friend's handsome face. One that was more serious than ironic, and it made me wonder. Em bent to her notebook and scribbled hard but, I think, smiled under the amber gaslight.

'Hello, Bob,' she whispered, and then greeted Brutus and Nero with a familiar fondness. Will was watching her, and continued to watch as she followed Miss F from the stage and opened the door for her. Then he examined his boots, and glanced at me, and muttered, 'She is a lovely girl, Bob, and dash my rags if I am not completely devoted to her.'

I could not look at him.

Finally, when I had spent my holiday in watching and wonder, Mr Carrier called me and my fine fellows to perform, and there was much interest in it, for most of the company lingered when they could have made tracks to the Bell and Leper. Instead, they decamped to the pit or the stage side and settled down to hear Mr Carrier describe Trim's 'dog pieces'. I had to concentrate upon Mr Carrier, for Mr Pocock's newly copied pieces were not yet to hand, and I learned that my boys must run onto a sandy shore, leap over rocks, bark at a pirate hiding in a tree, hunt out treasure buried beneath the sand (in fact, beneath the trap door in the stage), fell the villainous pirate chief to the ground and have him by the throat ('the seize', a trick all performing dogs should do, but at which many fail), open gates and carry lanterns and, finally, accompany the hero and heroine and the children's ballet in a grand and triumphal procession through the village, each dog carrying the flag of St George in his mouth! We went through much of it easily, and received appreciative applause. But there were some tricks, such as hunting out the treasure and appearing to dig for it, which would need practice. Nevertheless, I was pleased with it all, and had Brutus and Nero bark and lift their paws in acknowledgement, which was universally admired. As the company dispersed, Mr Carrier clapped me upon the shoulder.

'Marvellous, marvellous, Mr Chapman. A remarkable display of training and obedience. I think we have a success here. We will far outshine Mr Hennessey and his pyrotechnics! When Gouffe, our man-monkey arrives, we are complete, but you and your remarkable animals will be the stars in the Pavilion's firmament!'

I was so proud, I felt I should burst! I was given my own parts (copied cues and the ink still wet) to take with me, and Mr Carrier shook me by the hand and then departed, talking earnestly to Mr Pocock. I thought I heard Mr Carrier say, 'Excellent, excellent, Pocock,' and imagined he was talking about me.

The great black mouth of the theatre was now fallen silent, for there had been a wholesale exodus to refreshment houses and nearby lodgings, and the stage labourers were at their rest before the evening performances began. Only Mr Lombard and a handful of scene-shifters stomped about, dragging off the makeshift scenery my boys and I had used, and dragging on the rocks and boulders necessary for *Perilous and Drear* that evening. They were soon done, having turned down the gas and lowered the great chandelier in readiness for Mr Pilcher to test it. But I could have stood on the stage until the first customers wandered in, and would have done had not Mr Lombard shouted to me, 'You! Dog-man! Mind yourself!' and dropped the curtain with a heavy 'whoosh'.

And with that, the magic was gone.

Outside, the winter afternoon was transforming, like Mr Lombard's scenery, into evening, and with it dropped that bone-chilling cold which settles in streets and alleyways. I had not thought that the theatre passage would still be populated, but it was crowded with chattering ballet-girls and young women, hopeful of catching Mons. Villechamps and begging him to 'consider me, sir, if you have any opportunities'. Little children were there also, stamping their tiny feet and rubbing their hands and arms and waiting, waiting. There were little pockets of mothers, all wrapped against the cold, and they turned to look at me, at anyone leaving the theatre, and then turned back. I was a dog-man, of no consequence. It was as I passed the last clutch of mothers and their shivering off-spring, that I thought I heard a familiar voice, and stopped to look. And saw – but surely I was mistaken – Mrs Gifford amongst them. It could not be her! And yet her tall, spare shape was unmistakeable, despite turning her back into the shadows. Trying not to be seen. But perhaps I was mistaken, for when I reached the road and looked back, I saw only the dark shapes of the waiting mothers and wisps of shadow clutching their skirts.

CHAPTER 7

PILGRIM – A COPY-CAT

A visitor was waiting for me at the Aquarium: Pilgrim. His exotic headgear was replaced by an old-fashioned tile, and he was wrapped up in a long and rusty Benjamin that might have belonged to a guardsman many moons ago. Other than that, he appeared as always – as dusty as his books and much inclined to be incomprehensible. He was perched on a chair by Pikemartin's box, and had been refreshed by a glass from the Two Tuns and had no doubt returned the favour twice over, for he was tipsy: his small, pointed face was flushed at its extremities – nose tip, ear tips, chin. Also, he was argumentative with his other self.

'Now then, Bob Chapman. I'm not your errand boy.'

('Who spread it about that you were? I'll draw claret if I hear it!')

'I have a business to mind and no leisure to be your lad.'

('Give it over, Pilgrim, and let me at him! Give me a pint of his cochineal dye!')

'Down with you, you beggar! Bob Chapman's a pal!'

It was an exhausting business when Pilgrim was in this mood, but I have learned to watch and wait and let him settle his two selves and trust that sense will prevail. He wrangled and wrestled with himself for some minutes, and even hit his palm hard with his fist, twice or three times, and threatened to spit in his own eye and choke himself to death. And then, finally, he subdued himself into quietness.

'Bob Chapman, I have a message for you from next door.'

('For him? Who wants him? Is it the mummers?')

'They don't *want* him, you fool! They already *have* him, according to this!'

Pilgrim drew from his pocket a thin, folded sheet of paper. A playbill of the humblest quality. One that would dissolve into paste at the first drop of rain. He spread it out upon his knee and pointed a trembling finger to a black and inky line.

'Bob Chapman? In a place like this?'

('My eye! Yes he is, you dog!')

'Never he is! Scoundrel.'

I took the bill from him and read it carefully. From crown to foot. There was a real crown, indeed, with sparks of illumination bursting from it and balancing upon the words 'Royal Crown Theatre' and 'Fish-lane' under which, in smaller letters, the legend:

Where the Old may laugh, the Young may sigh,
The Student improve, the Romantic cry

sat hopefully in roman italics. Below that, the blurred image of a man in armour wrestling with a piebald dog and the striking announcement:

TALES (from popular Authors) adapted to
delight all who may visit this
TEMPLE OF THE MUSES
To the lovers of CANINE SAGACITY,
CHAPMAN'S DOGS
BRUTUS & NERO
Who have trod the Stages of all the principal
Theatres in the Metropolis
In the well-known Entertainments of
THE FOREST OF BONDY
PHILLIP AND HIS DOG
THE SMUGGLER AND HIS DOG
THE PIRATE AND HIS DOG
And their able Master
Mr BOB CHAPMAN

Doors open 7, 9, 11, &c. Admission Id.

Best order. No spitting.

Pilgrim had slipped into a doze as I read the bill once, twice. Turned it over. Shook it. Looked at Brutus and Nero and even showed it to them. And then read it again. I have heard of impersonators, and even imitators, but never considered myself important enough to be their subject! In truth, I felt put out and not a little irritated. There was a bouncefulness about the bill which rubbed me up the wrong way, and rather than feeling flattered, I had an altogether contrary impression and would have liked to have met the man who had the nerve to so ill-use me and poke him in the eye!

'I said it wasn't you, Bob Chapman,' piped up Pilgrim.

('You never! You bad-mouthed him all the way!')

'Give over, you! Bob Chapman is a pal! But our neighbours – they are a gang of thieves and mountebanks and no surprises.'

('Quiet, you!')

'Now, will you take advice from an old friend? Don't be precipitate!'

('Bash 'em up, Bob! Draw claret, I say! Make a fist of Bordeaux!')

I have to say, I was much inclined in that direction, and was debating whether to make a snack of it now or later, when Pikemartin appeared and squinted hard at Pilgrim and nodded towards the door – they seemed to know each other – and before I could make anything of my annoyance, the party, as they say, broke up. But I folded the bill carefully into my pocket, and the memory of it stirred about my head the rest of the day, for it was a matter that needed attention. What would Mr Carrier say if he thought I was moonlighting in a gaff! What would my new friends – my old friends – say!

But work needed my attention: I had been away from my stand all morning and some of the afternoon and, according to Mrs Gifford, who appeared suddenly (but with the cold whiff of the outdoors still upon her) and lost no opportunity in bringing me up when we passed on the stairs, there had been enquiries about me and if I was ever going to return.

'I said I didn't know,' she told me over her shoulder, snapping on her gloves as if they were manacles. 'You might have disappeared for the duration, for all I was aware.'

Which wasn't true, for I had left a notice prominently displayed. But I wanted to savour the pleasantness of my holiday at the Pavilion, so I did not let her spoil a shred of it, and marched her off to a prison ship, there to lock her up and bolt the door! It is a fancy I have employed all my life – this picture of locking up my troubles, in chains or stocks or, most recently, in the hold of a prison ship, which I then cast off upon a high tide. That prison ship had not been a busy one until these past few months – when I had been visited by unpleasant dreams and memories of my childhood – but, since the episode with the Nasty Man, it had done a couple of turns of duty and would come back in flotilla if I was not careful.

So, another good reason for keeping busy. And

why I was grateful for my new work at the Pavilion, and my good health (which I have not always been able to rely upon) and my good friends. By the time Pikemartin had drawn down the shutters and blown out the lamp in his box, I had completed four good exhibitions, had a handful of coin and the makings of a light heart, and as I tidied my stand, put the eggs in the correct box and hung my hat upon its hook, I contemplated treating myself to a chop from a supper-shop, even though the risk was hours of indigestion and wakefulness.

This was my little life and if I could so order it, there would be nothing to disturb its pleasantness. I would have my show at the Aquarium, regular as the army, and take my breakfast at Garraway's and an occasional supper at the Cheshire Cheese with my friends. For amusement, I would enjoy my new acquaintances and the changing vistas at the Pavilion Theatre, and for the future, anticipate a life of cabbages and peas, early mornings and crisp country air. I went through the list like a catechism, and could almost believe that if I said it over to myself, I could keep unpleasantness at bay. I was saying it as I turned down the gas and summoned my two boys, as I avoided Mrs Gifford when our paths crossed once again in the hall, and even as Pikemartin handed me a note, it was turning in my head.

To my dear Bob Chapman.
Please to attend upon the Princess at yr earliest.
For cups of tea.
I thank you.

It is the smallest note you have ever seen, a fairy note on fairy paper, the draught from mice yawning under the wainscot would have blown it away. But in its power to command, it was a royal summons, written on old-fashioned parchment, stamped with red wax and ribbons and delivered by a six-foot guardsman! It was the Princess's pleasure to 'take tea' late in the evening when it had, certainly upon me, such an enervating effect that I was guaranteed not to sleep at all that night. But she could not be refused, so of course I turned about and presented myself and my two freshly groomed boys at the door of the attic, what Will called the 'top drawing room', where she had her strange little 'palace'.

Princess Tiny was twenty-three years of age, stood only twenty inches high, but was the most perfect creature. Her skin was as soft as a child's and her hands the size of a doll's, each finger so fine it might break simply by breathing upon it, each nail like a piece of pearl. She had pale-golden cobwebs for hair, and the face of a fairy angel. But if she looked and sounded like a child – for her voice was no stronger than a newborn baby's – she had the wit and cleverness of an educated man. When Herr Swann, our seven-foot giant and the Princess's devoted slave, remarked once, 'Princess, you are a divine creature,' she instantly replied, in her high bird's voice, 'Then you are the more divine in divining it!', at which we all laughed, and none more heartily than the Princess, who put a tiny hand to her mouth and wiped tears as fragile as dew from her eyes!

What's more, she is, as we say in our profession, 'a great draw' and although she had been at the Aquarium for quite six months, visitors still queued around the corner to see her exhibition when she introduced a new song or wore a splendid new gown (which she was very fond of doing). But Mrs Gifford, when she was not bustling to and fro between the Aquarium and some other places (which she kept to herself), had taken over her supervision and kept her toiling until the poor little creature almost dropped through exhaustion. I have seen that woman stand upon the landing and actually call down to the rabble in the hall, 'Hi! Hi! Hi! In here! Come and see the Princess Tiny! Just about to begin!', when 'Hi-ing' and 'Just about to begin!' are universally regarded as very common and more suited to the fairground. 'Shake hands with a real fairy princess!' she would bawl. 'Only a penny extra to pick her up and see how light she is!'

Of course, she had no business letting any ruffian off the street handle the Princess, whose tiny bones are as fragile as a baby bird's. But was Gifford concerned about that? Not a bit of it. I think she would take over the Princess entirely if she could.

'You should be more agreeable with the gentlemen,' I heard her say one evening, between performances, talking to the Princess as if she was a child. Or an idiot. 'Gentlemen would like it better if you would sit on their knee and let them hold your hand.'

'But I would *not* like it,' returned Princess Tiny, rearranging her dress and refusing to look Gifford in the eye.

'That is neither here nor there. You will do as you are told.'

'You do not tell me what I should do,' retorted the Princess in her bird-like voice. 'You are not my employer, and Mr Abrahams would never ask me to do such things.'

'Don't give yourself airs, my lady,' snapped Gifford. 'You're an exhibit. Thru'pence a time, and don't you forget it.'

It was a cruel thing to say, and from that moment Gifford was banished from the Princess's attic palace, though it didn't prevent her from loitering about the door, from where she would try to peer into that fairy land whenever she could. And for that I would not blame her. It was enchanted, a place like no other, and fitted Princess Tiny, as Trim once remarked to me, like fairy wings.

'For,' said he, 'she has everything here exactly to her own size. And how pleasant it must be to sit upon a chair or reach a shelf without anyone's assistance. Here she has her own stove, and pots and pans and cups and saucers, just as anyone would have in their own room.'

It was strange, however, to wander in this fairy world under the great Aquarium roof, lit by many skylights and, at night, by twinkling lamps, and hear, like a faint hum, the London streets below. She had a little sitting room in which her own comfortable chaise and Herr Swann's plump cushion were placed on either side of an antique stove. Her *boudoir* was a bower of soft curtains and silken pillows and charming miniature pictures of sunny landscapes. Another little stove burned and the lamps (there were many of them) glowed warmly. Brutus, Nero and I discovered her in her bed, regally propped up by satin cushions, and resplendent in a tiny fur mantle and bonnet, quite as though she was ready to take a sleigh ride. On her bed, close to hand, was a pile of penny magazines, her only reading (for she was no scholar), but oh! how much she relished those tales of highwaymen and lovelorn maidens. And no wonder she gazed wide-eyed and blushing upon Will Lovegrove, and was very much inclined to giggle and hide her face when he whispered charming nonsense in her ear. Trim, she was in awe of when she learned he was sometimes the author of this nonsense, and would ask him, ever so modestly, to tell her, if he would, 'how the beautiful princess won the heart of the handsome pirate'.

But although she was comfortable in her little bower, outside she wheezed and coughed constantly, complaining that the damp London weather turned her lungs to water.

'You see, Bob, I am a child of summer, of golden hills and tall black *cipresso*. And blue skies and winds like baby breath, warm and sweet. This London is wet and dark, and my feet and hands, they are never warm. Always like – how is it? – *ghiacciolo*.'

I had no idea and shook my head, so she appealed to our giant friend – '*Herr Swann, wie übersetzt man bitte Eiszapfen?*'

He frowned and wrinkled his nose. 'I believe,' said he, after some moments of deep thought, 'that it is the icicle you refer to, meine *Prinzessin*. *Eiszapfen*. Ah, how many years since I have seen the German icicle, which is much superior to the English. Much bigger and colder.'

'The English *ghiacciolo*, he is big and cold for me,' piped up the Princess, pushing her tiny hands into the furry depths of her muff. 'Now, my sweet Anselm will make us tea while I chitter-chat with Bob,' and without another word Herr Swann lumbered away to the little kitchen, from where the tinkling of crockery could soon be heard. The Princess settled herself and allowed Brutus's golden head to lie upon the bed next to her.

'Now, Bob, I must be quick before Anselm returns. I need your help tomorrow. But it is secret.'

This was a surprise to me, for Herr Swann was so completely her guardian.

'I wish you to take me to the Pavilion Theatre tomorrow morning. Very early, Bob, so you must collect me from here in good time.'

I could hear the little kettle whistling upon the stove as the Princess leaned forward and whispered.

'I must meet a friend, Bob. He *is* a friend, you must believe, who needs my help.'

Of course I agreed. How could I refuse her! And she turned her radiant smile upon me, as Herr Swann broke into song: *'Meine Lieber! Meine Lieber!'*

'Anselm is a dear, good man, the best of men,' she whispered, 'but he will not understand. You *will* understand, Bob, *mia cara*, and that is why I ask you this favour,' and she took my hand, just as Herr Swann, doubled like a spring, staggered in with the tray of rattling cups.

We made our farewells late that evening, for the Princess and the giant were good company, and insisted on schnapps 'to complete the evening, no?' Herr Swann sang more German songs, which became sadder and softer as the schnapps in the bottle grew less. And the Princess sang in a strange language, well suited to the chirrupings of her thin, bird-like voice. Even my dogs showed their tricks, Brutus picking up from the tray one of the Princess's tiny, fragile cups, and Nero allowing one of her tiny white mice to sit upon his coal-black head. This last trick filled us all with great delight and the little woman clapped her hands and shouted '*Bravo, signor Nero!*' until she was overcome with a fit of coughing and lay back, panting, upon the pillows.

'I am well,' said she, waving away our concern, 'much better for seeing my handsome boys – Brutus and Nero, of course!' and we all laughed as though we had no cares in the world.

CHAPTER 8

TO THE PAVILION THEATRE –
BARNEY – THE NASTY MAN –
WILL LOVEGROVE, HERO

Pushing the Princess in her chair to the Pavilion Theatre was such a novelty. We bounced along like a little empress and her court, both of us enjoying the 'Good morning, Princess' she attracted from early risers. Her chair was a remarkable and sturdy machine, with wooden sides and large wheels and coiled springs to stop it lurching over the cobbles and bumping its fragile passenger about. Its seat was made of red leather and padded with cushions, and there was a hood which could be raised or lowered to keep out the weather. Princess Tiny sat high upon her throne, tucked around with rugs and resplendent in her white bonnet and muff, waving and smiling, and singing a cheerful little song in her own language, which she said was about 'beautiful Santa Catharina, happy to go to her death on the wheel'. Of course, if Mr Abrahams had known about our excursion, perhaps his feelings would have been mixed. Whilst he would never deny the Princess her dose of fresh air, the

127

showman in him might be troubled lest the gratis exhibition of his star attraction in the streets affected the coins in his pocket.

But he need not have worried, for there were few enough people out in the bright morning air and, scurrying around the back streets, we arrived at the Pavilion early, long before any performer (let alone any spectator!) would contemplate rising, though Mint, the doorkeeper, was already about and bustling in his cupboard – and, according to him, had already been in that enclosure for some hours. Through the cloud of smoke from his briar, that estimable man read to us, unprompted, the list of 'orders' he had for rehearsal today, which included the cast as well as the children's ballet, myself and boys ('teatime-ish, I would say, Mr Chapman'), and Mons. Gouffe, the man-monkey, who had yet to make an appearance, being unavoidably detained in South Islington.

We escaped, after the Princess had given free Aquarium passes to Mint and the four little Mints, and made our way to the side of the stage. The Princess was much taken by everything, and looked with interest at those theatrical effects which are so shabby in the half-light, but look magnificent from the auditorium. I mean the wood and plaster throne, which appears to be carved out of stone, and the heap of rocks, which look heavy and jagged, but which the stage hands carry with one hand. I wheeled her about the stage and she leaned out of her chair, eagerly touching the curtains and the great swaying roll of canvas scenery on which was half-painted a view of Greenwich by night.

Suddenly, the Princess plucked my sleeve and I was aware, as was she, of someone standing in the shadows, quite still and reluctant to be seen. She was eager to be lifted out of the carriage and I did so, putting her very gently upon the boards. She tottered to the centre of the stage, calling out like a baby bird, 'Barney mio, will you come? Do not be afraid. I am here, Princess Tiny.'

Who could mistake her poor, thin voice calling like a bird's into the darkness of that place? It was very affecting and no empty performance, either. When the boy stumbled out from behind the scenery and dropped to his knees at her feet like the convict son in *Ben Brown, the Shepherd's Lad; or Whistle o'er the Downs*, that picture could have done good service as an act two *tableau* – the one where the errant daughter (or son) returns to the crofter's lowly cottage, and begs his (or her) mother's forgiveness. I was moved, and wiped a tear, and coughed. Then his face was caught suddenly lit up (the theatre door must have been opened), and I was surprised to see it was *that* boy. It took me by the throat, for certain sure, and brought back unpleasant memories.

Did I, then, stride out upon the boards and firmly take the boy by the collar, deaf to his protests and ignoring his kicks and threats? Did I show a little slack, perhaps, and offer to set him upon the right road at Mr Fishburn's Ragged School and Industrial Farm, where boys in his situation might be 'saved' before they were 'spent'? Or did I clout him soundly about the head and introduce my shoemaker to his tailor on the way to the door?

Not in these boots!

I quickly tiptoed from the stage to seek out Mint, for if there was going to be trouble – and the boy seemed to be brother chip with it – I wanted seconds. He was not in his box, so I poked my head out of the theatre door.

'Mr Bob Chapman,' said the Nasty Man. 'A pleasure – indeed, a pleasure. And Brutus and Nero, no doubt? Handsome fellows all!'

I tried to shut the door, but he was there already. And how was he there? If he had followed the Princess and me through the early street, then he was uncommonly careful, for I swear I never saw him, and my boys, pressing close against my legs now, had given no sign that they knew he was near. But here he was, with an elegantly booted foot in the door and wiping his mouth with his terrible red handkerchief.

'Now then, sir, I am come to ask you "Any news?"' he said, so amiably that I might have smiled back. 'Not to beat about the bush, as the magistrate said to the pretty girl.'

This cat-and-mouse game evidently gave him

much pleasure, for he struggled to hold back his laughter.

'I wonder, do you have the packet? No? Oh dear. That is, as you theatricals say, a tragedy. Really it is.'

I gave the door another shove, but he was already halfway in. He licked his fat lips.

'We should go in, my dear. No sense shivering in the cold. Shall we join them? The boy and the tiny creature?' He giggled. 'Ah! I know her well. *Mia cara?*' And he mewed the Princess's little endearment like a cat. 'Oh naughty, naughty! She didn't tell you we are acquainted? Oh shame! Oh, silly creature!'

His smile was, as before, as mild as a priest's.

'Shall we go and find them? But don't alarm the boy, will you? I have business with him.'

Through the mist of his silky words, I was still wondering how I could keep him away from the Princess and although blood did not rush to my head, nor courage to its sticking place, I thought once more of Mr Mint, the Cerberus of the stage door, and a man who would allow no one through it with whom he was not acquainted. If he could be summoned, he would certainly bar this creature from his theatre. But even now, the Nasty Man was ahead of me.

'And Mr Mint – ah – excellent man! Shall we apply to him? Oh look, my dear, he has run away! Like little Freddy Forskyn. Naughty Freddy tight in lamb-skin / Cook him up a good

131

lamb pie! / Give everyone a *slice* of Freddy / Good and rare and toby-red . . . Know that song, sir? A naughty song? Oh yes, sir. Very.'

He must be mad, I thought, for he had pushed the door wide open and was dancing on the very edge of his toes with delight and relish, humming and reciting the vile rhyme over and over. Whilst he was so distracted, here was my opportunity to summon Mint and have him marched away. But his cubbyhole was locked and dark, and pinned to it was a note.

'Called away. Back soon. P.M.,' chanted the Nasty Man, without looking at it. 'Peter Mint. Brave soldier, stalwart chappie, but now the castle's unguarded – and pity the poor Princess and her young prince!'

The merriment was over and he pressed me towards the stage, his breath hot and sweet upon my neck. I wanted nothing so much as for him *not* to touch me, and the thought of those fat fingers and fleshy lips was quite terrible. In the dark regions of the stage with the swaying canvases and a labyrinth of passages, I had a fleeting notion that I could escape him, but it was a desperate thought and a forlorn hope for, as we approached, I could hear the Princess's tiny voice and the boy's urgent tones. They were where I had left them, only he had fetched a chair for the Princess – in fact, had dragged out the property throne – and was sat at her feet with her tiny hand in his. At any other time, it would be a touching scene, but not now. I waited for the grampus to make a dash at him and grab the boy by the collar, the advantage of surprise being all on his side. But he didn't. He stood at my shoulder, his breath coming in short whistles, breathing through those baby teeth.

The Nasty Man was listening.

His head was cocked as he strained to hear what they were saying and he leaned forward, putting his hand upon my shoulder. I flinched and, whether we made a noise or he sensed we were there, the boy suddenly sprang to his feet with a terrible cry and was across the stage and had shinned up a rope as high as the battens before anyone moved.

'You!' he cried, hanging like a monkey above the stage. 'You shan't get me, you devil! And I shall serve you out! For my father's sake!'

His voice rang out across the blackness of the theatre, but the Nasty Man was undeterred. Laughed, indeed, at the boy's boldness with a childish giggle, which he tried to hide with the back of his hand.

'Serve me out, will you?' he taunted. 'Son of George Kevill, the murderer, the thief! *And* filthy dog, so I've heard!'

The boy cried out again, slipping a foot or so down the swaying rope, but recovering enough to wrap his thin legs around it when his chorus began again. 'My Pa done nothing wrong, you villain! I'll serve you out, see if I don't!'

'Oh, Barney, take care!' cried the Princess.

133

'Barney, is it?' said the Nasty Man. 'Better come down here then, Barney Gallows-bird, and look after your little friend.'

'Don't you touch the Princess,' cried Barney.

'She's my friend,' mimicked the grampus in a high and childish voice, and wobbled his head. 'Oh, Pa! Oh, Pa! I'll serve him out!' and he laughed until I thought he would burst, but then suddenly turned off that wild laughter like a tap, and his face was set and terrible.

'Serve me out, will you?' he spat. 'And how will you do that, Jack Ketch's bait? I want the pictures your Pa gave you. You know where they are. Or did you give the packet away for someone else to keep? To this dog's-face, perhaps? Which is it?'

'What pictures? I don't know about any pictures!' cried Barney.

The Nasty Man took half a step and raised his cane. Nero, braveheart that he is, growled.

'You, dog-man,' said he, 'keep your curs by your side, sir, or I'll knock their brains into their arses and you can lick 'em clean! Heard that one?' Then he rapped the ebony cane upon the boards, and fixed me with that half-smile upon his face. 'Where are they, then? Pictures? And a letter perhaps? You know what I want. Give them here!'

He raised the cane once more, and as he did so, a door slammed behind me.

It was only when, some time later, I replayed these events, did I wonder how it came to be that the person who did that slamming and clattered

134

onto the stage, and greeted Brutus and Nero with a cheery whistle, was Will Lovegrove, elegant as ever in a rusty Benjamin and old slouch hat. Nor did I ask myself why he should be at the Pavilion Theatre at this early hour. I could only guess that he had not been home, and certainly from the dark rings beneath his eyes, he had not slept.

'Bob!' he cried, hanging his arm about my shoulders. 'Here's luck! Now, join me at Garraway's if you and your boys have not breakfasted, for I had the devil's own fortune last night and – Hello!'

What did he make of the extraordinary scene? The boy hanging from the rope? Princess Tiny trembling upon the massy gilt throne? The Nasty Man, forcing an amiable smile, politely saluting him and extending a gloved hand?

'My dear sir, may I shake your hand? I do not believe I have had the pleasure?'

Will's face was impassive, and he kept his arm about my shoulder.

'Not yet introduced,' effused the grampus, retreating only slightly. 'Quite understand. Not done. Precipitate upon my part. Am merely trying to recapture my young – er – apprentice, here, who will keep running away, sir.' He raised the cane. 'Naughty boy. Needs a thorough dry-beating, eh? You and I, sir? We might – enjoy – giving him a shirtful of sore bones?'

We stood in silence, as the Nasty Man looked from Barney to Will.

'*He* is party to the business, also,' the grampus

135

said finally, pointing at me. 'I hope he is not a friend of yours, sir. The boy gave stolen property to him. Outside this very theatre. I saw it. He should give back what doesn't belong to him.'

Will glanced up at Barney, still dangling from the rigging, and addressed the Princess. 'A runaway, eh? An apprentice, he says. And a thief to boot,' he said. 'That would make him an apprentice thief. What do you think, madam? He certainly looks like a pincher. If that is so, I must assume that, as his master, *you*, sir, are an adept yourself.' He wheeled upon the puffing grampus. 'What would you recommend, Bob? Shall I call the constable to arrest the boy for absconding and this master for procuring? Or shall I simply knock seven bells out of him myself and save the blue-bottles the trouble? What do you say, sir?'

And with a sudden flourish, he struck the Nasty Man a glancing blow upon his shoulder that sent that black stick clattering across the stage. It was surprising to see Will Lovegrove angry, and he clearly was. His face was pale and his eyes flashed, and he seemed six inches taller, whereas the Nasty Man was reduced to grovelling for his cane and squeaking threats.

'You have no notion, sir, who you trifle with!'

'Trifle, eh?' Will cried, advancing upon him. 'Let us review that when I've given you a regular good kicking, sir!'

The Nasty Man backed away, filling the air with threats and vile curses.

Then there was the slamming of the theatre door, and he was gone.

Will's only concern was for the Princess though she, shaken and trembling, expressed herself 'perfectly well, thank you, Mr Lovegrove' and even managed a smile as my handsome friend knelt and took her hand. Barney, who quickly let himself down the rope, professed himself fit as a trout, Princess, no worms'.

What a strange group we must have made for any ghost of a spectator sitting, that morning, in the pit of the Pavilion Theatre. Handsome Will Lovegrove, with his long, curling hair and actorly dress, and the boy Barney, begrimed and ragged. Then the tiny Princess, elegant in her dark-green walking outfit and a miniature hat perched upon her bird-like head. And, me, Bob Chapman, wrapped in my one good coat (a little out at the elbows, but still serviceable for another winter if I am careful with it) standing apart with Brutus and Nero, and taking in the scene as if it were one of Trim's dramas.

Will took charge, asking no questions (though he must have been consumed with curiosity!), and insisting that the Princess was returned, post-haste, to the Aquarium.

'Roll out my lady's carriage, Chapman!' he cried and, in stately procession, we went back to the Aquarium, Barney pushing the Princess's chair, Will walking by her side and my dogs and I keeping rear-guard. The Nasty Man was nowhere about, but when we arrived at the Aquarium, Mrs Gifford was in the hall to greet us, looking more pinched and unhappy than I have ever seen her, and anxious to remind one and all that the Princess was delicate and should not be 'traipsing the streets in the early morning or be thrown about like a sack of sugar'. Taking the Princess's hand and hurrying her through the waxworks chamber to the back stairs, she announced, with an imperiousness that set my teeth upon edge, that 'Princess Tiny will be resting for the duration, but she'll work as usual that evening, conscious as ever of her devoted public and the respect they hold for her.'

Aye, I thought bitterly, and the sixpences they drop you for extra favours, I shouldn't wonder.

I set up my platform quickly, and, with shaking hands and a sweating brow, brewed my first pot of the day. Almost before the kettle could sing, the salon door opened and my boys were on their feet in readiness for our customers. But Nero, poking his head around the screen, began to wag and *that* is a sign for the arrival of a friend rather than a customer. Two friends, in fact. Will and Barney, the latter with a scrubbed face and hands, courtesy of the Princess, and a clean shirt and breeches, courtesy of the waxworks wardrobe, hence their fashion of some distant century. We sat cosily behind the screen, and I put another two spoons of tea in the pot. Will was thoughtful.

'Here's a nice kettle of fish, Bob, and young

Barney here is the sprat caught in it. From what he has told me, and those details which our Princess has added, it is clear to me that Barney is the victim of a misunderstanding.' Will laid a friendly hand upon my arm. 'And that you, my friend, have been drawn into the business also.'

Barney nodded and rubbed an already red eye.

'As I understand it, the story is this. Barney's Pa was a peep-show man. He and Barney travelled the country fairs, where they met our fairy and giant, Princess Tiny and Herr Swann. They come to London from the country to make their fortune but, like many others, find it not so easy. Wherever Barney's Pa puts up his show, someone turns him off. He has to buy a pitch, and pay bullies not drive him out. He has a son to look out for, and not enough coin coming in.'

'It was a good show,' piped up Barney. 'We gave the Battle of Trafalgar and the Parting of the Red Sea, with the best coloured pictures to be had anywhere.'

'Then,' continued Will, 'the show is smashed to flinders by some drunken roughs. How does George Kevill earn a living now?'

'He goes to see the Princess!' said Barney with a smile. 'I thought she lived with the Queen, but Pa said she had an out-of-town residence. He called her our Fairy Princess, who saved our skins and put bread upon our table.' He rubbed his eye. 'She gave Pa some money to buy a photographic concern going cheap. She bought machines and

139

plates and a stock of pictures. My Pa said, "This could be the making of us, Barney!" He said, "By Christmas, we shall be as rich as the Queen herself, and twice as happy!"'

Silence dropped like a stone. The boy rubbed his eye hard with the heel of his hand, and Will looked away and gave Nero's ears a good scratch. Then, half-glancing at the boy, cleared his throat.

'I'm guessing that as soon as your Pa's photographic business started making money, someone else wanted a share. Or perhaps your Pa found that he owed someone else some money.'

Barney nodded his head.

'The Nasty Man. And an uncle.'

'Perhaps the Nasty Man offered your Pa a chance? Do this for me, he said, and I will ask my principal to look again at your debt. Your Pa had no choice. He went along with it, though he didn't like it much. But he had a boy and not enough chink, and London is a wicked place.'

It was quiet in the Aquarium, just the sounds of the animals in the menagerie, the rattle of feet below in the waxwork room, and a murmur of voices.

'My Pa wasn't a thief,' said Barney, suddenly. 'And he wasn't a murderer, like the judge said.'

'I believe you,' said Will. 'But he offended someone, Barney, for they fitted him up most thoroughly.' He frowned. 'What did the Nasty Man want? A packet? Like the one you gave to Bob and I gave it to Trim? Good Lord, that wasn't full of notes, was it? Or coin?'

Barney shook his head.

'It was just the packet your pal dropped when he tripped over me. Nothing in it but paper, so I brought it back.' He gave me a faint smile. 'I seen you with Mr Trimmer, coming out of the theatre. And the Cheshire Cheese. And I seen you talking to Mr Lovegrove, so I figured you were all pals together.'

Will patted Nero affectionately and raised his eyebrows at me.

'Remind me how Mr Trimmer came to trip over you, Barney.'

'I was in haste, wasn't I? From the Nasty Man. It was the morning when my Pa had been – well, you know. And he came up to me and said he wanted the pictures and if I didn't hand them over, he said he would – well, what he would do to me.' Barney bit his lip. 'He said I could keep the money what my Pa had stole. He just wanted the pictures. But my Pa never stole anything.'

'Of course he didn't. But these pictures? You're sure you don't know where they are?'

Barney shrugged his shoulders.

'I never saw anything.'

'Perhaps he left them with a friend?'

Barney scowled. 'A friend! Don't think much of his friend. He was supposed to send a letter to the Queen about my Pa so she would set him free, but he never.'

Will smiled. 'Sometimes friends are not all they're made out to be, are they?' He looked

141

thoughtful. 'Perhaps your Pa gave this friend the pictures, or the money. Or whatever it is the Nasty Man wants.'

Barney shrugged.

'Perhaps he kept the pictures in his photographic shop? Where was that?

'It's a emporium and I dunno where it is.'

'Certain?'

Barney frowned and looked irritated. 'Why do *you* want to know? You're as bad as the Nasty Man, you are, with your questions about my Pa. I'll serve him out, you mark me!' he muttered. 'I promised my Pa I would,' and looked mutinously at us both.

'Quite right,' said Will, solemnly. 'Too many questions. My mother always said I was a regular Boy Jones, and too nosy for my own good or anyone else's. But one last poser. Is your Pa's photographic business still there? Where he left it?'

'No more questions!' cried the boy, and he screwed his fists into his eyes and ground his teeth. 'I don't know! I don't know!'

Will put a strong arm around his shoulders and Brutus, of course, pushed his head under Barney's arm. I busied myself with the tea and soon had the pot filled, but then discovered I had no milk. (I am a devotee of tea with milk and cannot now abide it in its raw state.) It was but a step, with my little can, out of the Aquarium to the dairy shop, four doors away.

I went for milk, but did not return so soon.

142

CHAPTER 9

ROUGH-MAKING

I am not a violent man and, indeed, hate violence of any kind. I avoid it. Have sometimes been called a coward. But I cannot help my nature. I once contemplated joining the Society of Friends when I learned that they embraced mildness and shun aggression, and I think they would have suited me. Perhaps in such gentle company, I might have put behind me the brutality which marked out my childhood in pain and fear and which, even now, stalks my dreams.

When I am asleep, I see my father. A small man with rough hands and arms covered in scars. His profession was to mind furnaces and kilns. Especially brick-kilns. Any brick-kiln, he was not partial. My mother and I trailed the country with him, living in cheap rooms when he had work, and in sheds and under arches when he was out of a shop. He was a brute, both in word and deed, and my memories of him (for he died when I was six years old) are of his fist, hard and cracked like old wood, the snarling twist of his mouth and his boots.

Yes, when I dream, I see him, and hear the roar

of his voice and feel the thud of his fist and boots.

Much as I do now, as four roughs deal with me. They have dragged me into the narrow passageway at the side of Climmber's chandlery and, business-like, have set about me with their stampers and fives. My little milk can, about which I am very anxious, skitters away down the passage, bumping against the sides and performing somersaults. I watch with concern as it comes to rest upside down against an old ship's figurehead, like a begging bowl.

The roughs are thorough in their work and take pains to leave no part of my body unattended to. Indeed, they go over it twice. To be certain. And only when I am curled in a ball and a pool of blood has begun to gather beneath me, do they stop and survey their handiwork. One turns me over, and another inspects the job with a practised eye.

'He's had a fine gruelling,' says the last. 'A neat piece of work. Enough.'

'Indeed,' says another, rubbing his fist, 'and only one blue knuckle to show.'

Finally, the first crouches down and puts his mouth to my ear: he has the foul breath of long-eaten meat and onions.

'Now then, small beer. Unless you want your dogs poisoned and their legs broke as well, you will give up them properties what are not yourn when next applied to.'

He nudges me with his boot and a shaft of pain tears through my chest. Then it goes dark and quiet.

Mr Climmber came out of his shop only once (to fetch a bag of chains or something that rattled). He stepped over me very carefully. I was glad of that for when I didn't move, the pain was not too great, and I could doze and wake, and spend what seemed like hours examining the mossy ranges of the cobbles with one eye, the other having closed up. How long I lay there, I don't know. Hours or days, it was all the same. Sometimes I slipped into childhood again, and dreamed that I was in my mother's arms. But the smell of the cobbles, as powerful as sal volatile, awoke me to those nights when I hid from my drunken father, when, as my poor mother, rubbing her bruised face, would say, he was 'on a certain rampage'. Then I listened for his heavy step and the tirade of words and fists with which he battered every face and door, and squeezed myself into the smallest crack and held my breath. But, no matter how quiet and careful I was, he always found me. Then came that hard hand to prise me out and those wicked boots kicked at my refuge, and I retreated, like a mouse into a hole, until I was squeezed so tight, my knees pressed hard into my chest, that I couldn't breathe. He waited, I think, until I was overcome with panic. Only then would I allow myself to be dragged out, and his boots were the last things I saw before the rain of blows and the pain.

When I saw boots before me once again, I started, but I knew these were not my father's. They were dusty and shifted this way and that, and they were followed, not by blows and curses, but a murmur and a gentle hand upon my shoulder – I prayed that the hand would not move me so much as a hair's breadth, for moving my shoulder produced a bolt of pain which shot through my neck and coursed around my skull and left me gasping for air. But whoever it was left and I was pleased, for I could sink back into the oozy darkness which had enveloped me. Then came a clatter on the cobbles, like an army marching past my ear, and all light was suddenly blotted out, and I believe I panicked and thrashed about before I heard Will's voice, coming from a long way away.

'By the Lord Harry, Bob old fellow, what have you been up to? Look at you. Dear God, what has the poor devil suffered? Now then, I've told you before to leave those rowdy bob-tails to me, you naughty fellow! See, your two fine friends have come to look you over . . .'

And indeed, here were Brutus and Nero, nuzzling my aching hands, and knowing, somehow, to be gentle. But though I was more glad to see them than the sun in the morning, I was also fearful for their safety, given what the roughs had threatened, and as Will raised me carefully to my feet, I made certain that they were at my side. To be sure, they never left me, and Brutus, with a gentleness that was so affecting it brought tears to my eyes, by turn licked my hand and breathed upon it as if to reassure me that he was my protector.

Though Mr Climmber remained within his dark shop, with the door shut, at the passage end a little crowd had assembled, and I was greeted by oohs and aahs and kind words, as well as jests.

'Take more water with it, mate!' cried a barrow-man.

'Not Aldgate water!' cried another. 'He'll be dead before morning!' and other less charitable jibes.

Most were sympathetic, though, and bemoaned the violence of the streets and how 'an honest man couldn't fetch a can of milk these days without being robbed'.

Mr Abrahams called a cab to take me to my lodgings and in the same breath summoned constables to look for the bashers who had attacked a valuable employee. Will had to lift me into the cab and insisted on coming along.

It is strange how impressions run in moments of pain and distress. As I clung to the window sash, trying to shut out the agony caused by the cab's shuddering wheels on the cobbles, the scene in the street seemed to play before me at half speed: Mr Abrahams on the kerb, frowning and shaking his head, Pikemartin in the doorway of the Aquarium still and blank as a statue, the boy, Barney, on the steps rubbing his eye. And

Mrs Gifford, in widow's black, scurrying around the corner and, seeing my face at the cab window, stopping dead.

My lodgings – I never invite anyone there – are in Portland-road, in a row of quiet houses, all three-storeys with adjoining areas which at one time, perhaps seventy years ago, might have been smart, attracting nice families or a solicitor on his way up. Now they are, as Mrs Twentyfold, the lady of the house, put it, 'not of a piece', by which I think she meant all in different states of repair and use. Certainly, the upper end, nearest a pocket park, was tidier and better kept than the farthest end, where lodgings rubbed shoulders with houses in which every room was let to a copyist or scribe, the cellar to a noisy shoemaker and the attic, of course, to as many tailors and their boys as could be shoe-horned under the skylights. Mrs Twentyfold's establishment was snug between two similar houses, one taken entirely by clerks, and the other by a roaming community of commercial travellers, those cheery men who are as attached to their bag as they are to their regular enquiry of 'What do you travel in?' addressed to anyone carrying a card or a parcel. According to Mrs Twentyfold, I am something of a flamer; that is, I am unusual, but not in a good way. Mrs Twentyfold did not take in 'theatricals' as a rule, neither did her neighbours, but her second-floor back room had stood empty for three weeks and, as she said, pocketing my week-in-advance and removing the cruet, 'beggars can't be choosers'. Nevertheless, she looked upon me with a steely eye and my two boys also, and I think was only awaiting a lawyer's clerk in search of chambers, to find an excuse to turn me out. Given her already strong prejudices, she was none too happy at the sight of me in single mourning with a bloody nose and limping, when she opened the door.

'I want no trouble here,' she began in a low voice, which was for my ears only. 'This is a quiet house and respectable. I already put up with your animals and your unnatural hours. I won't have trouble as well. Think on, Mr Chapman, and mend your ways, or you'll be looking for another room.'

I tried to ignore her and Will nodded and tipped his hat, but it did not silence her, and we were accompanied by a monologue concerning the tribulations of being a landlady as we mounted the stairs to my room. I was not ashamed of it – I keep it neat and clean, and it is *my* room, *my* corner of the world which, for the first time in my entire life, is my own. I would rather it remained that way, but at this moment, unless I determined to crawl up, step by step, on hands and knees, I had to lean upon Will and allow him in. My eye was swollen shut and the other throbbed, and there was a swelling upon my cheek and around my jaw which was hard to ignore. I would very much like to have lain down, but that could not be, said Will, until he had attended to me. He unlocked my door, threw up my blind, raked out my fire, laid a new one and put a light to it. He filled my kettle and lit my lamp. Then he sat me on the edge of my bed and took a few steps back to give me a good once-over and, after helping me off with my coat, found a bowl and water and some cloths and set to work. He had gentle hands and talked constantly, to distract me from the pain.

'What did they steal from you, Bob? I've never seen you with a watch and chain and if you're harbouring a bag of treasure, you must have swallowed it!'

He frowned and I winced.

'Did that hurt, old fellow? I'm sorry.'

He worked in silence for a while and then began musing upon Barney and his father's difficulties. 'I wonder who George Kevill had put out,' he said. 'It must have been someone significant, otherwise why would they want to destroy him? You know he was pinched for murdering a lady-bird? The boy says that was a put-up business, that witnesses were paid to finger him.' He was silent for a moment. 'It was only a few weeks back that he danced the Newgate jig, as they say. And left the kid to shift for himself.'

Will went to pour the bloody water away in the scullery downstairs and boil some fresh. It was not a pretty tale. Even Trim might think twice about making a story of it. And though perhaps

I did recall reading about a hanging, those desperate men who make light of the Newgate jig are common enough. Men like the Nasty Man. Danger made them bold. So that if the Nasty Man believed that Barney had passed to me something *he* wanted or believed was his that morning outside the Pavilion, if he thought I had some association with the boy or his father, well, I had salt on my tail, like it or not, and that man would pursue me through hell and high water. And, if any were persuasion was needed, well my cuts and bruises were evidence enough.

I jumped when Will opened the door, and again when someone knocked upon it. And I was relieved when he cried, 'Look here, Bob, who is come a-visiting you! Your friend and that famous pen-driver from the Pavilion, and soon-to-be Albemarle-street, Fortinbras Horatio Trimmer!'

Trim smiled faintly, enquired after my injuries, shook his head in sympathy and lapsed into awkward silence, perched on the only chair. Will brought more fresh water and dealt with my swollen knuckles, at the same time recounting the strange events of the day to Trim, who was as mystified as we were. Finally, when he could get a word in between Will's, Trim said, 'You were in the soup for a while, Lovegrove. You didn't say where you'd gone, and when the Gov sent around to the Aquarium to see if you were there, and Mrs – What's-'er-name? – Gifford? said you were in a bad way, Bob – well, everything was sent awry.' He laughed. 'We were forced to have costumes instead of rehearsals, Mr Pirate Hero, and you missed the attentions of Miss Pikemartin.'

Will never raised his eyes, but I thought his cheeks coloured at the mention of her name.

'Bob Chapman has been wretchedly knocked about,' he volunteered, dabbing at my knuckles, 'but he is a stalwart fellow and a true Englishman, and never let a comrade down, or dropped anchor in another man's port. Do you think your excellent landlady might have some witch-hazel in her cupboard? That is a sure way of treating fighting injuries.'

She had – for a penny, of course. And would send out for anything Will required – for a consideration. But the witch-hazel was sufficient.

'I'm afraid you won't do much damage with these fives for a while, Bob,' Will said, shaking his head. He was right. My hands were more badly injured than I had at first realized. The knuckles, where I had tried to fend off the roughs' kicks and blows, were cut and broken, and so swollen that I could not flex my hand at all, and my fingers were red and tight. Besides, every touch and movement pained me now, no matter how careful Will was. And he did seem to know about bruising and swelling and breaks – though he thought I had none of the latter – and I wondered whether this was another of his dark secrets, particularly when he said, with a wry smile, 'I remember the great Tom Spring would swear by witch-hazel. Said there was nothing evil about the way it mended his fists after he had smashed Jack Langan! So I think it'll do for you, Bob, my friend.'

Finally, Will declared me 'well and truly doctored' and announced that now he really must return to the Pavilion. He had a performance of *Perilous and Drear* that evening and, of course, if Miss Fleete and her assistant were still on hand, he said, he should attend to his costume. Trim smiled faintly, and I followed them downstairs to the door, though they urged me to stay within. But I was eager to breathe the outside air, and with my dogs at my heels, we stood on the top step of the house and watched our friends disappear into the gloom, having agreed that, if I felt more like myself and was desirous of company, I should meet them at the Cheese that evening, though they wouldn't blame me if I didn't.

They are kind friends, I thought, as I slowly climbed the stairs, watched from a crack in the door by Mrs Twentyfold, but I was glad they had gone. I wanted nothing more than to shut the door and light the candles – I prefer candle-light to all others – and with Brutus and Nero taking their ease on their rugs either side the crackling fire where the kettle hisses, to sit, warm and quiet.

I looked around my little room, with its comfortable corners and familiar objects. My little shelf of books, the pictures (cut from the illustrated papers) tacked to the wall, my collection of treasures gathered from the wasteland and displayed for my own pleasure on a table. Candles burned with a pleasant bright light. The fire sputtered, and sparks flew merrily up the chimney. The kettle stood ready. The tea tin, with its pink Japanese flowers, was in its usual place. A cup and saucer. A plate of bread and cheese in the cupboard. My bed was made, my dogs in their places. Everything was in order.

But not quite. For, like a button in the poor box, something had crept in uninvited. And it was not that Will and Trim had been here, had disordered my bed and the little rug before the fire and left their footmarks upon the floor, the impressions of their fingers upon the window pane. They would soon fade and be gone. Nor the ugly slops of bloody water, the bottle of witch-hazel. No, it was as if fear itself had taken shape and walked in with me, and was now, like a shadow, behind and before me. Even the air was fouled by it, and suddenly I felt stifled and, panicking, stumbled to the door and down the stairs, to the street steps where I clung to railings and breathed as deeply as my injured lungs would allow. Which was where I was discovered by Mrs Twentyfold. After some moments' scrutiny, she brought me water in a chipped cup, and then wrestled with the dilemma of whether to offer me consolation or complaint. In the end, she settled for an equal distribution of the two.

'Of course, I shouldn't wonder at you getting knocked about, Mr Chapman,' she began, 'given the company you keep and the visitors you get. Why, I have been to the door a dozen times this week with people asking for you, and I won't have it. This is a respectable house and your callers were *not* all respectable people.'

She looked up and down the street and sniffed. 'They leave no card nor message, and that does not signify respectability. Mind you, neither were they theatricals. My late husband was one of the first Buffaloes – the Buffs they were known as – him being a stagehand at the Drury-lane Theatre. So there is little you can tell *me* about theatricals. Now, your Mr Lovegrove – he *is* a respectable theatrical, and a man my late husband would have opened a door to. And your Mr Trimmer, who I hear is a dramatic author, though not quite of '*the calibre*', as my late husband would say, but is still a respectable person. Both of them I am willing to allow over my doorstep, though not regular. This is a lodging house, not a cutting-shop.'

Sometimes Mrs Twentyfold's associations were difficult to follow, but her chatter was strangely calming and lapped over me like waves.

'Of course, there are some – in this very street – who are not so particular as I, and who will rent a room to any hawcubite, as my late husband used to say. But not I, Mr Chapman. This is a respectable lodging house. I know I repeat myself, but if it's true, it's worth saying over. It may not be a prince's bedful, nor even a queen's cup of malt, but it *is* respectable.'

Weary to the bone, I clung to the railing, but she didn't appear to notice.

'I have no objection to the very large gentleman, Mr Chapman,' she continued. 'He claimed to be a friend of yours, though I don't recall his name.' She mused, 'A refined gentleman, I thought, perhaps a Buff, though not a theatrical, that was very clear. As you are aware, I have lived among theatricals all my life, and need no introduction. My father was a stroller in Mr Whiston's company. The King's Lynn Circuit. And my mother, before she married, was Miss Flygrove.'

But I didn't hear any more. I was too struck by her revelation that the Nasty Man had been here. I realized then that he knew where I lived, where I worked, the names of my dogs, my friends. He could find me at any time, rough me over and poison my boys. He could be just around the corner, now. Or creeping up the area steps and waiting for me in the darkness.

I should jump upon a cart and be far away before the sun rose. I should do it to have an easy mind.

The air was dropping colder, and with it the pains in my back and chest increased. I gasped. Stumbled. Mrs Twentyfold clicked her tongue, and hurried me inside. Having me collapse upon her front step would do nothing for the respectability of her establishment.

In my little room, Brutus and Nero snored, the fire glowed. Somewhere in the street, voices were raised and doors slammed. The heavy clump of

156

footsteps and the smell of chops and kippers began to announce the return of my neighbours. In their lodgings, actors would be rousing themselves, eating their bread and butter and drinking their sweet tea, conning a few lines at the last minute. At the Aquarium, Alf Pikemartin would be turning up the lights and giving the entrance hall a sweep. Conn would be inspecting the menagerie, looking to the poorly lion cub, tending to the apes. Moses Dann, the Boneless Man, would be getting up from his mattress in the cellar (where he slept every hour he is able) and calling for his pot of ale. Every day the same.

But not for me, I thought. Everything is changed now.

CHAPTER 10

ONE DAY – TIPNEY'S WONDERFUL GAFF AND EXHIBITION – BARNEY'S PLAN – MURDER

I should have put on my coat and muffler and left that very night. Strong's Gardens were not so far away. With a steady walk and a couple of stops, I could have been there by morning.

But I stayed in my bed that night. And the following day. And the one after that. I slept and woke and stared at the wall, but I did not stir. I lay until the sheets stank and I with them, and the mattress was stained into the outline of my body. My boys were anxious, only leaving me to visit the area and then hurrying back to lie at the foot of the bed. Mrs Twentyfold called through the door and Will rattled the handle and begged me to come out, but I did not answer it. I could not bear their company. I wanted nothing to do with the world.

As my bruises turned from black to purple and the pain eased, I forced myself to get up. I did not want to think about Barney and his troubles, the Nasty Man and his roughs. They were nothing to do with me. I went unwashed and unshaven for days, and if it hadn't been for someone (Will or Trim, I expect) paying Mrs Twentyfold to put bread, tea and milk outside my door, I believe I would have starved. And, with nothing to occupy me, I could have taken to my stew of a bed again, if it hadn't been for a change in the weather. Standing at the window one morning, I saw that there had been a fierce frost during the night, both outside – where the bushes in Mrs Twentyfold's area were dusted white – and inside, where it lay thick upon the glass. My room was bitterly cold too, and I lit a fire (which I never did as a rule before the evening) and wrapped myself in my coat and scarf until the warmth had spread. The stale stink of illness floated in the damp air, the ice on the window began to melt and drip onto the floor-boards, and I was fixed by the mournful eyes of my two faithful companions. This would not do! And within a quarter of an hour, I was outside, on Mrs Twentyfold's top step.

We avoided the wasteland and the Aquarium, and those other familiar places – the chop house, Garraway's, even the Pavilion – and wound our way through squares and back streets in the direction of our country retreat. It would be just a visit, I thought. But if Titus Strong begged me to stay and help with the cabbages and look out for Lord Bedford, then, since he was such a good, old friend, how could I refuse? I hoped he would beg me to stay.

We made good time, despite my injuries, and I

was even enjoying that familiar bite at the back of my throat from the bitter, acrid air. Brutus and Nero trotted in front, eager to inspect the usual posts and walls but, when I stopped to ease my aching ribs, they stood patiently by me, waiting until I was ready to continue. I felt stronger, and more certain that today my fortunes would change. Then, turning a corner, I was brought up sharp when I spied my name, in two-inch capitals of dense black ink, hallooing me from a wall. It seemed like a year ago that I had found Pilgrim in the hallway of the Aquarium waving just such a bill as this at me, but without doubt it was one and the same: the Royal Crown Theatre, otherwise known as Tipney's Gaff on Fish-lane, the very one, next door to my friend Pilgrim's bookshop. It still roared a programme of kingly proportions and startling celebrity. Mr Macready's name was almost as large as mine, and the dramas of *Othello, Richelieu* and *The Miller and His Dogs* were given similar bravado. No one who reads these bills is duped. Everyone knows that it is all guff: Mr Macready (if he did but know it) merely 'recommends' the Royal Crown Theatre and *Othello* will be done and dusted in twenty minutes! In fact, the company consisted of only a handful of performers – Mrs Dearlove, Mr Crowe, Mr Tafflyn, Mr Corney Sage and Miss Lucy Fitch, Les Trois Acrobatiques, Senor Spaniardo and the Infant Prodigy, Little Louisa Penny who, but seven years old, will dance and sing – and, of course,

Mr Bob Chapman and his excellent hounds, Brutus and Nero. The street was liberally pasted with these thin bills, which were doing their job and attracting much attention, particularly from crowds of boys.

And there was my good friend Pilgrim, out upon the step of his establishment, anxiously inspecting his neighbours. The building work seemed to have been completed, and the whole shopfront, even up to the gutter, was covered in bright flapping bills announcing not only the Royal Crown Theatre and Bob Chapman, but also an Exhibition of Waxworks and Novelties and one for which the artist had exercised his brush and a great quantity of red paint. In particular, the execution business of the waxwork show was most carefully attended to, and almost every bill had a picture of a man being stretched, and a grinning madman holding up a bloody cleaver or a rope!

The shop was transformed. Where its front window had been, was a brick wall and a second entrance (or exit) had been put in on the opposite side to the present door. I've seen these places many times before. They are what the showman calls an 'in-and-out' show, and do exactly that – let people in one door and out the other, swiftly and without a crush. This in-and-outer had a penny theatre at the rear, the Royal Crown no less, and while one slack-jawed youth announced the bloody delights of the waxworks ('The reeel choppin' block, and reeel blood'), another was

161

roaring out the improving drama of 'Maria Marten and 'er 'orrible murder by the willain Corder in the Red Barn! Just about t'begin!'

Poor Pilgrim was in a state of terrible agitation. 'You see how it is, Bob Chapman! Thieves and wagrants on my very doorstep!'

('Quiet, you! I'll tell him, John Pilgrim!')

'Not you! Day and night that commotion is murdering my ears. And now it's underground.'

('I've told you. Buried treasure and pirates.')

'And Bob Chapman appearing next door! What did I tell you? Did you believe me?'

('We have the bill to prove it, don't we? Shove him out, you waster! You frog-taster! What're you afraid of, John Pilgrim?')

'Not you, cat-sick-man! Bob Chapman is our friend. No gaff-acting for him. An impostor, that's who it is.'

He thrashed wildly at himself and pinched his own arm and kicked his shins.

('Bob Chapman should smash the man who has been taking his name, damn him!')

'He's right, for once.'

('Smash the man!')

'Not with those hands,' and mad old Pilgrim nodded at my poor bruised mitts and hooked my two boys into his shop (to feed them sugar and biscuits), slamming the door behind him.

I was eager to be on my way, and my ribs were aching so that I could hardly breathe, but being, so to speak, in the business, I am never too proud to look into a penny show, nor even a gaff. They are not all as bad as people claim. I have seen conjuring and balancing, as well as singing, dancing and acting in these places that would not disgrace the stages of some of our nobbier theatres. Of course, not all are up to the mark, and many are the last resort of the mummer turned to drink. His cobweb throat and dull eye single him out, and if he is not looking pale upon the stage, he can be found sweating in the gin-shop or sleeping in his costume on a sack of flour. But, when I see these unfortunate relics of the profession, I remind myself that, if ill-fortune had not been looking the other way when I found my present comfortable shop, I too could have been pumping the harmonium outside such a gaff.

If you have never been inside a penny exhibition, let me say now that it is not for the faint-hearted. Not that there are fearsome things to be seen, for anyone with half a cup of sense will know that the blood, splashed about like a pie man's gravy, is merely paint and water, and that the figures, all wide-eyed and leering whether they represent royalty or saint, are made of plaster and sawdust. That the 'terrible sharp sword' is fashioned from a roof-timber, and even the hangman's rope is worn to a thread in places, not from long service upon the three-legged mare, as the guide will assure you, but from hauling barrels in and out of Mr Publican's deep cellar at the Two Royal Children over the way. Gloom is the showman's friend. From the entrance, where it is so dark that you are forced to lean upon the greasy wall – greasy from the numbers of shoulders which have leaned there before you – you must grope your way into the nether regions, to a room lit only by a couple of naked gas flames (courtesy of the previous occupant) and a tuppenny tallow. What you cannot see, you must imagine!

But if it is not a familiar resort of yours, you will not be hardened to the celebration of crime and criminals to be found in a penny show, and it will shock you to see how casually people enjoy scenes of murder and execution. How they will stand for minutes before even the roughest tableau of a man cutting his wife's throat, having already banged his infant's head against the hearth stone. And though the waxfigures are awkward and hardly resemble the living or the dead – a change of costume next week will transform the Empress of Russia into William Tell or Springheel'd Jack – people will still relish, for as long as the showman allows, the scene of outrage and the blood splashed liberally all over. And once outside in the street, they will straightway pay a penny to see it over again!

Today, a lanky youth, a mere streak of water, described the exhibits for general edification. ''Ere,' he says wearily, 'are the very stones under which poor Mrs Vowles was buried. They was lifted from the 'ouse and brung 'ere with the dust and blood still upon them.'

164

A murmur of interest goes around, for the so-called 'Deptford Murder' was of recent and terrible notoriety and the audience of wide-eyed boys shuffle forward to see it better and have to be restrained from dipping their fingers into the gore.

'And 'ere h'is the wery plaster wall agin which Mr Vowles, h'in 'is fit of h'awful temper, slung 'is beautiful child an' dashed 'er very brains upon. 'Ere you may h'observe the drips of the brains as they run all-a-down the plarster.'

There certainly was a disagreeable stain upon the wall, on which was also the engraving of a dog begging for a bone, torn from a picture paper, and two tickets for a distant tea-gardens, 'to include band, dancing platform extra'.

The other waxwork tableau – comprising a scene from *Hamlet* showing the appearance of the prince's father as a ghost (a very pale figure in a large hat gesturing to heaven) and the murder of the poor little princes in the Tower of London ('Look at that old feller, a-smothering them to pieces!' cried one boy. 'Wouldn't I like to find out where he lives!') – were only part of the show. In another corner was a talking fish that was brought out of its dark and narrow box to blow out a candle and count to five in a strange coughing voice, and rewarded by being shoved roughly back into its box again before anyone could be more interested. In the final, gloomy alcove was a display of antique swords and knives (labelled 'INSTRUMENTS OF

TORCHER FROM ITALY' and all very carefully fastened down), after which we were emptied into a passage, one way leading out into the street and the other to the back of the house where, according to a swarthy man lashed by a wide belt into a uniform several sizes too small, 'Here it is! Just about to begin!'

All, here they were! The villain who had taken my name, installed in the gaff theatre and ready to do his show. I handed over another penny and traced another dark and greasy path to the theatre. This had evidently been the back room of the shop, for there were still traces of it left – a fireplace, a cupboard (without its doors), remnants of pictures pasted to the walls, and gas mantles (without their covers) doing service as lights on a stage raised up no more than a couple of feet, and draped with ill-matched curtains. And, what with the heat of the gas, the closely packed audience (we were crowded as tight as herrings in a barrel, standing room only) and the air thick with 'Black Jack' and 'Old Moley', it was a veritable inferno.

I stood, shoulder to shoulder, with a stern-faced coal-heaver, his hands – if he had any, for I never saw them – thrust into his trouser pockets, and for the duration of the entertainment, he neither moved nor spoke. He was exceptional, however, because the rest of the audience was in a state of excited fury, which erupted at every moment with shouts and roars of laughter. Boys were mostly responsible, and seemed to count it as a point of honour to jump upon the back of their nearest neighbour at every turn, and call, at their utmost volume, obscenities which would make the roughest cazzelty blush.

A roar of applause greeted the sheeney who crept in and took his place at the piano. When he ran his fingers up and down the keys, you would have thought he had played a symphony with his feet, and when he struck a chord and from the side of the stage a dark, lean mummer in high boots and a mouldy velvet cloak swung out and stood, bandy-legged, with his hand held up for silence, it was as though Mr Macready himself had appeared, just for a day!

'Gentle friends,' he cried above the tumult, 'today – some tumblin'-an'-balancin'.'

'Where's the dog-man?' cried someone.

'Where's Chapman and his dogs?' cried another.

Yes, I thought, I'd like to see that man too!

But the mummer was having none of it.

'Singin'-an'-dancin' – great drammer of King Richard – what lorst 'is 'orse when most incon-wenient to 'im.'

'Chapman!' went up the cry. 'Bring him out now!' was followed by a wholesale stamping of feet and under different circumstances, I might have felt flattered! But the mummer held up his hand and looked mournful. 'I regret – Chapman and dawgs – indisposed – on account of bad meat.'

And that was that. My namesake was dismissed, the mummer disappeared with a flourish and on shuffled a stout fellow in dirty pink tights, who juggled four ill-matched balls and quickly wore out the patience of the audience, who were still baying for Chapman! Finally, the cry of 'Hook it, macaroni!' was joined loudly in chorus, which immediately unbalanced the juggler, who lost his nerve and the balls. The ivory-thumper filled the interval and then on scuttled three white-faced clowns. Tumblers. *Acrobatiques*. It was soon apparent that they were only boys, but not half bad, and they started off with some simple balancing and flip-flaps. The smaller lads were unsure of themselves, and looked to their older friend to take the lead, and he was certainly the most impressive, quite a pro, though still young. He stood on his head, balanced on a barrel and turned a somersault with ease. Even the crowd were half-appreciative and the jibbing was replaced by encouraging cheers and then by stamping feet in time to the music, which produced not only little flurries of dust and plaster from up above and a shuddering of the floor-boards beneath our feet, but also the lean mummer, who stopped the show by holding up his hand.

'Appreciative of your goodwill,' came the phrase.

More stamping and shouting. The mummer's hand went up again.

'But deee-sist from stampin' – will yer!' He drew a great arc with his arm. 'Bring the 'ole 'ouse down! – all perish in consequence—'

Laughter rocked the audience, and there were more intervals of wild cheering and stamping, and roars of approval. It was a welcome hiatus for the tumblers: the air was hot and thick, and they were breathing heavily. Sweat melted the whiting on their faces, which were soon streaked and dirty, and when the older one screwed his fist into his eye much of the paint came away. Then I realized I knew him.

It was the boy. Barney.

I watched him with renewed interest as he threw himself into the remainder of the act, and then, standing on his two hands whilst the boys carefully balanced an upturned champagne bottle on the soles of his feet, he walked from the stage to raucous applause. It was a clever trick, one he must have learned whilst on the fairground with his Pa, for it was well-taught and showed a deal of skill. Indeed, he was a boy the circus-folk might have looked twice upon and taken up, but now, here he was, in Tipney's Gaff, a shop no professional would choose unless he was on his uppers. Or unless his Pa had been stretched.

I mused upon this while the next performer, a little girl in short skirts and wearing a smile that only her mother could have beaten into her, pranced heavily around the stage. Small, dark-eyed and dark-haired, decked out in the ribbons and glass beads that mothers believe enhance their child's beauty, she registered hardly at all with the audience who wearied of her immediately. And I recognized her also. She was the little child so cruelly rejected by the dancing master at the Pavilion and, I suppose, in consequence forced to earn a penny for her family in this place. Another child put to this hard life of labour for little reward. I felt sorry for her, but also for Barney Kevill – that was his name! – alone in the world and playing here in this gaff. The last time I'd seen him, weeks ago it seemed, was from a cab through a rapidly closing eye as he stood on the steps of the Aquarium.

Enough. Strong's Gardens called me.

I pressed through the crowd and, feeling a blow of cold air, I followed it. But I turned, not into the street, but the back yard. After the fuggy gloom of the theatre, it took a little time for my eyes to accustom themselves to the glare of light. The yard was small and cobbled, with walls on either side and a building at the back which might once have been a stable. The backs of shops were always a mess, but the outbuildings, if the owners (or tenants) were cute enough, could be rented out to make a pile or more. On one side, beyond the wall and through the gate, were the tumbledown sheds which made up Pilgrim's yard. On the other, behind a shop selling anything from cabbages to candles, were outhouses in which a couple of pigs and a family of four shared equal space.

There was no sign of my namesake, and no evidence of Brutus and Nero's canine impersonators either, just a gaggle of mummers in their stage clothes, sitting upon the upturned buckets and barrels, ready to perform *Richard III*. They paid no heed to me, nor to Barney who, with his shoe bag over his shoulder, sauntered over, rubbing his eye the while and looking carefully about him.

'Here you are. Them bashers made a mess of your face.'

He seemed unsurprised to see me. Indeed, his small, round face was almost blanked of expression. He nodded at the stable.

'I found it. That's it. That was my Pa's shop, Kevill's Photographic Studio and Emporium. I got to thinking when Mr Lovegrove asked me. I asked the Princess if she knew. She said she thought it was hereabouts. Fancy you coming here. Was it on account of the dog-bloke taking your name?'

He didn't wait for an answer.

'I've seen the Nasty Man too, but he hasn't clocked me yet. I got to be careful. Still, I'm going to serve him out.'

There was a roar of laughter from within the gaff, which broke like a gun-shot upon the quiet of the yard.

'It don't look much,' he was saying, nodding to the building, 'but my Pa set it up like a reg'lar shop inside. There are proper winders in the roof, you know, with shutters over them and a big photographing machine with a cloth. It's still there.'

It was a sizeable building and I could see that

it had once been smart. A flag fluttered on the roof, and there were even the remnants of old advertising on the door – 'Quality Pictures' – 'Latest Styles'. But it was run down now, the wooden walls rotting and full of holes. I was surprised that the photographing machine was still inside. In this district, it should have been stolen in a blink, and so in spite of my haste to get out of the city and into Titus Strong's cabbage fields, I was curious and wanted to see for myself.

But Barney grasped my arm and held me back, frowning and listening.

'Not yet.'

And then he pushed me hard into the shadow of the building.

'It's him! The Nasty Man! He mustn't see us!'

I was so surprised that it took me a moment to realize what he had said, and another to register that the voice, getting louder as it emerged from the gaff, was indeed the Nasty Man. He was holding a child by the wrist – it was the little creature I had just seen dancing on the stage – and looking about him. To make sure no one was here.

'Listen to me,' he whispered in that familiar, soft voice. 'When you have danced your next little dance – which you give so beautifully, my dear! – don't run away, but come to me here and I will take you to see the fine gentleman and he will give you a present!'

The child shook her head.

'I would rather go home, sir.'

'Dear child, you'll come to me. Here.'

He was bending down to speak to her, leaning upon a black cane. The child struggled against his grasp.

'My ma will wait at our street end for me. I have to go to the theatre tonight. She'll give me a whipping if I don't go home.'

'And I will give you a whipping if you do. How would that be? Don't you remember how I punished you when you disobeyed me last time?'

The child was silent. And had stopped struggling.

'Don't you remember how it hurt? And how the nice gentleman comforted you and rubbed your little red cheeks better?'

She was perfectly still now.

'Perhaps another whipping?' said the Nasty Man, straightening up and drawing the cane across the cobbles of the yard. 'We'll see what the gentleman says, shall we?'

The creature regarded her, as a cat watches a mouse, and then, as though he was considering every moment, leaned towards her and whispered in the little one's ear. She gasped and began to cry, which seemed to be his purpose for he slowly took off one of his pale gloves and, with great care, pinched the skin of her chubby arm between the tips of his fingers. She squealed and cried and rubbed her arm.

'There! Like a kitten!' he mocked. 'It shall have a hard lesson if it isn't a good kitten!' He pinched her again. 'Now it knows what to do. It'll come here, won't it, and be good!'

He pushed her ahead of him into the gaff and stood for a moment, pulling on his glove, and looking about him. If he saw us or heard our hearts slamming in our chests, he showed no sign of it, but simply rapped the stones with his cane and strode back into the gaff.

Barney and I stood in silence. He was breathing hard through clenched teeth.

'Hear that, Mr Chapman? What was that about then? Something dodgy. Stealing off little kids, by the sounds of it. I will serve him out, mark me, I will. For my Pa's sake. And hers.'

What I had heard, I didn't understand. What I had seen, the Nasty Man's careless cruelty to a child, I could well believe. But I didn't want to know any more of it, and neither did I want the Nasty Man to see me again in the company of Barney. Even more reason, I thought, to collect my dogs and hurry to Strong's Gardens and safety. I started for the gate, the one that led into Pilgrim's yard, but Barney clutched my arm urgently.

'Will you help me serve him out, the Nasty Man? I've got a plan. All it needs is for you to come back here with your dogs when I send for you, to make sure of it. I mean to have him – look at this! – I've got a stopper.'

His eyes were bright as he produced from his shoe-bag a small gun, what the hunting brigade call a cripple-stopper, used to put wounded birds out of their misery. What it would do to a man, I had no idea. He shoved it back into the bag.

'It won't be any trouble to you. Or your dogs. I'll send for you. All right?'

He didn't wait for an answer, but disappeared into the gaff.

If I had taken Barney more seriously, if he had told me his plan at that moment, I would have persuaded him against it and, indeed, would have refused to be part of it. But I was eager to get out of the gaff and Fish-lane and any chance meeting with the Nasty Man. I gave not a second thought to Barney's scheme to serve out the Nasty Man.

My dogs were in Pilgrim's yard when I opened the gate. I wanted to be on my way quickly and Brutus, clever dog, seemed to understand and came to stand by my side and leant gently against my leg, ready to be off. But Nero had gone exploring. He had discovered the tumbledown shed of rotten wood and sacks and barrels (home to rats, without a doubt) which lay at the bottom of my friend's yard. This was once quite a nobby street, popular with tradesmen and, with market gardens at the back growing vegetables and orchards full of fruit trees, a jolly place to live. But that must have been a long time ago, I thought, for now it was a crowded street and not at all nobby, and the backs overlooked not gardens but high walls and fences. Pilgrim's yard was piled with rotting books, all stacked and messed together by rain and damp. Great mouldering heaps, about to fall apart or fall over, making good nests for colonies of rats and mice. It was little wonder that the Growler from the gaff had not brought in some dogs. This would be an ideal ratting ken. But what interested Nero seemed to be beyond the book heaps. He was intent upon squeezing himself behind the paper mountains and, fearing that he might stray and wanting to be away soon, I went after him.

It was a foul place, full of scuttling creatures and quite treacherous. Any slight disturbance caused the book heaps to sway and slide. Piles of newspapers gave way underfoot and my boot disappeared more than once into a slimy porridge of rotten paper and crunched down upon nests of sleeping snails. Of course, the terrain presented no difficulties for Nero, who was intent upon following the scent he had picked up. He disappeared for a moment, and although I could hear him, snuffling and scrabbling, I couldn't see him, so I scaled yet another mountain range of paper, stumbled and overbalanced and, crashing heavily into the shaky fence beyond the sheds which immediately gave way, I tumbled forward, onto my knees, grabbing at the thin air, and almost diving into the railway cutting below.

I had not realized! I had no idea that the railway had come this far, and was taking its destructive course behind the yards of Fish-lane, thirty feet below. Already the rails were laid and the tunnel, a little way distant, was being cut and covered. It was no wonder that nearby houses were leaning over and falling down, that the floor of the gaff was unsafe, and the thunder of the workings and the stink of old earth hung in the air.

I caught my breath and looked about me for Nero, but he was nowhere to be seen. For an awful moment, I thought he had disappeared over the edge of the precipice, but the sound of his snuffling told me that he had gone in quite another direction. Over the dividing fence. Into the yard next door. It was his wagging tail I saw first, and I thought he had sighted a rat and was excited by the anticipation of the hunt. But then I saw that he had squeezed himself between the panels of the fence and those of one of the buildings. The gap was probably no more than a couple of feet wide and full of leaves and dead brambles and I balked at the tightness of it, but Nero was ahead of me, and was now pressing his black nose against a gap in the wall of the building and snorting hard. If he attracted attention, if the Nasty Man were in ear-shot, we would have trouble on our hands, so I followed, to grab him by his scruff and pull him back. It was then that I heard voices inside the building. And realized that we were behind George Kevill's Photographic Studio and Emporium.

I listened, trying to make out who was speaking. I recognised the child and the Nasty Man. And the voice of another man. Perhaps two men. I held my breath, signalled to Nero to be quiet, and listened to the scuffling and sounds of movement within. A mild, musical voice was speaking, unfamiliar, and I could only hear snatches of what he was saying.

'. . . won't you sit here, my dear . . . yes, by me . . . much better . . . like to drink this? . . . (A laugh.) . . . yes, it does burn your lips . . . such pretty lips . . . ah, now then . . . take off that pretty mantle . . . yes, and your dress . . . let me help . . . don't struggle, my dear . . . come, sit here, on my knee . . .'

Nero lay awkwardly at my feet. He would stay there until I told him to move. But if we moved, we would be heard. There was no possibility of shifting silently in that cramped place.

So I waited.

And listened.

There were thuds inside the stable. Everyday noises. Furniture being shifted, perhaps. Someone walking about.

'Put the machine there.' It was the Nasty Man, his voice was unmistakeable. 'Yes, it will do well there.'

Somebody mumbled, and the voices were suddenly clearer.

'Good. Is everything ready?'

A pause.

'Is she drowsy, sir?'

Mumbled reply.

Another pause.

A child's moan.

And then broken words.

'. . . exquisite . . . like a bird . . . a mouse . . .'

'Good, good.' The Nasty Man. 'But . . . don't linger, my lord . . . the show will finish soon . . . people in the yard.'

A muttered exchange, laughter, the sound of glasses.

There were gaps in the wall where the wood was rotted through. I pushed my finger in to make it wider, and pressed my eye against it. I could see the edge of a red chaise and its twisty feet. And the legs and booted feet of a man. The naked legs and tiny, slippered feet of a child. I saw a man's hand upon the pale leg. I guessed she was sitting on his knee. The skirts of the Nasty Man's coat passed back and forth, the hand stroked the child's leg, and then, suddenly, darkness. I strained left and right to find another gap in the wall, but someone or something was in front of it.

'Ow! Oh! Sir, please. You're hurting me . . .'

I held my breath, and tried again to see.

A pause, and then more of the child's pitiful cries. 'You stop that!' and 'Oh, I don't like that!' and cries of terrible distress.

'Shall I bind her mouth up?' It was the Nasty Man.

'No, no! Let it be. I like to hear her.' The other was breathing heavily, excited.

'But, if she makes too much noise . . .'

The child cried out. 'That hurts!'

More movements, hurried this time.

'Do as you're told and it won't. Now, lie still . . .'

'No! No!'

More sounds of struggle.

'You'll have to hold the bitch still, sir. Otherwise the picture won't be a good one.'

There was silence, then a small voice crying, 'Sir, please. Oh, sir, it hurts! It hurts! I want my mother.'

A surge of laughter broke in, the Nasty Man's high and shrill. 'Mama! Mama! She wants her mama!'

'Please, sir. Oh no, sir! Please don't do that!'

'Keep still, damn you!'

'Oh! Oh!!! Sir, sir, please, no! You hurt me! You hurt me! Let me go!'

I clapped my hands over my ears to shut out the horror, but it came anyway with a voice roaring, 'Damn her! The bitch has scratched me!' and the sound of a slap – once, twice, three times and the child's terrified scream – 'Hold her down, can't you! Hold her legs!' and then, 'Now I have you! Ah, yes!'

And on it went until I thought I would go mad – the child screaming, begging to be allowed to go, promising to be a good girl, and the Nasty Man's laughter, rising like a wicked song above it all.

Suddenly, there was a pause. A breath. A cough. Someone shifting about.

I put my eye to the gap again, but it was still dark. There was the sound of footsteps upon the floorboards.

A child's voice crying: 'Oh, it hurts, it hurts,' and 'I want my mother.'

There were murmurs, a hurried conversation. I couldn't hear it, or see beyond the chaise. But then the Nasty Man said, 'This is a tidy mess. I think you've cramped it, sir. Look at the blood everywhere.'

'If she hadn't struggled so . . . It wasn't my fault,' said the other. There was fear in his voice.

'All the same, sir. My lord.'

'What are we to do?'

The child moaned in pain. The murmur of conversation. And then the Nasty Man again, 'Well, of course, I can do it. But it will cost you.'

'Anything.'

'An extra – ten pounds.'

'Yours,' said the other, 'when you've done it.'

'What? Kill it *now*, sir?'

'Here. In front of me, man. Get it done.'

The Nasty Man laughed, but there was no humour in it. 'I am at your service, of course. But there'll be no pictures of *this*. You – put the machine away.'

I put my eye to the gap. The chaise and its twisty legs. The Nasty Man's light-coloured britches and another man, standing close by. And the pale legs of the child and its bare feet and curled toes. I looked away. What did I need to see? Now I could hear everything that was happening and put pictures to it in my head – her cry of fear and panic, a thud as she fell to the floor, the sound

181

of a struggle as she tried to get away, the feeble kicking of her heels. A beat of four. Or was it the sound of my heart thumping in my chest? Then someone cleared his throat and spoke in a voice trembling with emotion – or excitement?

'Ah. Perfect.'

Another beat. Then people moving about.

'You. Get rid of it,' said the Nasty Man.

Sounds again of movement. A cough.

'She scratched my face. I think there's blood on my face.'

'Hers, I think, my lord.'

'My pictures? You did make them, didn't you?'

A third man spoke, but his voice was so low I could not make out what he said.

'Collect them at the usual place. From him.'

The door opened and closed. Once, twice. There was the sound of footsteps receding.

I waited. Nero shifted and looked at me, ready to go. Inside the shed someone was moving, breathing heavily. I forced myself to look through the gap, but it was black again. If I stayed here until the door opened, I could see who was inside. And then – what would I do? Run to the magistrate? Fetch Tipney and his mummers? Rouse up Pilgrim? A child had been killed. Someone must want to do something.

Nero, however, had other plans and, though he didn't move from my side, he was tense and set up a low growl which would soon be heard within, so, risking all, I touched his head and we made a mad dash, scrambled frantically out, over the Alpine range of paper, slipping and sliding and causing great avalanches and disturbing a nest of rats which ran squealing across the yard, chased by Nero and joined by Brutus.

I peered over Pilgrim's fence. The stable was quiet, the door shut. There was no one in the yard, and stillness settled over everything, as though the world was holding its breath.

Pilgrim stood in his doorway, frowning.

'Where have you been, Bob Chapman?'

('Over the fence and far away.')

'What did you see?'

('You should have told him, you devil!')

'How should I know he would go poking about over there? We don't go any further than here!'

Pilgrim shuffled towards me, then stopped and drew a line with the toe of his boot upon the brick cobbles.

('Death to go further! That's what the big man said!')

'Didn't he just? But didn't *you* sneak down there, along with the rats, to see the amusement?'

('Not I.')

'You know you did.'

('I'll bite your tongue out, you.')

'Listen to him.'

('You lie as fast as a dog can trot.')

'Listen to me! Corpus delicti!'

('Baw baw!')

'*Corpus delicti*, Bob Chapman!'

('Beggar me! You're another!')

I couldn't bear to hear him a moment longer. With his voices ringing in my ears, I ran through the shop, scattering books left and right, upturning tables, tugging at the door and breaking the latch. I ran into the street with Brutus and Nero at my heels, and down Fish-lane, like a madman, and kept running, knowing that if I had stayed a moment longer, I would have beaten my brains out upon the very stones of the yard.

CHAPTER 11

NOWHERE TO HIDE –
THE AQUARIUM –
RETURN TO TIPNEY'S GAFF –
INTO THE DARKNESS

I have given up Strong's Gardens today.

I turn my face to the Aquarium. A safe haven. Balm in Gilead, as Titus Strong would say.

A cup of tea behind the screen. A moment or two to consider – the magistrate or the police station?

I try to picture my workplace, its warm calm, as I walk briskly to it. In my head, I count down the boxes and their contents – the eggs, the balls, Brutus's lantern, the kettle, the teapot, cups, the tea box, the tray on which they stand, my coat, my hat. I hold the image of my stand before me, and put aside everything else. I put my mind and my thoughts in this quiet, safe place.

I hurry down street after street, Brutus and Nero trotting at my heels. Walking helps, the rhythm is a comfort, but I am sweating with exertion and shaking and must dig my hands into my pockets to keep madness from breaking out. Dodging through the crowds, I slip on the cobbles and the pain has me hugging my ribs and gasping for breath. But I don't stop, not for a moment. Through the afternoon streets, where clerks are hurrying back to their desks and early-morning carters are propped in a doorway catching ten minutes' sleep. A baby squalls on its mother's hip, a drunk clutches at a lamp-post. I take it all in, but I do not see it.

Around a corner, and there it is, the Aquarium, with the familiar banners flapping upon the walls and a gang of sharp-faced boys crouched around the door. Every day they call to my dogs and I wait whilst they pat and stroke them and call them 'reg'lar spankers', just as their fathers would. Not today, though.

Ignoring their cries of 'What's the row, Sam?', I hurry inside. The hall is cool and dark and quiet. Conn is manning Pikemartin's box, is rocking to and fro, and I hurry past him. But he sees me and calls and I stop at the bottom of the stairs, but don't turn around.

'Bob, Bob, she's done for me,' he wails, and arches his spine with a grimace. 'My back is breaking out again. The wounds are opening up. Blood everywhere.'

I take the stairs three at a time. He calls after me. 'Bob! For the sake of the Holy Child, show some pity to a broken man!'

I hurry to the salon but, putting my head around the door, I see it is crowded with people. Some are in front of my stand, waiting, looking at the clock, gazing about them. A man peers behind

186

the screen and shakes his head and says something which makes everyone laugh. He resumes his place and waits.

All I want is a moment's silence. Just to think. To consider what I should do. To force the child's cries out of my head.

I close the door quietly and go up to the menagerie, passing a gaggle of young women on their way down who nudge each other and say 'aah!' when they see Brutus and Nero and whisper behind their hands when they see me. The door is half open and I step inside, leaving my boys on the threshold. There is a pleasant animal smell of straw and warm bodies. Bella comes to the front of the cage, and the cubs mew. She bares her teeth. The room is crowded, but I go in anyway and walk about like a customer, stopping in front of the birds and squirrels, the badger, the snakes coiled in their glass box, trying to feel calm, like the average man.

But, no. The everyday world continues out of my grasp. I am looking through a window at it, can see it, but cannot be a part of it. For I have heard a child killed and I don't know what to do about it.

I start down the stairs again, and meet Mr Abrahams, coming from his little office at the back of the third-floor landing. He is surprised and doesn't realize it's me at first, and then calls out. 'Bob Chapman! My dear friend! How are you! When will our customers see you again? And your fine animals?'

I don't ignore him, but I am already at the first

floor, where the board stands showing times of performances. It is a large slate upon an easel, and on it Mr Abrahams announces the special exhibitions and their times:

11.00	Moses Dann, the Skeleton Man. Before the grave consumes, Dann will amuse. Bones visible. Skin like paper.
12.00	The Prussian Giant, Herr Swann, will speak on various subjects and sing songs from his native region of Warmia.
1.00	Princess Tiny, the Smallest Woman in the World, will sing and entertain. (Entrance 3d)
1.30	Moses Dann performs again.
2.00	The Prussian Giant – songs of Warmia.
2.30	Princess Tiny. The Aquarium's resident fairy.

And so on, until the exhibitions end at half past ten in the evening. At the bottom of the board, in pink chalk, is the legend:

> The East London Aquarium is sorry to announce that Mr Bob Chapman and his Clever Dogs, Brutus and Nero, are indisposed for the duration.

Indisposed.

I want to laugh but, turning the corner of the stairs, I am caught in the ribs by the elbow of a stout lumper, sending a raft of pain through my side and down my arm. He looks at me curiously and enters the salon, still eying me over his shoulder. Mrs Gifford pushes past me with a smartly dressed gentleman at her elbow. She is nodding and talking to him, but I know she has seen me. The stairs are crowded, and the jostling is a trial. It's mid-afternoon and early workers, who have already finished their day's labours and bought their ticket, chatter in the hall and look at the coloured floor-plan on the wall and wonder what they shall see first. In every room, on every landing, there is something remarkable – swords and helmets, phials of fairy-tears and eleven-breath, cabinets of wax anatomy – hands and noses and ears – drums from African and shrunken heads from the South American Amazon. I have not seen half of it, Mr Abrahams once assured me. It rivalled the British Museum for its antiquities and curiosities.

It will not do.

None of this humbug, these gew-gaws.

Someone shouts.

'Hoi! Hoi! Bob Chapman!'

It's Trim.

'I wondered if you might be here,' he says breathlessly, coming after me. 'How are you? I've just sold a marching song to your friend the Giant for five shillings! And what do you think it's called?' He threw his head back and laughed! '"The Dutchman's leetle dog." It's a comic song. Your Giant's not a Dutchman, of course, but that don't signify!' He roars again, and even slaps his thigh with delight. 'What an excellent fellow he is! And what do you think of your old friend Trimmer turned librettist now? It's talent, Bob, nothing more or less. How are you?' he says again. 'Not working, I see from the board. Not going home, though? Out for a walk? Taking the air? It's good for you.'

He is bright-eyed and agitated, excited. He can hardly keep still.

'Not going home?' he asks again, and before I can respond, 'I have an urgent appointment in – you'll never guess, Bob! – Albemarle-street! Yes, Mr Murray! Well, perhaps not Mr Murray himself – but, then, you never know!'

He is so happy, so animated and full of optimism! I should have been able to shake him by the hand and clap him on the shoulder. Instead, it is Trim who takes my hand and pumps it hard and lifts his hat to Conn, who still hands out tickets, and hurries across the hall and out of the door.

The world has turned upon itself.

I am pushed about again, this time by Mrs Gifford, who shoulders past me a second time and cannot resist a jibe, 'If you're not well enough to work, Mr Chapman, you're not well enough to be loafing about here, watching them as must.'

She adjusts her hat and pulls on her gloves and makes a show of the little reticule on her wrist. She wants the world to see her and take notice of her. Brutus and Nero have placed themselves, like bookends, on either side of me, and they regard her with unfriendly eyes. But she's done with me; I'm beneath her notice.

'Is Pikemartin not here yet?' She addresses Conn. 'What's keeping him? If anyone asks for me—' She looks about her, 'I am gone upon an errand. That's all. Do you hear me?'

'I hear you, ma'am,' says Conn, with a curl of his lip, and curses her beneath his breath.

She leaves behind her a trail of stale sweat and indignation.

Everyone is busy. The Aquarium is bursting with people and noise, not at all the still and quiet place I hoped it might be this afternoon.

Conn beckons me over. He has taken a mouthful from a bottle in his pocket and his breath is thick with gin.

'If you see Alf, give him a nudge, won't you? *She's* on his tail. Tattling to the Boss about him. She'll lose him his job. And this job's his life, Bob. His very life. Like it is mine. Though Bella would have my blood first.'

I cannot bear to hear him talk so, and I escape into the street and turn my face to Fish-lane once again. For I have resolved. I must make sure.

I walk swiftly and with a purpose, and I'm at the gaff within half an hour, have paid my penny and been nodded through. I ignore the exhibition where the languid youth is still describing Mrs Vowles and her sorry end, have pushed through the boys trying to go round twice, and I'm fetched up in the yard again. A handful of tumblers and mummers stand around a smouldering fire, smoking pipes and passing a stone jug from hand to hand. They glance at me but make no move, which is fortunate for I haven't considered what I shall do if anyone challenges me.

I have only one thought, and it has plagued me since I ran away: that I must see inside the place with my own eyes.

And it is as if I had made an appointment. The lean mummer comes out of the gaff and rounds up his troupe to do battle with the tragedy of King Richard once more. The stone jar is left on the wall. The door to the gaff is banged shut. The yard is quiet.

It is greasy and paved with mossy stones. Remnants of scenery – a badly painted woodland scene, a withered tree-stump with a hole bashed into it – and heaps of bricks and timber clutter it from end to end. I pick my way through the debris and skirt the stable once again. I can see the trampled brambles and dead grass where, only hours ago, Nero and I stood, listening to a child being raped and murdered.

I put my ear to the stable door and, when I am certain there is no one inside (it is a risk I don't consider for long), I pull it open a little way to peer in: it is empty. If it hadn't been, and the Nasty Man or some other had been silently waiting for me to betray myself, I don't know what I would have done. Except that I felt a different man since this morning, and that the rules about everything I ever knew had changed. Brutus and Nero stand behind me, sniffing the air. I think they might have protected me. But I don't know.

I step inside.

It is a small, mean place in which to die. Rotten from roof to floor, underfoot the wormy timbers sink and, though at some time it has been patched, the drapery pinned to the walls does little to stem the thin draughts of cold wind. There is a grey light from the half-open roof shutters falling on a few rough pieces of carpet, a three-legged table, but the chaise I had spied through the gap in the wall is not there, and though I go about lifting the curtains and peering behind them, I only disturb colonies of spiders and rattle a nest of mice. It might have been simply another wretched building, falling down through damp, neglect and the undermining of the diggings nearby. There is nothing here to show that a child had died.

I wonder why I bothered to come here. I wonder what I thought I would find.

My dogs sniff about curiously, and while Brutus (who quickly loses interest) lays down upon one of the carpets to take a nap, Nero has his nose pressed to the floor and is scratching, then sniffing, then scratching again. Lifting the carpet,

I see that it covers a hole where the floorboards have rotted through and that underneath is a void and probably rats' nests. Nero is very excited, though, and will not come away, and I have some difficulty in holding him back from scrabbling the rotten wood. He is determined to discover the source of the scent he's picked up, I suppose, and he would, I am sure, have investigated further if there hadn't been steps on the yard and the door suddenly tugged open. I hurriedly throw the carpet back and drag Nero away, ready to run or defend myself, for it is certain there is nowhere to hide.

Barney Kevill must be surprised to see me and my dogs in this place, but he is not about to let me know. A startled look is enough.

'You back again, Mr Chapman? You after me?' and then, without waiting for an answer, 'By rights, this should be my gaff. Kevill's Photographic Studio and Emporium. I thought my Pa might have left something for me,' he says. 'Hid it. But I've looked top and bottom and there's no chink.'

He frowns.

He produces some cabinet cards from his pocket and thrusts them at me.

'Found these behind the wall. They've got my Pa's name and everything printed on them.'

They are regular cabinet photographs and some trade calling cards. The sitters are decent tradesmen photographed with the emblems of their trade: an undertaker posed with a shiny coffin, a haberdasher

194

with some bales of cloth surmounted by cards of buttons and lace, a butcher with a leg of lamb on a plate. As calling cards, they were unusual, a novelty. George Kevill could have made a good living from them, but perhaps he chose another route.

'Nasty Man's had a clear-out,' Barney says matter-of-factly, poking the curtain again. 'There *was* an old chaise in here, but I saw someone burning it out in the yard. 'Spect it was full of mice. And a nice bit o' carpet too. That's gone.'

Barney casts about again, and kicks up the carpets.

'Holes in the floor. Look where they've been pulled up and put back. There's a regular cavern down there. I'm going to get a lantern and have a proper look, see if my Pa left any coin underneath. And will I let the Nasty Man have it? Not I.'

He lay on the filthy floor and peered into the hole.

'There might be something down here, you know,' he says, shoving his hand through one of the gaps. 'If I could just pull up the boards. Yes. I can feel something. Like a roll of carpet.' He shuffled and stretched, turning on his side to get the better reach. 'Ner, can't get it. Have to come back.'

Nero joins him, sniffing excitedly at the hole.

'Hold up! Your dog's got a nose on him. And another half.'

He is right. Nero is anxiously digging at the rotten floor and the scraps of frowsy carpet as if

195

they were rabbit holes, and then sniffing long and hard.

'I reckon there is something, Mr Chapman, don't you? Perhaps it's chink. My Pa's fortune!'

He lies beside Nero, and puts his scruffy head against Nero's dark fur.

'Yes, there is. I'll come back with a lantern and a forcer and take up the floorboards. Then we'll see. Your dog's a good 'un, ain't he? He knows what's what.'

He rubs Nero's ears, and pats him hard, but even then Nero is reluctant to give up and I have to drag him away, and hold him back while Barney covers over the hole carefully with carpet, and then, brushing the dirt from his short trousers, as if they were quality, he looks about him.

'Yes, I'll serve the Nasty Man out, Mr Chapman. You still willing?'

He takes me by surprise. I wonder what on earth he thinks he can do, what either of us can do.

There is a noise outside and Barney pricks up his ears, almost as quickly as my two friends. Nero sets up a growl, a warning, and Barney puts his eye to a hole in the wall and steps back smartly.

'Look out! Someone's coming out of the gaff. Might be just one of the mummers, but I don't know. We don't want to be in here if *he's* coming. We should go. Come on.'

Outside, the cold of the winter afternoon is starting to drop, and the lights in the gaff are lit. Barney takes my arm.

'We can't go through the gaff. I'm not clowned up, and he knows you and your dogs. If *he's* there – or his bullies – they'll catch us. If you want, there's another way out. Only – are your dogs good at climbing?'

We clamber over the rotting book mountain and squeeze ourselves behind Pilgrim's stable. Barney deliberately moves the fence-palings away, one after the other, slotting them behind the shed, until a gap is revealed, large enough for us all to squirm through. We are perched, it seems to me, on the edge of a precipice. Below us is a cliff-side of dirt and stones, of tufted grass and scrubby bushes, all lightly sprinkled with frost, plunging down thirty feet. This chasm alone is terrifying, but even more so for me, as in the near distance, is the mouth of a great tunnel, looming round as a cry, and black to its depths. I cannot help but recoil and begin to post myself back through the fence. But Barney grabs my sleeve. 'Look, I know a way down. It's safe. Come on.'

We scramble along the top. The frost, which has never really disappeared, has made the narrow ledge slippery, so where Barney walks and Brutus and Nero trot, I crawl on my hands and knees, trying not to look below, as the tunnel mouth opens wider and closer. I try and distract myself by thinking and calculating. I reckon that we must have covered the length of Fish-lane, perhaps further. That the building beyond the fence is the abattoir, that I cannot support much more of this anxiety. We are now almost on top of the tunnel, looking sideways down upon it. It is half complete, still shored up by a skeleton of planks and wooden pillars, and slotted through with temporary platforms where the bricklayers stand to work. There is a rough, steep path cut into the side of the gorge, and while Barney scuttles across the tunnel's half-covered roof and waits for me, my two dogs scamper down the path and stand, panting, at the bottom, sniffing out rabbits.

I don't know what I'm running from, but panic is contagious and I follow the boy anyway. His head has already disappeared from view and he is clambering down the ladders and along the platforms, and calling for me to do the same. Though he is fleeing from the Nasty Man, I think he's probably enjoying the adventure. I follow him blindly. The ladders are rough and flimsy, with rungs missing, and slimy with the damp. The platforms are the same, boards unsecured and liable to move underfoot and, with a layer of mud and grease upon them, every step becomes treacherous. But it is the descent into that thick darkness which terrifies me. The dense, dank gloom of the tunnel swallows me up, but I dare not look back, for the sight of the grey sky disappearing far above will, I know, send me into a panic and I will dash up the ladder and run into the arms of the Nasty Man rather than plunge any further down. Just as that blue funk begins to rise out of control, though, my foot finds the ground, and the wet noses of Brutus and Nero find my hands.

'Come on,' Barney says anxiously, and takes my sleeve again. 'It's all right. I know this tunnel like my way home. Keep close to this wall. The other side isn't properly finished, and there's another one dug below us, so don't stray or you could fall in and I wouldn't be able to find you. No one would, 'cept the rats.'

Once we are in the tunnel and there is no prospect of going back, I give myself up to it. I stumble along, scraping my knuckles along the brick wall and trying not to fall. And I think perhaps Barney is right, for I do hear someone behind us. But it is not the sound of a chase, not the footsteps of someone trying to catch up with us. For when we stop, it is often perfectly silent except for the steady panting of my dogs and Barney's occasional whispered caution to 'Watch it! There's a dip hereabouts!' and 'Hold up, don't fall over this heap of muck!' Only every now and again do I think I hear someone. The crunch of stones, a cough. But I hope it's because I'm horribly nervous. I am like a blind man, clinging to the wall or the scruff of Brutus's neck, unable to call out and almost paralyzed with fear. More than once, Brutus and Nero disappear for a long time – to chase a rat, I suppose – and I think I've lost them, until they push their soft heads and wet noses into my hand and I hear them panting and sniffing. Then I breathe again, but it is a long and frightening expedition in the darkness that seems never-ending.

When I see the prick of light, so small at first that I think my eyes are playing tricks on me, I try not to look at it, for it fills me again with inexplicable horror. But then we race towards it and it becomes larger and the air colder, and then the great round O of the tunnel casts us into a strange landscape of brick heaps and piles of sleepers and rails. The air is dense with frost and, the cazzelties having finished their labours for the day, it is silent here also. But where we are I have no idea, that is until I look up and, seeing the hoardings and that familiar smear of red and blue bills, and realize, to my surprise, that we are in the wasteland. Barney is ahead of me, scrambling along the trackside and disappearing around a bend, and I run to catch him up, not wanting to let him out of my sight with the tunnel so close behind me. He is already clambering up the bank, where the sides of the cutting are at their gentlest and where a track has been roughly hewed out and laid with steps made of stones, bricks, planks of wood. The route, of course, that the cazzelties take, every day, to their grim work.

We stand, panting, at the top of the gorge and the wind whips across the wet ground. Barney rubs his eyes and then his nose, and squints at me.

'I sometimes come this way 'cos I like the adventure of the tunnel. You know what I mean?'

I nod. He is only a boy after all.

'Only, don't let anyone know about it, will you? 'Cos I shall need it to get away when I serve him out.'

He gives Brutus and Nero a final pat and salutes me.

I watch until his figure is lost among the heaps of mud and soil and remember how once, a lifetime ago, he burst in upon my settled life in this very place.

CHAPTER 12

THE SEIZE

I am all to pieces and want my bed.

My dogs are foot-sore and hungry.

After such a day, I shall lock the door.

I will count up my coin and buy a cart and horse in the morning, whether they are broken-backed or no. Or I will just leave.

Above all, I will try and forget what I have seen. But that cannot be.

No. Apparently, tonight is just the night for a mutton pie and a round of acrobatics and melodrama at the Fish-lane gaff. Such is the message delivered by the lanky youth, who introduced himself with a shake of the hand as Half-pint. He came out of the shadows like a shadow himself and plucked at my elbow. Said that young Barney urgently requested my presence, as agreed, and that if we made haste directly to Fish-lane, we should still be in time.

For his own part, he said he didn't usually carry messages from 'kids', but he felt sorry for him, knowing that his father had been stretched at Newgate only recently. And he gave him sixpence too. But, as we turned our faces into the biting wind and flurries of snow, he reminded me that he was only the messenger and wasn't party to any of the business, but he thought that if I considered myself any kind of a friend of Barney's, I should advise him against what he was planning to do.

'But then,' he said, not looking at me, 'you might have put him up to it. Perhaps you want a piece of the chink yourself.'

Fish-lane was still open for business. The Wretched Fly was still buzzing, Mimm's Pie Shop still baking, even the street-sellers were still calling up their 'Potatoes 'ot!' and 'Peas, all green!' But the Royal Crown Theatre and Waxworks was the loudest and brightest of them all. Not only was a harmonium out on the street, which Half-pint quickly appropriated, but an assortment of skinny youths and heavy men, all dressed in left-over costumes and second-hand boots (mostly with their toes hanging out), were pacing upon the pavement under the naphtha lamps, shouting in passers-by with that old-fashioned showman's promise of 'Just about to begin!' and 'You'll regret it if you miss it!' and 'Never to be repeated wonders!'

Another penny got me into the exhibition (how many had I spent these last few days!), and nothing much had changed except that, in the interval between my last visit only hours before, the scenes showing the Deptford murderer, Mr Vowles, now included his terrible execution ('only this morning'), and 'the actual hangman's rope what was used, still warm'! I shuffled through and paid another penny to go into the theatre, where the show had begun. Barney and his two young companions were already on the stage, giving their flip-flaps and preparing for the pyramid. A few minutes and the pianist played them off, the mummer striding on to announce, as before, the drama. I edged out of the door, into the dim passage and then the dark yard, where Barney was waiting, breathless, and grabbed my arm.

'I've got it worked, so don't get exercised. He's here.' He nodded to the shed. 'I'll serve him out easy as an old shoe. All you have to do is get your dogs to fetch him down. Snap!'

He gave me no time to think about it.

'Half-pint's slipped some liver in the Nasty Man's pocket. Only a button's-worth. But I recollect Mr Lovegrove telling me that your dogs are so good at the seize that they don't hardly need any meat at all. Just your say so.'

He was right. Brutus and Nero learned that staple of the theatrical dog's repertoire, the 'seize', when they were very young, and quickly too, because they were so adaptable and wise. A piece of meat, liver usually, is hidden at the actor's throat – or hand or leg, tucked into a scarf or a sock or a sleeve – and, because they are trained to take the meat and not injure the actor, the dog will leap and knock him to the floor and appear to have the man by the throat – or the arm or leg –

when he is merely taking the bait. Brutus and Nero are past masters of the 'seize'. Indeed, as Barney rightly said, they hardly needed the lure of meat and would go and knock a man down and appear to have him by the throat just at my command. It is a trick which looks very well upon a stage. But that is all. It *is* just a trick. And although it might shake the Nasty Man and take him by surprise – and who wouldn't be surprised to be felled by two snarling dogs! – he would suffer no harm. It was poor punishment for the injuries and suffering he had inflicted, but Barney was only a child, I thought, and to him it might seem enough.

Revenge was a dangerous game.

Full of misgivings, I went back into the theatre to await Barney who would come and get us, he said, when he was 'certain' of the Nasty Man. It was still only half-full of an audience only half-interested in the bloody exploits taking place on the stage – a highwayman drama, I guessed, given the cloak and roaring voice of the leading mummer. Even when the company stepped to the front of the stage to bow and curtsey at the end of the play, no one noticed. They were much too busy fighting and passing around jars of juniper and ale and hallooing their friends, who were pouring through the door. The gaff was filling up as wave after wave of boys and young men crowded in. If we left now, I thought, under cover of these rowdies, we could get away unnoticed, and be out of the plot. The boy would feel let down, of course, but there would be other opportunities for him to serve out his enemies and revenge his father. Ones more likely to succeed than taking the starch out of the Nasty Man with a theatrical trick. And I could seek advice from Will and Trim and perhaps find my own way of bringing him and his terrible business to justice.

My dogs and I edged towards the door, but it was immediately blocked by another surge of bodies and we were pushed back. The audience was being 'packed'. An old showman's trick, it worked on the principle that if an audience had no room to move, then it had no room to fight! And there was no escape, either. Once you were in, you were in. Heaven help us if there was a fire!

A chord from the pianist, and a red-faced mummer strode out, held his hand up for silence (which was generally ignored), and cried above the throng, 'And now to conclude our superior entertainment, The Little Wonder, Miss Topsy Truelove, will dance the schottische and give us a comic song.'

Another child performer, she tripped out upon the stage, and curtseyed low. Plump and clumsy and no more than seven years old, she bared her teeth into a forced smile, prinked and posed, assumed postures of coyness and knowingness in grotesque parodies, paused for the required counts of five and ten, and finally bobbed a curtsey, as if she had been doing it all her life. The audience roared and stamped its feet, pushing and punching itself and laughing wildly at its own wit. Brutus,

Nero and I hugged the wall, as far from the stage as we could press ourselves and, with a crowd of youths in front of us, we were hidden from view when the Nasty Man and his companion slipped through the door. Huge as an overfed turkey in his pale Benjamin and red waistcoat, he elbowed his way through the mass, his reputation preceding him for, though they spun around ready to take him on and some had their fists raised, when these young roughs saw who it was, they turned away quickly. His companion was smaller and much muffled-up, clinging to his side like a limpet, and showing interest only when the child began to sing, and when the audience yelled its approval. It was a vile song, though it began innocently enough:

> *Apples and chestnuts, walnuts and pears,*
> *Are poor little Jenny's humble wares,*
> *She stands about in the mud and murk,*
> *And no one there is going home from work*
> *To buy from poor humpbacked Jenny.*

And the chorus, apparently well-known by everyone in that room, was roared out with great gusto and much stamping of feet:

> *Pipkin ripe, pipkin round,*
> *Get it while it's fresh,*
> *Oh, poke my pipkin, if you like, sir,*
> *With your tosh, tosh, tosh.*

Oh, how heartily the Nasty Man sang! As if it were the most beautiful song in the world! As if he were centre spot at the opera! He swayed and roared, and his strange voice, high and thin, soared above all the rest. As the child piped up the many verses, he was in unison, conducting an invisible orchestra rather than a little girl, and although the roughs around him nudged each other and winked and smirked behind their hands, no one, not a single one, made fun of him. For the final verse, which was slower than the rest, he stood like one in a trance, with his eyes shut and his fat, pink face turned up to the ceiling:

But one kind gentleman stopped and said,
'What, no one buying your pipkins, my poor little
     maid?'
And stroked her hump and called her lady
And had her ride on his nag for a penny
And gave her – the clap, poor humpbacked Jenny!

His companion stamped and hallooed with the rest of the company (though not quite so familiar with the song), but when he roared out the final chorus – 'Oh, poke my pipkin, if you like, sir, / With your *handsome* tosh, tosh, tosh!' – the Nasty Man clapped him upon the back and, as the little mite curtseyed, they pushed through the crowd, hurried up the steps of the stage and followed her behind the curtain.

In that moment, seeing him in all his repulsiveness, I warmed to Barney's plan. Small justice to soil his white coat upon the yard stones and worry his smooth features compared to what he had done, but then perhaps the boy would be satisfied. Nevertheless, it was not without its perils. If the Nasty Man summoned his roughs we would be trapped. And where could we hide so that he would never find us?

Another act appeared on the stage – a natty little comedian with a shock of carroty hair dancing in clogs and singing 'The Industrious Flea' with much energy, who was too good for this place – and then an interval when the ivory-thumper did his best. But the din was quite hellish and no one could hear anything above the row. More noisy roughs charged in at intervals, packing the place to bursting, and amongst them I recognized Barney, completely transformed by his street clothes and looking every inch like one of them. For a few minutes, he laughed and jossed with them and then pushed through the throng and pulled at my arm. 'It's all set. Go on. I'm behind you.'

We pushed our way out and, with Brutus and Nero on either side of me, I waited in the yard like a man condemned, not knowing quite what to do. I think my dogs knew something was not as it should be, for they stood very close and Brutus pushed his head under my hand. I waited, and looked for the boy, and tried not to look at the stable where slivers of light, dancing on the ground, showed that someone was within. It had grown cold and my boys were restless before the door eventually opened. The Nasty Man stood, framed there for a moment, looking around and glanced back inside and nodded to the other, a pinch of a fellow, who stepped out, buttoning his coat and pulling on his gloves. Anyone could see he was anxious, urging the Nasty Man in a not-especially-hushed voice to 'Make haste!' and 'Get me away from here quickly!' But the grampus would not be hurried and gave instructions to someone within the stable to 'Call the minder!' and 'Make sure all is sweet and tidy!'

We were pressed hard into the shadows, whilst the Nasty Man and his companion paused in the middle of the yard in close conversation. It was in that pause that I felt a touch on my arm and Barney's whispered 'Go to it, Bob!'

I gave my dogs the signal, the one they knew for the seize. Obediently, Brutus and Nero ran forward, and their keen noses lit upon the Nasty Man and the tasty morsel that Half-pint had laid upon him. Just a trace of it was enough and they went to work with a will. He was startled and sprang back whilst Brutus lunged at him, paws high and Nero barked ferociously, knocking him to the ground. My dogs were used to this! They set on and Brutus gripped the sleeve of his coat, whilst Nero worried his boots. The Nasty Man writhed on the greasy cobbles, shrieking 'Mad dog! Mad dog!' at the very top of his voice. The commotion brought out a crowd from the gaff, who packed into the doorway and quickly began to cheer, and my dogs, who enjoy appreciation, went to it again with a will, though never with their teeth. Barney, hanging upon my arm, cheered wildly. 'Go to it, Brutus! Have his throat, Nero! I'll serve him out, you see! I have him now!' and the crowd quickly took up the cry, 'Have his throat! Have his throat!'

I laughed, thinking that they, like any gaff audience, were entering into the spirit of the scene and, really, it did my heart good to see the creature rolling in the dirty puddles. But as the cheers rose in volume and urgency and I saw the faces of the crowd, livid with drink, I realized with horror that they were in all seriousness, and that the cry of 'Blood! Blood! Blood!' was no jocular call from enthusiastic spectators, but real and insistent: they expected to see a real fight. Perhaps it happened regularly in this yard, a man set upon by dogs! I have heard of it, but never seen it. What would be their reaction when they discovered – when Barney discovered – that this was simply a stage trick! There would be no blood, no serious injury, and certainly no death. The moments sped by and Brutus and Nero, though they continued to leap and bark at the Nasty Man, were wearying of the business, for being theatrical dogs, they knew it should be over by now. The crowd too were becoming restless, and many had left. And, having overcome his original surprise, the grampus was now kicking out frantically and had twice caught Nero a hard thud in the belly with his boot, which made him yelp.

Enough.

I whistled them to me and my dogs bounded across the yard to my side, wide-eyed and panting, and eager for their reward. The roughs roared and cheered: 'Brutus! Nero! Brutus! Nero!' and 'Chapman! Chapman! Chapman!' Even though there had been no blood, they were, thankfully, not at all put out. They had seen my name on the posters. Perhaps they thought that this was part of the show? A song, a dance, a jaunty rendition of 'Alonzo the Brave' and then a man set upon by dogs in the yard! 'Send them in again!' cried someone. 'Finish the job!' cried another, and they laughed and cheered and someone clapped me on the shoulder as though I had done something very clever.

Barney was nonplussed and, with child-like disappointment, frowned mutinously. As I received yet another offer of a drink at the Wretched Fly and my dogs were petted within an inch of their lives, he punched me so hard in my ribs that I gasped.

'What you doin', Bob Chapman? I thought they was goin' to 'ave him. The seize, it's called, because the dogs seize the man's throat and rip it out. But they was just playin'! They warn't goin' to serve him out ever, was they?'

Half-pint had dug his way through the crowd and was at Barney's shoulder.

'Now then. Someone's gone for the coppers,' he said, looking at me. 'They're saying a man's been set upon by savage dogs!'

The Nasty Man had been helped to one of the barrels and was sitting nursing his arm. His hat had rolled away, his gloves had already been pinched. He was streaked with mud and his coat was torn. And he was very, very angry.

'I will burn this place down. You can tell Tipney that for nothing. He can expect a visit.'

The crowd murmured. Someone brought the Nasty Man a bottle and, as he took a long draw upon it, he fixed his eyes upon me.

'And you, Chapman. I will have your skin for this. No, better. I will have the skin of your mongrels.'

Silence dropped.

'I know you, dog-man. I know your friends, where you work, where you live. I know the soil-shoveller you visit, I know his slut of a daughter and his trollop of a wife. I know what you are and how to get you, and I will make you suffer for this. You cunt-face. You slit-jammer. You kid-stretcher.'

His voice was low and deep, and his fleshy lips twisted about the curses as though he had eaten them and was now vomiting them back. The yard was still, struck dumb, fear bristling the air.

'I told my Pa I would serve you out,' came Barney's voice. 'I will too,' and he stepped forward, pointing the stopper at the Nasty Man. I tried to

213

snatch it from him, and Half-pint too made to grab it. But the boy was too quick. His hand wavered, there was a click, followed by a breathless pause.

'It's bunged,' murmured someone in the crowd, and the whisper went round, almost like a sigh of relief. Barney shook the gun and tried again. A click. He bit his lip and screwed his fist into his eye.

'I will – serve – you – out!' he cried, vainly trying to fire the gun, click after click. 'You killed my Pa!'

The Nasty Man cast a contemptuous look at the crowd, though I am certain I saw fear in his eyes when Barney produced the gun.

'Someone make him safe, before he hurts himself!'

There was a ripple of laughter, and Half-pint drew Barney away into the gaff, and at that same moment a cry went up from the front of the house that police officers were even now turning the corner and would be here in minutes.

I didn't wait. I signalled Brutus and Nero to heel and we barged through the crowd, through the gaff, sending tables and wax figures flying, and when we reached the street I ran, once more, like a madman, taking turn after turn through narrow alleys and courts, and stopping only when I thought one more step would have my ribs burst through my chest. Brutus and Nero were also panting, and Brutus was limping. We were a good distance from Fish-lane (though I had no idea where we were) and I hunkered down in a passage to get my breath. Still as the stars we waited, as a pack of roughs raced past, calling to each other, excited and ready for the chase. Perhaps they weren't chasing us, but I was too scared to risk discovery.

We crept home to Portland-road by more back streets and dark lanes, and when we arrived, I closed the door firmly and thankfully behind us.

I lit the fire and fetched water to bathe Brutus's wounded paw and bandaged it carefully. He lay on his rug in front of the fire, shivering slightly, and his companion, seeing his pain, lay close to him. I sat on the corner of the bed, tormenting myself with the thought that these two animals were kinder companions to each other than I had been to them, involving them in danger, and now the revenge of the Nasty Man. For I had no doubt it would come.

CHAPTER 13

INQUEST AT THE TWO SPIES –
A DEAFENING SILENCE

Sleep used to be my nursemaid. If I was troubled, she would come to me and I would hide away in her dark arms.

But she must have been attending to some other poor soul, for she would not visit me, and after a sleepless night, I was up early to scour the newspapers. I found a butcher wanting to sell, cheap, a nag and wagon, but when I had found the shop and then peered through the yard fence and saw them – a poor, broken-winded old horse and a cart with more holes in it than a trinkerman's net – I made a quiet exit.

And I kept quiet, terrified of every knock at Mrs Twentyfold's door, slinking out to eat, wandering the streets during the day, and lying sleepless in my bed at night. Besides, Brutus's paw was more badly injured than I had thought, and the poor creature was forced to limp slowly and painfully at my side until it healed.

The Nasty Man had me prisoner.

A dull and frosty morning, and Brutus, Nero and I were dining in Garraway's on our 'starve' fare of tea and bread and butter. I had not seen Trim or Will since the gaff incident, but they knew all about it. Trim sent a note asking if he could help, and Will called at my lodgings two or three times whilst I was out wandering. Ours is a small neighbourhood, and it is not just the theatre and the Aquarium, where everybody does indeed know each other's business. This patch of ground, though I cannot put borders on it, and though it mixes a rookery or two, a theatre, three or four gaffs, drinking houses by the dozen, and churches hiding in corners, and though its population has more creeds and nationalities than Botany Bay, is still as tight a community as you could find in any village. Every face and voice is as familiar as every narrow alley and court. We might not know them by name, but we know of them, and that is the point.

I am on the very borders of this community. By my profession. By my disposition. By choice. I like society, but not familiarity and I live in Portland-road for that very reason. And whilst I was sorry to have missed my friends and I wondered, with more than a little concern, where Barney had disappeared to, I now wanted, more than anything, to get away from here.

I indulged in another cup and another slice, and drew my chair closer to the fire (coals were a sacrifice I currently was forced to make at Portland-road). Christmas approached and the daily sheets were full of the season's 'forthcoming

217

attractions', and these half dozen or so columns eagerly anticipating the theatres' production of the 'Christmas Novelties' I would normally read with pleasure and excitement. But I avoided them and I have not replied to Mr Carrier's letters of enquiry either. Although he assured me that my position was safe, that he was confident of my ability and that of my dogs, and that I did not need to attend the Pavilion until the very last, when he and the entire company would rejoice to see me, I have remained silent, not wanting to betray my intention of leaving. And, for that same reason, I did not want to see the names of my old friends listed in the 'Christmas Novelties', knowing how disappointed they would be when they discovered me gone and untraceable. So, every day, I deliberately turned to the classified columns and scanned them. This morning, I noted two likely carts and horses and, memorizing their addresses, was preparing to go and inspect them, when my eye was caught by a paragraph entitled 'Royal Crown Theatre and Waxworks' on the page headed 'Police News'.

PENNY 'GAFF' – RUINOUS EFFECTS UPON THE RISING GENERATION
Eleven persons, male and female, four of them children and one a Negro, were brought before Mr Brunswick-Hill, charged with being concerned in the performance of dramatic pieces in an unlicensed place

in Fish-lane, Old Martin's-road. The court was crowded to excess, in consequence of the majority of the prisoners being led along the streets and confined in the police station cells overnight in their theatrical costumes. Mr Superintendent Hughes, together with Wilton 163 D, and other constables, gave evidence in the court, and Mr John Bunyan Pilgrim said that his bookselling business in a neighbouring shop had been quite ruined by the persons occupying and frequenting the 'gaff' named. The whole of the prisoners were taken into custody while the performance was going on, the piece being that of *Six-fingered Jack, or the Knight of the Road*. They included: Mrs Dearlove (40), Mr Crowe (56), Mr Tafflyn (45), Mr Sage (38), Miss Fitch (20), Mr Garcia (37), Joe White (16) and 4 children under the age of ten years. It was further shown, by the evidence of Wilton 163 D, and other officers, that at the rear of the place in question was a building used for the making of indecent photographic images. A play-bill, of which the following is a copy, was handed to Mr Brunswick-Hill – 'Novelty, on Wednesday, for the benefit of Gupta Percha. To commence with the drama, entitled *The Farmer and his Dogs*, in which Mr Chapman and his Sagacious Channies will demonstrate their skills; a comic song by Gutta

Percha; a dance by Mrs English; and a glee by Mr Gutta, Mr Corney Sage and Miss Fitch. To conclude with the laughable farce – *Come Early – Good Fires.*' Mr Hughes said he had caused frequent visits to be made to Mr Tipney, the owner of the 'gaff', in the hope that he would put a stop to the unlawful practices which he had carried on. He was called to the 'gaff' in question only last week, there having been a complaint about some vicious dogs. 'Are they among the company now?' – No, sir. 'Were they apprehended on the occasion in question?' Mr Hughes – No, sir. Chapman and his hounds had escaped before we had arrived. They are notorious in the area and attacked a gentleman that very evening in the yard. Mr Brunswick-Hill was of the opinion that the demoralizing consequences of penny gaffs upon the youth of the district was a more serious issue than the habits of an unruly pair of dogs.

Nevertheless, the neighbourhood had to be made safe, and it would not do to have people attacked. If the complainant cared to present himself at the conclusion of the proceedings and still wished to bring a prosecution against Chapman, who had still not been apprehended, then he would consider it. Turning to the business of the prisoners who were still shivering in their stage clothes and causing amusement in the courtroom, he inflicted a fine in some of the cases, and in others the parties were discharged. Mr Brunswick-Hill added once again that such places as the Royal Crown Theatre were demoralizing in the extreme and gave a bad reputation to the district and made intolerable the lives of the tradesmen who lived and worked there.

I wished Will Lovegrove was sitting across the table from me at this moment! With his good sense, he would know what to do. He would frown, grow thoughtful and then, with a thump of his fist upon the table, would cry, 'I know, Chapman! Let us go and consult Mr Clerk – or Mr Magistrate.' Or even, 'Don't give it a moment's thought, Bob! The case has no legs and couldn't even hop into the court room!' I've heard him cry that many times! But left to myself, I fell into a panic, and it took some effort to order up another cup of tea and read the paragraph again, and not dash into the street and run away, as I was very much inclined to do.

I read it four times, and by the fifth, the only thing that stuck in my mind was that I could expect an action to be brought against me by the Nasty Man. How he would relish that! He said he would have my skin, and he would do it. Even at the risk of standing in a courtroom, he would be unable to resist the pleasure of causing me pain, savouring the opportunity to parade me in court, perhaps even having me sent to prison. And for the vile practices in that stable, the murderer of the little child – he, the Nasty Man – would go unpunished, for who would take my word, a convicted man, against his?

Now it was imperative to lay hands upon a half-decent cart and horse, and quickly. The Nasty Man could not bring his action against me before the morning, by which time I would be safe. And Brutus and Nero also. And if he came to Strong's Gardens – I could not forget that he knew even that about me – well, my good friend would be true to his name and protect me and my boys. That was a sensible, calm plan, one worthy of Will Lovegrove, I thought as I buttoned my coat and stepped outside.

It was very cold, frost still lying heavy upon the housetops, and the pavements slippery where over-zealous housemaids had thrown their scrubbing slops before dawn. I kept to back streets and passages and, before the church bell had struck the mid-morning hour, had inspected a couple of broken-down horses and three wormy carts (one only fit for the fire-back), and came away with nothing. I was almost despairing, and walked the streets – I was fearful to return to Portland-road – until the smell of dinners drew us off-course, down a dark and narrow passage ending in a thin building, wasting away in a thin yard.

Out of my little community, I was a foreigner,

but even within it there were unfamiliar streets and closes, ones that I had never set foot in. This was one of them. I had never been in Favour-alley, nor Dolour-court, and the Two Spies tavern was a stranger to me, but the aroma of gravy and cabbage was the same everywhere and as we turned into the court, from out of an open window steaming plates of chops and potatoes were being passed to a bandy-legged boy, to hurry across the cobbles and post to unseen hands through another window. Brutus and Nero's noses rose to follow the fragrant course, and it did smell so savoury and appetizing and, advertised at only fourpence, it was cheap also. And it clearly had a good name, for a little cluster of men were waiting for it in the yard. Even so, I still found a spidery corner in the bar parlour and anticipated a tasty chop dinner. But after ten minutes, when not even the usual servant in a greasy apron came to look down upon us, and the room was filling up with people who were clearly not waiting to dine, I realized that the chop dinner was not on this menu and, overhearing a conversation between two lumpers on their way to work, found we had come un-invited upon an inquest hearing.

It was one of the qualities of our neighbourhood that word of mouth served better than any number of notices, and if I had been my usual self, trot-ting between Portland-road and the Aquarium and the Pavilion Theatre, there is no doubt I would have heard of it. But I had been laid low for some days and the world had passed me by. And if I had known that the object of the court hearing was the mysterious death of a child, I would have put many streets between myself and the Two Spies, and would not have looked at a hoarding or a newspaper for a week. As soon as I discovered my mistake, I tried to leave but, unless I wanted to draw attention to myself, it was impossible. The parlour and snug were packed to the rafters, the windows were opened and the doors propped wide to admit as many heads and shoulders as possible, and they were lined up, six deep in the little court, determined to hear the proceedings, by proxy, if necessary. And there was now a small cohort of policemen, back and front, ready to put themselves in the way of anyone entering or leaving.

A long table had been brought in and chairs set about it, a large Windsor with a cushion drawn up to the head – for the Coroner, I assumed. He was a small, morose man, and was contemplating the present proceedings from the doorway leading to the yard which today had been pressed into service and, in the shadow of the closely packed buildings around it, contained a table on which a small, white-shrouded object lay. The crowd, entirely male, was mostly silent or quietly respectful, labouring men in shirt-sleeves and heavy jerkins. When the room and yard were full to capacity and the landlord, with brimming jugs ready and eager to serve, only awaiting the appropriate moment, the Coroner took his Windsor, the foreman rounded up the jury and swore them in, and the proceedings began in their customary fashion.

Amidst the lingering tobacco smoke from the previous night and the sweet and sour smell of spilt ale from but half an hour ago, Mr Coroner began in the time-honoured way, intoning the sombre phrases – 'to inquire in this manner', 'to know where the person was slain', 'if they can speak or have any discretion', like a clergyman, reading out the verses and responses. Then he stopped and looked about the room.

'One of our duties this morning, gentlemen, is to try, if we are able, to identify this child. No one has yet come forward to claim her. She has no name. She may or may not be from this district.'

His pale fish-eyes ranged about the room.

'If anyone here has information which might lead to an identification at any time during these proceedings, I must remind you that it is your duty to lay that information before the court.'

The silence continued, broken only by the creak of working boots and a phlegmy cough.

'Very well,' said Mr Coroner quietly, 'then we will proceed.'

The foreman gave summary information – the body was discovered at such and such a time on such and such a day and immediately the police were summoned.

'Let us hear from the officer, then. Stand up,

address the court, speak slowly and clearly. Don't omit anything. Give it all.'

The policeman stood up, a young man with a fresh face and tidy manners, holding his hat hard under his arm and balancing a scrap of paper in a trembling hand.

'I was called to the railway diggings at the back of Marlpit-road. The labourers had come to their work and discovered a child's body thrown in the tunnel about thirty yards along. It was wrapped up in an old rug. One of the labourers, stopping for his dinner and seeing the rug, said he thought he would take it to sit upon rather than the wet earth. The child's body dropped out of the rug as he picked it up and he had a start.'

'Is that man here?' enquired Mr Coroner.

A large man, with a dirty face, hesitantly held up his hand.

'Aye. Here, master. Sir. Yer 'onner.'

A cazzelty.

'Sit and wait. Now, constable, continue.'

The young policeman looked around the room, swallowed hard and began again.

'Well, sir, I was taken to the mouth of the tunnel and given a lamp and I made my way along.'

'And where is this tunnel? Where does it lead?' asked the Coroner. The policeman was nonplussed, and so was everyone in the room, including the clean-faced workman who shook his head when asked. The inquiry went back and around and out of the door into the yard a couple of times before it brought back with it another cazzelty, who had the bearing of 'one in charge' and, with his hat in his hands and refusing to blink (as if he were incapable of blinking and speaking at the same time), he informed Mr Coroner that the tunnel 'was for the railway, sir, leading up as far as Tiber-street and down as far as the Medway-road, and cutting under "thorinfares" both major and minor, sir.' Mr Coroner was satisfied, as was the assembly, who nodded and murmured, and someone patted him on the shoulder and said, 'Well spoken, Charlie.'

'Now then, continue,' said Mr Coroner, and the young policeman, who seemed to be hoping that his part in the proceedings had finished, was forced to get to his feet again and resume. 'Well, sir, I found the – the body – and it was just as they had described it. Wrapped up in a piece of old carpet, and looking more like a roll of carpet than a body, if you get my meaning, sir. It was up against the wall, lying flat.'

'Had there been any attempt to hide it? Perhaps to bury it under stones or earth?'

'No, sir. It was just a-lying there.'

'What did you do when you came upon it?'

The young policeman swallowed hard. 'Well, sir, I stooped and unwrapped it—'

'Was it secured? By cord or rope?'

'No, sir, it wasn't. The – body – flopped out as I unwrapped it.'

'Flopped out?'

227

'Yes, sir. That's what it did. And rolled upon the earth.'

'I see,' said Mr Coroner, making notes. 'And was the piece of carpet collected from the tunnel when the deceased was removed?'

The young policeman, increasingly pale now and anxious, didn't know. Perhaps it was left behind, he said. He hadn't seen it. Mr Coroner frowned and expressed the opinion that though they had very many admirable qualities, the police were sometimes lacking that attention to detail which might assist the judiciary in the administration of their duties. And also in the catching of the perpetrators of the crime. Had it not occurred to anyone that the carpet in which the body was wrapped was as important as any of the evidence?

The young policeman looked shamefaced and said in a quiet voice that he was most sorry, but he wanted to remove the child from that awful place and he couldn't think of anything else. It was a response which met with general approval, and there were nods at him and at the Coroner, who was then more inclined to let the matter go and move on from the business of the 'where' and 'when' to the 'how'. Here the medical man was summoned, Skinner, the police doctor, who was irritable and in a hurry to have it over with for he had 'four suicides and a public hanging to deal with before I can hope to eat my dinner tonight'.

The medical questioning necessitated the jury, followed by the other spectators, trooping out into the yard 'to view the deceased'. If there was a little crush and a few remonstrations of 'Mind yer elbow!' and 'Watch it! My plates!', it was all done quietly.

Skinner cleared his throat. 'The child is female, eight years of age, of fair general health. Not overly underweight.'

He drew back the white cloth – the landlady's third-best tablecloth – and looked around the assembly of crusty, tired faces and then, in an unusually hushed and gentle voice, said, 'Mr Coroner, I say this because there are no females within earshot, and what I have to say is not for female ears. This child was violated and strangled. I cannot tell which, at this stage, was the cause of death.'

There was silence, broken only by the squealing of pigs in the nearby abattoir.

'I examined the body earlier, as you requested, and the evidence seems pretty clear to me. I will, of course, need to perform a more extensive examination at the mortuary, but I cannot imagine that my findings will alter materially.'

Mr Coroner nodded sagely, and the jurors, with serious faces and some licking their lips nervously, followed his lead.

'There are,' said the doctor, 'signs of a struggle, pathetic though that probably was. She has, for example, broken fingernails.' He frowned. 'I would hesitate to suggest that this injury was sustained in an attempt to fight off an attacker. It is difficult to be precise. One might arrest a suspect on the evidence of claw marks, perhaps to the face or arm, but a conviction on those alone would be difficult to secure. Let us say that the victim struggled in an effort to escape the outrage and in that struggle sustained some damage to the phalangeal extremities.'

There was an angry murmur and shaking of heads, and an almost wholesale attempt to retreat within the Two Spies, for we all knew the child was dead and how, and anything else which the doctor was moved to offer seemed unnecessary. But Mr Coroner would brook no retreat and waved Mr Skinner on.

'The extent of the injuries, gentlemen, both – er – within – and – er – without, are consistent with that of a mature individual applying – er – considerable force.' He hesitated. 'Do I need to elaborate, Mr Coroner? This will all be detailed in my report. It seems superfluous in the present circumstances . . . Very well. Suffice it to say that the deceased met her death in a violent manner due to substantial internal injuries which were inflicted by an as yet unknown assailant. And, I would hazard, against her will.'

Again we tried to put the horror behind us, and again we were called back. 'One last thing,' said Mr Skinner, 'which I believe should be drawn to the jury's attention. The manner of strangulation. The child was young, small, not at all robust. A grown man would have no difficulty in extinguishing life with his hands. And yet the mark upon the throat suggests to me – and I confess I have only ever seen it upon adult victims – the application of a garrotte.'

A red handkerchief flashed before my eyes like a curse. We filed into the parlour and I took my seat next to a pale man, perhaps a wharf-man or a street-porter. He turned his hat in his hands for some minutes and then, along with others, could be heard to swear, to the foreman and to anyone else who might care to listen, that he could not endure any more of the doctor's medical talk, and that it was enough to know what he knew without some jumped-up medico telling him in a hundred different ways. Then the conversation turned to the manner of the child's death and while the violation was sickening, they were most terribly angered by the garrotting. It was a punishment from which women and children were exempt. It was a vile and cowardly crime. There was talk, from the collection of lumpers and haulers at the window, of calling up some assistance – there was no shortage of volunteers – to 'find the devil what done it and do for him, well and good'.

Mr Coroner seemed to have some sympathy with us, for he allowed the company to speak out their anger and threaten parliament and the 'upper ten' (for having caused it) and the police (for not having prevented it). Then, in the hiatus and having ordered his papers into piles and single sheets in front of him, Mr Coroner cleared his throat and began again.

'Thank you, Doctor Skinner, for that illuminating account. Gentlemen, I think we need little occasion to debate the cause of death and, indeed, that subject is beyond our resource at present. Yet there are still matters to be dealt with. We have heard from the police and the medical profession. But we have not heard a word from witnesses who might know the child. Who have seen her playing in the street, perhaps, or walking to church with her parents. This child – a pretty child, as yet unnamed and unclaimed – is a mystery. Surely someone has missed her? Some mother has surely been searching the streets for her and enquiring at hospitals and police stations?'

And so it went on until the Coroner declared the business concluded, pronounced 'Unnatural murder, by persons unknown' and the room emptied. I had not disclosed what I knew. Had sat in a corner, listened and held my peace. But now that everyone had left and I was alone with the doctor or the Coroner, perhaps now I could do it. Not in front of a crowd of strangers, but in the quiet of the parlour or the yard.

The doctor was still there, lathering his hands vigorously in a bucket of water and talking to a small party of clerks in rusty black, all eager to be gone, but too polite to leave.

'A tragic case,' he said. 'It's no secret that these young ones are sold for the purpose of violating them, though one would hope that few come to grief in this manner.' He shook his head. 'What mother could sell her child to this? I would give my fortune to discover who did it and bring him to justice. And those who are behind it. As would all decent men,' and he frowned and scrubbed his hands dry on the landlady's towel.

Then he drew back the cover and I looked upon the child's face for the first time. Dark curls, matted now, and a begrimed face, the blue eyes half open, the mouth fallen into a smile in that strange way the dead have of reminding us of life. A sweet face, limbs still full and round, baby features made more childlike by those cheap glass beads and ribbons with which poor mothers deck out their child because it earns money.

I didn't know her real name. It might have been The Little Wonder, Miss Topsy Truelove. She might have been sister to Little Louisa Penny and Happy Rosy Banks, and cousin to Sweet Carrie Honeydew and The Mother's Favourite Jenny Brighteye. There were so many. The supply was endless. Daughters of poor families, with a grain of talent and a winning smile and, if they are lucky, join the ranks of a children's ballet. Those less fortunate haunt low concert rooms and travelling shows, little mites with bare arms and thin dresses, dragged about this city to find one night's work in the pleasure gardens and two at the gaff so that the family can eat. This child was perhaps the only one keeping the rent-man at bay and her father in the gin-shop.

I must have been staring at the child's face, for

the doctor touched my arm and the clerks drew closer.

'Do you know her? It is your duty, man, to say if you do, and a crime if you don't say what you know. Withholding evidence, it's called, and the law will send you down if you're discovered.'

He rolled down his sleeves and a clerk held his coat for him. They bustled back into the parlour and I saw him have a word in the ear of Mr Coroner, who looked hard in my direction, and I think they were about to summon me, but their attention was drawn to the dark-coated gentleman who had come into the room and was taking a glass with the landlord. It was his horse and wagon drawn up in that tight little square to fetch the child to the mortuary where the doctor would attend to her again. She had been violated and killed in that cold and shabby place; she was bundled into a scrap of mouldy carpet, filthy with the dirt of the street, had been left in the cold and dark. She was stared at, not as in life, prancing and singing and smiling, but lying cold and still on a table in the yard of a tavern. And finally, she was to be rattled and tumbled about upon the back of a cart and then laid upon a cold, hard bed.

I should have waited, I should have made them understand what I know.

But alone, I could not.

I would find Will and Trim, and together we would go to the magistrate where he would learn of the Nasty Man. I would point out the shed at the back of Tipney's-gaff, I would show them the carpet and the hole in the floor where the body of the child was stuffed. I would take them to every place I have ever seen the Nasty Man and, with the resources of the police and their agents, they would track him down. Barney need not fear him any more. Nor poor, pretty children.

I hurried from the yard, glad of the company of my two dogs and hating my own fear and cowardice more than I have ever hated the world for its careless cruelty. I hardly noticed when I shouldered someone and I didn't hear the abuse they roared at me. For I was locked in my silent world, with only the beat of my own footsteps in my head and as I walked, head down, unwilling to meet the eye of anyone, I was once again a child. But for good fortune, my dead body could have lain upon a table in a tavern yard whilst well-meaning but indifferent strangers gazed upon me and wondered who I was and if anyone cared for me. For if my mother had felt love or concern, she never spoke it and rarely showed it. She was a gypsy woman who never mastered anything but the rudiments of the English tongue, and spent all her days trailing after my father and waiting for him outside taverns and shops, club rooms and dens. Even keeping watch whilst he worked at tending the kilns, keeping them stoked and the fire alive. Whilst he followed the flames and made them roar or simmer, she followed him, making sure that she got some of the money he pocketed before he drank it away, and I followed her. Our only connection, it seemed, was her shadow. As a child, I was always in someone's shadow. My mother's. My father's. Never in the sunlight myself, seeing an open road and wondering where it might take me. But always in the wake of my mother's ragged skirts or my father's clumsy boots. Always with my head down, waiting for that skirt or those boots to stop. And always ready to retreat when those boots turned upon me.

Then one day, my mother didn't get up. Every night for the best part of a week we had lain down to sleep against the low wall of a brickworks. The kilns were close by, and the earth and the walls were warmed by the constant heat. It was a comfortable spot, though the ground was hard. I was a little chap, no more than six years old, but I think I looked much younger. When I woke, I nudged my mother, but she didn't stir, and I thought it must be too early to rise, so I curled up next to her, like a little grub, and waited. And watched the sun climb higher. It was very quiet, only church bells ringing. And when I couldn't wait any longer, when I was bursting to piddle and my stomach was aching with hunger, and my mother was still, as I thought, fast asleep, I got up and walked about a little. It felt strange, for I was used, as I have said, to following, and now the world seemed great and grand and wide. I explored the street and a little patch of rough ground, keeping my mother always in my eye. Finally, I was adventurous and climbed into gardens and peered into windows, and watched birds bathing in a puddle. I had never before felt the luxury of simply watching.

But when I was caught peeping through a window to watch a family eat their dinner, and chased over a fence with the cries of 'Piker!' in my ears, I was driven, shaking and terrified, back to the wall and the still form of my mother. And there I stayed, and she grew stiff and cold. I passed one night there until hunger forced me to go out early to find food and drink and when I returned, saw a crowd had gathered around her. I hid and watched her wrapped in a blanket and taken away. I wanted to cry out, but thought better of it and instead trailed, again, in the wake of the party, to a little public house. She was put in the stable, I think.

I was sure my father would know what to do, but I couldn't find him. I knew we had been waiting for him in that warm place because he was at work within the furnaces, and so I went back to the wall and sat, day and night, and once even peered through the gate, but he never came. A week passed. My mother was buried, and I followed at a distance, and hid behind a gravestone to see her, wrapped in cloth, lowered into the ground, along with five others. A pauper's grave, and nothing wrong in that. Going to eternity in company.

Every night, after my wanderings, I returned to the furnaces, always hopeful that my father would be there, and I became a familiar sight to those who lived around and worked in the brickyard, for there were no more cries of 'Piker!' and one day a blanket was left upon the wall. I didn't take it straight away, in case it belonged to someone. But after a few days, I realized that it was meant for me. Little packets of food also appeared and were placed on the wall, and one day a pair of boots. I never discovered who left them, but I am always grateful to those kind people, and hope that life has dealt fairly with them, as they did with me.

One morning, returning to my makeshift home, there was a change. The gate to the brickyard stood open and the yard was full of people, all clustered about one of the kilns. I was curious and someone, turning round, saw me and nudged his neighbour. They strolled over and, being always wary of strangers, I was ready to run.

'Now then, young 'un,' said one, 'where's yer pa, d'ye think?'

I remember he was an old man, with no teeth and a very red mouth.

'At work,' I said, and wondered at the sound of my own voice, which I hadn't heard for a long time. 'In the kiln.'

They looked at each other, the old man and his neighbour, a smart journeyman, with a round hat and a blue kerchief.

'In the kiln, ye say? And when did you see him go in there?'

'I didn't see him, but that is where he works. His name's Mr Frederick Chapman, if you want to know.'

They nodded gravely and strolled back again, and went up to a man in a dark coat, who turned to look at me, and then at the kiln. I wondered if my father was in trouble. My mother had always 'got him out of bother' (one of her few phrases), and that generally meant that he had fallen down drunk and was a danger to himself. Or had been brawling. Now, since my mother was gone, it fell to me to 'get him out of bother'. So, when no one was looking, I crouched low, I followed the wall round – I was clever at following! – and turned up behind the kilns. A scramble, a bruised knee and I was over the wall and scuttling, like a dusty crab, in the baked earth alongside it. There were four kilns, but I knew the one my father had been minding, for he had pointed it out to me. It was small and, because of that, not often used. He told me it had been especially built to make a batch of fine tiles – for the Queen's bathroom in one of her great palaces, my father said – and was known as the 'Royal Oven' and now it was only used for special jobs. Throughout his life, he had bragged that he was well-connected, and perhaps he *was* in the end, crawling in to lie amongst the Queen's tiles, and not discovered until a week later when the kiln was cooled and opened. That was the story I learned many years later. But as a child all I learned was what I saw.

A side flue stood open, letting out the final draught of warm air, so I scrambled in easily and, on knees and elbows, pulled myself into the chamber. It had been almost emptied of tiles, otherwise I could not have got so far, and only a bed of broken pieces remained and, in the dim, foggy light of the open door, a sack, left I supposed, to put them in. I looked about me and saw burnished brick and floating motes of brick dust, and breathed in the thick, hot air and wondered where my father was and what he could have done, for I was sure now that he must be 'in bother'. But there was nowhere in here he could be hiding, though to make sure, I inspected the shallow alcoves of the kiln and finally put my foot under the sack of broken pieces. Then I realized that it wasn't a sack at all, but a man for, now I was closer, I could see a coat and hair. It was someone lying asleep, and when I cast my eyes over him I saw that the man was wearing my father's boots! I was in no doubt that they were his, for I was very familiar with them and knew them, if not as old friends, certainly as close acquaintances. They were drawn up, one on top of the other, just like my father's boots when he was asleep. And I knew then that it was my father, lying fast asleep. The kiln had been carefully searched, and yet they had mistaken my sleeping father for an old sack, just as I had done. How

240

fortunate it was, I thought, that I recognised him and could wake him up, for no doubt he would be in bother over it. I put my hand on his shoulder and shook it gently.

'Pa?' I said, quietly, for although I didn't want those outside to hear, neither did I want to wake him up suddenly and be clouted for my trouble. 'Wake up, Pa.'

There was still no sound.

I shook him again, a little harder, and, though I feared his wrath and terrible boots, I rocked him by the shoulder.

He turned over, light as a cinder. His skin was drawn and brown, stretched tight over his nose and cheeks. His eyes were tight shut, but his mouth was wide open, black as a tunnel, and shouting – or screaming – silently.

I was paralyzed with terror.

I screamed. But although my mouth was open, not a sound came out. I screamed and screamed, and the noise in my head was deafening, though in the thick air of the kiln there was only the hum of voices drifting in from outside.

I was terrified that the doors would be shut and bolted and that I'd be unable to get out, so I backed away and posted myself down one of the flues. The last thing I saw was that black mouth, screaming, as the sides of the flue closed in upon me. Feeling their closeness, like arms tightly enfolding me, I wanted to turn round, but I couldn't. The flue was too narrow. Forwards took me back into the place of terror and, scrabbling backwards, I was almost insensible with panic.

Surely the flue was never this long?

Suppose I was stuck, and could go forwards or back and could not – ah, the horror of it chokes me even now! – could not turn round.

A sudden yell – 'You! Donkey's arse!' – hurtled me back to the present. I was pummelled by a man with a handcart. His potatoes and cabbages have been knocked to the ground. It was my fault. Couldn't I see him coming? He wasn't invisible, was he? I picked up the potatoes, the cabbages. I put them on the cart, carefully placing each one as if they might break. Finally, the man lost patience and, with another thump upon my arm, pushed me out of the way, declaring that the city would fill its mouth with empty spoons whilst he waited for me, and threw the remaining vegetables on the cart himself. His parting gesture was to hurl two potatoes at Brutus and Nero, at which they yelped, and one at me, which caught me hard on the side of the head.

'Donkey's arse!' he cried again. 'Tom o' Bedlam! Yah!'

I cannot answer him.

I have never uttered a sound since that day when my father's black and terrible mouth turned silently upon me. It is not that I do not want to talk, but that I cannot. The sounds do not spring to my lips. My throat is barren, though I have words waiting to be tried, many words which sound in my head but never come to my lips.

Words of love. If I could, I would be bold and declare to Em Pikemartin that I love her above and beyond all women. I would shake Will Lovegrove by the hand and say, 'Will, you are the best of fellows! Come to Garraway's and let us feast!'

But before any other sound passed my lips, I would say the names of my two boys, my Brutus and Nero, for they have never heard my voice. I would call them to me by name, and tell them they are good dogs, and teach them the words to 'Heel!' and 'Fetch!'

Only in my dreams do I have a voice, and then, why, I can bawl Will Lovegrove twice off the stage! Often, I wake with my mouth open and have the impression that words will leap to my lips. I wait and listen, but no sound comes. I wonder what my voice would be like now, for I have never heard it, a man's voice, except as an echo in my head. The last words I ever uttered, which no one heard, were to my father, who was already dead.

'Pa,' I said to him, 'Pa.'

And that was my childhood, snatched away. I have never sung childish rhymes nor played childish games, nor yelled and hallooed in the streets. Christmas songs I have never sung, nor Easter hymns, nor Harvest Home, yet I know every word and every note. And I have never called for my mother or my father since.

That ravaged childhood I re-live in dreams and in those dark places inhabited by my blue devils. My little life, when I begged and tramped, when I found kindness and cruelty. Children can make a home anywhere, even the gutter. If they have nowhere to go, they will crouch for hours watching the trickle of water, floating any scrap of dirt in that stream and make a boat of it. They will make the filthy gutter a home, rather than look up. For when the child raises its head, then it must see the world as it is: the boots that kick and the fists that strike and the mouths that roar and spit.

Who will care for this child? Who will take its part?

CHAPTER 14

SILENCE

There was a real commotion in Portland-road as I turned the corner, and all of it outside number twenty-two.

But I hardly noticed it, for I was bursting with new resolve. I had walked myself into the shape of a new Bob Chapman, who was a man of action and resolve. From this moment, Bob Chapman will come out of the shadows, and stand in the sun.

I would seek out Will and Trim. We would go to the magistrate. I would make him understand.

So I determined.

And then I turned my attention to Portland-road.

The front door of number twenty-two was flung open, wide open, in a very uncustomary way. The window of the downstairs front parlour, Mrs Twentyfold's private room, was also flung open and her good lace curtains were flapping about and dragging upon the dirty sill. I was uncertain whether to hurry towards or away from the house, but the decision was quickly made for me when Miss Slyte, one of our neighbours, a vast dumpling of a woman, who trimmed bonnets and kept cats, noticed me on her return from the gin-shop and waddled at me at an alarming speed.

'Ah! ye gob-shite, ye!' she shrieked, for she is of Irish ancestry and leaned heavily upon that accent. 'Look at the trouble you bring upon this house and this good lady wid yer evil friends and yer evil doings!' and she struck me hard upon the chest, pushing her red face, heavily perfumed with the contents of a gin-bottle, into mine. 'Look at the trouble, here!' she cried and she grabbed my elbow and steered me to the house and up the steps, as though I was the very criminal they had been seeking and she had caught him!

'Here he is,' she cried triumphantly, 'the sneaking dog-face, with his animals a-slinking behind him like the villains they are,' and we were all, Brutus, Nero and I, thrust into Mrs Twentyfold's parlour, a room which was so very closely guarded that I had never even glimpsed inside it before now. It was small, made even smaller by the quantity of people pressed in there. All sorts of unfamiliar persons were seated, standing, perched upon tables and sills, leaning and squatting against the walls and threatening to upset any number of my landlady's mats and doilies which covered every surface like a snow-storm. The air was full of heat and loud chatter, and in the midst of it all, on a hard chair, was Mrs Twentyfold herself, half a glass of gin in her hand and her cap lurching drunkenly over one eye. She gave me a curious look, which changed by the moment from curiosity to recognition to outrage.

'You!' she cried. 'This is all your doing, you and your – associates.'

Someone patted her shoulder, and another refilled her glass.

'They rushed her and knocked her to the ground in her own kitchen,' murmured a swarthy-chinned man with two fat rabbits slung over his shoulder, drinking gin from one of Mrs Twentyfold's best cups, 'and rumpaged therough the 'ouse.' If he had broadcast it in the street, with a band and cheerful banners, it could not have provoked more attention, for everyone in the room heard him and felt obliged to express their own opinion of me and my character, my friends and my profession loudly and vigorously.

I gathered – it was not too difficult – that there had been a burglary, outrageous and in full daylight. That the burglars – some agreed two, others three, all powerful and dressed as road-menders – charged through Mrs Twentyfold's area and kitchen, knocked her to the floor and went through the house 'like a hurricanoe'. It was a bold enterprise, and though my good landlady was unhurt – except for the damage to her pride in being tumbled to the flags and banging her elbow upon the fender – it came to something, everyone agreed, when a respectable house could be so entered and taken apart in the middle of a Tuesday morning. The police were summoned and had attended; the sergeant would see Mrs Twentyfold later at the station, but no one expected any great effort from them. My fellow lodgers had been discovered and brought back from their places of work; I had been sent for at the Aquarium and the Pavilion but could not be found.

'And no wonder, ye Ned Fool,' roared Miss Slyte, 'since ye were slinging about here a-waiting for yer thievin' pals!'

Did they really believe I had arranged the robbery? Or had anything to do with it? Perhaps my incredulity, writ large upon my face, satisfied some of them, but a rumble of suspicion still drummed about the room. The bag-man and the thin clerk who lodged above me (I never discovered their names) said they had already examined their quarters.

'Nothing missing from mine,' whispered the bag-man. 'But nothing in there anyway, except a tea-pot which belonged to the previous.'

'Likewise,' wheezed the clerk, who was anxiously binding himself up in his muffler preparatory to leaving for his desk. 'Turned my mattress for me. Dusted the mantle. *Nusquam captus.*'

The rabbit-man was on his second cup. His rabbits, having begged a ride upon his shoulder, were slumped there with an easy grace, glassy eyes winking at me.

'I've had a sniff round,' he said importantly, but

to no one in particular. 'Nothing taken, as far as I can see, though a deal of mess.' And then he eyed me. 'Except your room. Second floor? Back?'

An odd feeling crept into my belly, for an audacious robbery, in the middle of the day, nothing taken and Mrs Twentyfold, who wore a deal of jet and a purse snapped about her waist, only knocked to the ground, was more than out of the commonplace. Pushing through the casually curious who were not admitted to the inner sanctum and had taken up residence on the stairs, I hurried to my room, where the door stood ajar. As the rabbit-man had pronounced, there was a deal of mess. Everything had been turned over – bed, mattress (which was ripped apart and the flock bubbling out of it like porridge), shelves, even my coal bucket and the floorboards. I closed the door to the curiosity of people who would keep wandering in and looking about them and staring at me as though I was suddenly going be alarming. Brutus and Nero made themselves comfortable before the dead fire. The clump of feet and the murmur of voices echoed from below. I perched on the edge of the bed and considered. I must have been spied out on my errands, and the Nasty Man had taken the opportunity to organize a thorough search of my room. Otherwise it was a grand coincidence.

Perhaps this was the start of his campaign.

A regular turning-over, the destruction of my few possessions. And then one day me. Or my dogs.

I would leave for Strong's Gardens today.

I set to and put my room to rights. I cleared all my belongings, put them all in a pile on the table (it was a very small pile). Mrs Twentyfold could do what she wanted with them. I worked quickly and assembled the half-dozen penny novels, two cracked cups and a frying pan with a loose handle, a knife, fork and spoon, a tea tin painted with pink Japanese flowers.

It was done. I sat on my bed and contemplated my worldly assets. They were few enough, but nothing I minded leaving behind. The tea tin had but a single spoonful left in it and it was the appeal of a simple cup of tea to cheer me on my way that took me down the stairs to fill my kettle in the scullery and to let Brutus and Nero out into the area. In the hall was evidence of much to-ing and fro-ing, for Mrs Twentyfold's polished banister rail was dull and sticky, and there were drips and spots on the stairs. The painting of a watchful Saviour had been pushed awry and stray cups stood on every surface. From the parlour came the murmur of voices, and a knock upon the door went unanswered.

There came another knock.

I had been instructed by my landlady on many occasions not to answer the door upon any account, and I was still eager to please. I ignored it. But when the knock came a third time, and heavily, I wondered if it might be a policeman to see about the robbery, and since no one emerged from the parlour to answer, I opened it myself. Brutus and Nero were at my heels, curious to see the visitor.

It wasn't that the sun was bright, or that I was distracted by an insult or a blow on the chin, but for a moment I could not make out the two figures standing before me. Neither did I see the covered cart in the road. But suddenly I realized who and what they were, not because I recognized them, but because there was something terrible in their faces. I tried to shut the door. One had his foot already in, and the other shoved me hard to the floor, and by the time I regained my feet, they had grasped Brutus and Nero by their collars – the dogs struggled a little, but made no sound, for that was their training – and dragged them onto the pavement.

It all happened very quickly.

Now I know them. They were part of the crew who bashed me, and I think I saw one at the Fish-lane gaff. The thicker, darker, uglier of the two faced me from the pavement. He had Nero on a choke, struggling to get away.

'You had plenty of warnings, Mr Chapman, so now we're taking these beauties,' he said in a low voice, and then raised it for the benefit of every passer-by. 'For ill-treating these beautiful creatures! For training them up to be wicious curs! You ought to be ashamed of yourself! Why, they attacked a man only the other evening!'

A soberly dressed woman gave me an indignant look. 'Monster!' she cried. 'Shame on you!'

The dark man nodded his head vigorously, and put on an air of outrage.

'True to you, madam. Sure, shame upon you, sir!' he cried. 'And thank 'eaven for societies like ours what rescue these poor dawgs and give 'em a good 'ome.'

The woman agreed, and even gave him a coin from her purse, patted him upon the shoulder and raised her fist at me, which his companion found hysterically funny.

I lunged at him and tried to grab Nero's collar, but the man had attached – how had he managed it so quickly? – a rigid lead, with a choke upon it, so that my attempt to free him and every movement Nero made was strangling him!

'Give it up, man,' he cried, 'unless you want to kill the creature dead,' and he bundled Nero into the back of the closed black wagon. Brutus followed, his tail between his legs and, straining against the choke, he turned his head to try and find me. But he was roughly thrust into the cart, the door was slammed shut, the bolt pulled across.

I rushed into the parlour, knocking over a plant and rattling the china. There was a collection of half a dozen matrons gathered about Mrs Twentyfold's table, and they stared at me in amazement and anger. Miss Slyte, of course, rose to the occasion. 'Out! Out, ye heathen, ye! Don't ye even have the decency in ye to knock upon the wood of the door and wait for a lady to call you in!'

I tried to appeal to Mrs Twentyfold, but she

would not look at me. If only I could persuade her to pull back her lace curtains and look through the open window, she would see what was happening outside. But she turned her head away.

I opened my mouth, and felt my throat tighten, just as it does in my dreams, and I tried to shout. But there was nothing, not even a breath. I could not make a sound.

I ran outside again, and looked up and down the street. I was so completely associated with the robbery that our neighbours shunned me, and when I hammered upon the doors, no one came.

They waited until I was upon them before they drove the cart away and I ran after it for a long time. I think they deliberately drove slowly so that I could keep pace with it, but never quite catch it up. Then, when my strength was almost gone, it picked up speed and I lost it. It turned a corner, and I was stranded in the middle of the busy road, and was nearly knocked over by a cart. The driver leaped down, pushed me out of the way and thrust his ugly face into mine. But I didn't see him, and I think he believed I was mad, because my mouth was still wide open, waiting for the scream that would not come.

CHAPTER 15

PIKEMARTIN

MY DOGS HAVE BEEN TAKEN I have written the words on a card – the first time I have ever done such a thing, for I am ashamed that I never learned to write with a good hand and I hold a pencil awkwardly. When it becomes ragged about the edges (for I carry it around with me and show to everyone I meet) I make another, precisely the same. Most of the population of this great city have seen my card. I make sure everyone who passes me in the street reads it, and I have ventured further in every direction out of my little neighbourhood than I have ever been. I scour every passage and court. I search parks and gardens. I become a familiar figure on my strange errand. People are sympathetic and, every day, ask me if there is any news and promise to let me know if they see or hear of my dogs. Many people recognize me: Chapman, the dog-man, and those clever, handsome dogs, one golden, one black, Brutus and Nero. Of course, they remember them. And pretend to remember me. The questions come thick and fast, though they know I can answer only with a nod or shake of the head.

'Were they stolen?' Yes.
'Do you know who took them?' Yes.
'Do you know where they are?' No.
'Do you know what's become of them?' No.
'Do you know why they were taken?' Yes.
'Do you miss them very much?' Yes.

I go back to Portland-road – Mrs Twentyfold is persuaded by Will and Trim and another month's rent (courtesy of Mr Abrahams), to let me keep my room. I stare for hours at the rug where Brutus would lie and the corner of the hearth where Nero slept. I fill their bowl with water. I lay out their brushes. I look out of the window into Mrs Twentyfold's area at the bush where Brutus would always sniff, and the hole in the fence where Nero had once cornered a fox. I think of our happy times, walking to Strong's Gardens and our early morning breakfasts of milk and bread, our plans for a new and better life. I remember our small triumphs at the Aquarium and our hoped-for ones at the Pavilion. 'Clever dogs!' Mr Abrahams had said, beaming through his beard. 'Our new novelties! The best the Pavilion has ever seen!' according to Mr Carrier. Will, Em, Trim, the Princess – everyone loved them, and my boys gave their trust and affection freely and willingly. And no more so than to me, Bob Chapman, their trusted friend, who betrayed them. Because I encouraged them to perform that trick, a novelty on the stage, they were taken.

In truth, I am but half a man without those creatures who have been my constant companions since we were all young. Easy tears well up when I think of them, and I cannot bear to imagine where they might be or, worst of all that, before they died, they were harmed or cruelly treated and they thought of me and wondered why I had abandoned them. I am plagued by these thoughts worst at night and I have taken to going out walking, walking, until I am so tired that I fall asleep immediately I return. But I always wake up after only a couple of hours' respite, and then the images of their dear faces, their joyful bounding along the streets, their serious concentration as we practise new novelties, their delight in everything we do, all come back to haunt me.

Soon, no one sees me. The butcher, who would wait upon the doorstep to give Brutus and Nero a bone in return for a friendly paw, stays inside his shop and barely glances at me as I pass. At the dairy, the bowl which sat by the door and was christened 'Chapman's milk pan' because Mrs Harmer filled it with fresh milk for my boys every time we passed and would take nothing for her trouble, was still there, but empty now. A few wisps of straw and a skin of dust clung to it, and Mrs H stayed in her stall.

I do not expect to see them again. I think they are probably dead. Killed for spite rather than profit. I hope they were not put into the ring.

When I am in my room in Portland-road, I lock

the door and lie in bed, afraid to sleep these days, except when I have had a few glasses at the Two Tuns. Then I sleep like the dead. I am not a drinking man, but I found that gin and company help to chase wakefulness, and have kept up the habit. There is little left of my savings and all thoughts of the horse and cart and Strong's Gardens have receded. Besides, I was foolish and one day hired a man to search for my dogs. I was low and desperate, and when he pushed a notice under my door, saying that he had heard of my difficulties and offered to make a search 'for ready rhino', I gave it only a moment's thought. He took two guineas and I never saw him again. Will and Trim, seeing the notice and learning that I had been duped, went out three days on the trot to find him, threatening violence if they ever did, but of course he was long gone. Mr Carrier sent me a note by Will, assuring me that my place in the Pavilion company was still secure, and also that of my boys 'when they are found, which they assuredly will be', and that Chapman's Sagacious Canines still had their place in *Elenore the Female Pirate* and the programme. But I did discover that he had made enquiries of my rival, Mr John Matthews and 'Devilshoof,' and had asked Trim to work in some single-dog business.

The Princess was kind, and sent a fairy note every day. And Herr Swann and Moses Dann. Conn sent me a bottle and a message of 'good cheer' with Barney and, indeed, Barney it was who kept me from madness. One morning in the early days of Brutus and Nero's disappearance, when I was searching the streets around Fish-lane, he found me and said he would help. Though I was terribly occupied with my task, I could not but notice his shabby clothes and wasted cheeks, and when Will saw him, and questioned him over a plate of bread and cheese, he discovered that Barney was street-tumbling with another lad, and that both were sleeping where they could. A word with Princess Tiny and, of course, that was soon put right – Moses Dann, the Boneless Man, now had company in the cellar and someone to talk to in the night when his joints pained him. But when he wasn't street-tumbling or sweeping the Aquarium yard, Barney was at my side, interrogating boys like himself and charming maids and milliners. He was my voice, and untiring in his labours. I could not afford to pay him, but our companionship and daily treks through the neighbourhood and beyond seemed reward enough.

I have kept in work. Mr Abrahams, who daily shed tears over Brutus and Nero and called me his 'son in tragedy', gave me employment at the Aquarium. I sweep and dust and rearrange the exhibits, and one day he stopped me in the hall, where I was hard at work with broom and mop, to say that he had devised some plans for me to make a list of the Aquarium's collection.

'Dear Bob,' he said, with much shaking of his head. 'It will be a labour of love. Before she died, my Mimi said to me, Abby, you must make a list of the whole Aquarium, from the Alabaster Priapus to Wyld's Monstre Globe – we had no x, y and zs at the time, Bob, though now we could accommodate the whole alphabet!' He beamed happily. 'We shall do it, and make books of your list to sell. Pikemartin shall sell them.'

Pikemartin was silent in his box. Perhaps he thought he had enough to do.

He was certainly busy with the visitors who flocked to the Aquarium in their hundreds. Mr Abrahams, being an able showman, changed the exhibits every week, bringing out new wonders (though old acquisitions) from the cellar or the cupboards on the landing. And it was one of Pikemartin's duties to fetch them from storage and install them according to Mr Abrahams' instructions. Today there was a packing case awaiting his attention in the hall, transported early from Jamrack's Emporium by the river. Mr Jamrack is more usually associated with the menagerie trade, but occasionally acquired curiosities from sailors short of chink and willing to part with objects they have acquired on their travels. Mr Abrahams hovered over the box, rubbing his hands in excited anticipation.

'It is an Eternal Flame,' he said in hushed tones. 'Perhaps *the* Eternal Flame. Mr Jamrack purchased it from a Chinese captain who had bought it in Egypt. Or was it Greece? I don't remember. But it is a remarkable thing.'

Remarkable – and very heavy! It took Pikemartin

and me much effort and the best part of an hour to unpack and carry it up the stairs to the second-floor salon, with Mr Abrahams flapping his arms and urging us to keep it upright 'lest the oil slops about and the flame goes out!' Then we had to mount it upon a sturdy table – strong enough to bear its weight (and wobbling only a little) – and then be on hand as our employer arranged a display of ceremonial swords and daggers about it, secure them with bolts and pins and admire the effect. True, the lamp was a pretty thing of brass and ivory, and the flame burned blue and pink, depending upon where you stood. But Pikemartin was unimpressed, I think, and returned to his box without a word to anyone.

Never a jovial companion, of course, and devoted to drink, these days he was more morose than I had ever known him. He seemed deep in misery and would sit for hours at a time without saying a word, contemplating the walls of his box. Perhaps his misery was on account of Mrs Gifford's harrying of him, which she did for any small thing, and he seemed to be constantly at the end of her tongue-lashing and door-slamming. She always had something for him to do and, whether or not he was already occupied, would not tolerate my assistance at any price.

'Come here, Pikemartin and see the state of the windows in the front salon,' she roared, even before she had peeled off her gloves and unpinned her feather bonnet.

'Do you want to keep your position, Pikemartin? Shall I keep silent about the filthy floors in the waxwork room or will you fetch your mop now?' she squawked over her shoulder and, leaving me in his cubbyhole to deal with tickets and visitors, he crept after her, as meek as a kitten.

But it was curious. Although she was incessantly at his throat and seemed to dislike him almost as much as me, I saw them talking on the landing by the wax eyes and even outside, on the street corner. Barney remarked upon it too, and thought there was 'something rum about it', but he didn't know what.

It was one of the things Barney often talked about when we were on our expeditions, and he amused me by conjuring up all kinds of strange stories about Gifford and Pikemartin – that they were French spies, or coiners, or planning to rob the Bank of England. His stories were always fantastic, guaranteed to make me smile, but their essence – that those two were 'up to something' – never varied, and this was rooted in reality for it was clear that, whatever they were 'up to' caused them both no little anxiety and effort. Gifford had always been bad-tempered, but these days she was out on errands at least once a day and returned flustered and pale. Pikemartin was like a man with more worries than a rat in a dog-kennel, but even that did not explain his behaviour when I accidentally shouldered him in the street. Naturally, I would have taken a side step to avoid him as I turned the corner by the Aquarium, but I did not see him and knocked Pikemartin with such force that I was driven back and even caught poor Barney a glancer.

'Look where you're going,' Pikemartin cried, pushing me hard. 'Have you no eyes in yer head to go with yer ignorance, ye dummy!'

The shock of his anger – and his insult – was like a blow.

'Keep out of my way or, by God, I'll knock your face into the wall. And that young gallows-bait with you!'

He was pale-faced and white-lipped and stank of drink and ill-use. There was a trace of vomit on his coat, and his hands were cut and dirty. I had often seen him maudlin and miserable, tetchy even, but never in such a state as this. Even so, I was not about to retaliate. I laid my hand upon his arm and smiled in friendship, for he had been good to me recently, giving me a place in his box and occasionally sharing his bottle. But now he behaved as if all that had never happened. He lunged out, striking my hand away with a limp fist, and then he turned upon Barney. The boy dodged behind me, frightened, but Pikemartin came for us both again, swinging wide with arms and fists and roaring curses. They were a drunkard's swipes, easy to avoid, but his curses were a different matter.

'You don't know what I have to do, damnation take the both of you!' he cried. 'What I'm made to do! You and your father's filthy business!'

Barney retaliated; he would never hear a word said against his Pa. 'You don't know anything about my Pa! He was fitted up, everyone knows that!'

Pikemartin wiped his hand across his mouth and swayed.

'Aye, but does everyone know about his pictures! Eh? What was done to them little girls? Eh? What I have to see every time I'm summoned to that place! It's your father what started it! Curse you, George Kevill! I hope you're roasting in hell!'

Alf Pikemartin's face was pale, his eyes red. Spittle flecked the corners of his mouth and, struggling against drink and despair, he staggered, which was when our eyes met and everything slowed down in that cold street. If he had come and hit me then, a good sharp cut on the jaw, I would not have felt it more keenly than that moment's understanding. And if he had told me, in simple words, clearly, over and over, until I understood, I would have been just as wise as I was in that instant. For I knew then that he was the man in the stable. The one who made the pictures. The one who wrapped the dead child in a rug and put it under the floor, and then took it to the tunnel where the cazzelties found it. He inherited the job from George Kevill and it was driving him mad.

He swayed and wiped his mouth again.

'Ay, mash that, Bob Chapman! You think it's the world's end because he's taken your dogs? Look at me! He has my soul! He wants my daughter!'

That was how the Nasty Man worked! He threatened George Kevill with – what? Corrupting his son? Murdering him? If he didn't make the pictures and get rid of the children. And, because George tried to fight back, wrote a letter or told someone, he was strung up, dancing the Newgate jig. And now there were pictures – lost? destroyed? – and the Nasty Man would use any means to recover them. Even wrecking a man's life, beating him, taking his livelihood, stealing his dogs. Terrifying young Barney. And now Pikemartin was damned in the same way. Threats, blackmail, who knows what he suffered to protect himself and Em.

We might have stood in that street until the city fell about our ears if Mrs Gifford had not come hurrying around the corner. Busy as ever, rushing between this place and that, on this errand and that, she all but fell into us, and stopped herself just in time. We had gathered quite a little crowd about us by now, for Pikemartin looked set to hit someone and London folk are always up to watch a fight. But Mrs Gifford would have none of that and, against all advice, took Pikemartin by the elbow.

He was beyond reason. He pushed Gifford roughly out of the way, staggered backwards half a dozen paces and then, setting his eye upon Barney and me once again, lurched towards us with a terrible roar, and he would, I am sure, have felled us both if a burly lumper had not strode across, begged our pardon and caught Pikemartin a blow upon the jaw that sent him crashing to the ground.

'This is no sight for ladies, or young 'uns. He's the box-man at the Aquarium, isn't he?'

He threw the unconscious man over his shoulder like a sack of potatoes and set off down the road.

Mrs Gifford, her mouth straight as a puritan's eye, followed in his wake, but anyone could see that she was ruffled, and when Barney and I arrived at the Aquarium ourselves, he was nowhere to be seen and *she* was in his box – a thing never before seen in my time! – taking money and handing out tickets. But she called me over, and with an authority to which she had no right but which she assumed anyway, she instructed me to 'look after the box and make sure you're not short-changed' and directed Barney to the menagerie.

I took over his box sometimes whilst he was out on errands, or taking objects here and there in the Aquarium, and though it was a cramped and airless place and the smell of him lingered long after he had shuffled out of the door, even so, I envied Alf Pikemartin. For not only did he see his beautiful daughter, Em, night and morning, but he had a portrait photograph of her in his box to look at during the day. It was propped up against the wall on the bench and I admired it long and long during the weary hours I sat there. It was Em to the life, and if she looked over my shoulder as people in portraits do, I could still persuade myself that she might be thinking about me. And I developed a fancy that if I could only gaze directly into her face, her eyes would look directly into mine. I longed to have the photograph in my hand to test this out, but it seemed a liberty to remove it from where Pikemartin had placed it, and so Em continued to stare serenely at the wall behind me. So I contemplated her gentle features and thought how dreadful the hours must have been for him in this place, waiting for the summons to Fish-lane, and then, once there, knowing that he must come here and betray nothing of what he had seen. No one must know what he did. The image of Em was a constant reminder of that.

Suddenly, the front door opened and a flurry of milliners blew in and they, knowing no better, I suppose, let it slam, sending a veritable hurricane through the hall and up the stairs, rattling the windows and blowing about the tapestries. They giggled and shrieked (and never an apology to be had), and bought their tickets with winks and kisses (not real). But when I returned to Pikemartin's box, I realized that Em's photograph was not in its usual place. It must have fallen to the floor in the blast and I scrabbled around, under the bench, pulling out the bucket and the spidery pots and trays to find it, but to no avail. The only other place it could be was behind Pikemartin's cupboard, a rough, knee-high thing which stood on the floor and in which he locked his bottle of

Old Tom, his tobacco and anything he found whilst he was sweeping up. (He told me that he found a diamond brooch once, and a ruby bracelet, and that if I found anything I should show him, since I was doing his job and he should claim a share. But I have only ever found a ticket for the Haymarket Theatre and a glass eye and kept those myself.)

I dragged the cupboard out far enough to push my hand behind it, and I found Em's photograph immediately. It had suffered no ill-effects, or none that a quick dusting off with my sleeve could not put right, and I swiftly replaced it and shoved the cupboard back. But I pushed it too far back. A dusty line revealed where I had been exploring, so I tried to set it to rights, shoving and pushing it about, too far and then not far enough. There was something underneath that kept catching on the bottom, and it was when I tipped the cupboard back that I saw the key.

There were probably two bottles of Old Tom in the cupboard, for I heard them clink together and I suddenly felt a keen thirst for a glass. Pikemartin would count me as a friend when he was sober, I thought, and anyway would not notice, so I unlocked the cupboard and found the bottles and a cup, as well as an old briar pipe and a little tin of tobacco. I had a small taster, and then another as the warmth started to chase about my arms and legs. But I am not a drinking man and it was only like medicine to me, so I made myself comfortable on the floor and looked about me, and noticed inside the cupboard three packets, carefully wrapped in thick brown paper, tied up with string. When I took them out, I saw that each one was labelled 'To Collect', and then 'Farringdon', 'York', 'Purdoe', in a shaky hand. Inky spiders spreading across the brown paper. I opened one.

I wished my boys were with me, Brutus and Nero sitting by my side as I squatted on the floor. They would have been company and reassurance, would have sniffed the packets and inspected the contents and licked my face when I covered my eyes. They would not have flinched when I pushed the vile images from me, and Brutus would have sat close, and put his golden head upon my knee until I stopped shaking.

And Nero would have let me know that Alf Pikemartin was standing in the doorway.

CHAPTER 16

PIKEMARTIN AGAIN – PILGRIM'S SHOP IN THE DARK

In one of Trim's stirring Pavilion dramas, Pikemartin would have threatened me/broken my jaw/turned the air blue and black. Or, at least, demanded to know why I was sitting in his box with his cupboard open and his bottle of Old Tom half drained and his own property strewn across the floor. And the audience of the Pavilion Theatre would have jumped to their feet and roared, whilst he, the villain of the piece – often played by Mr Penrose, especially engaged for the part – would roar and shake his fist in reply.

At least they knew who the villain was.

Whereas I, unable to roar and very unsteady upon my pins (on account of the three cups of Old Tom), could only sit on the floor of Pikemartin's box. When he, after some moments, snatched up the packets and, saying nothing, sat wearily upon the bottom step of the great staircase, I was as calm as a dog in the sun.

He turned them over, and pushed his hand through his wild hair. He was still very drunk, but some of the madness had left him.

269

'These are for collection. Or for *her* to deliver to the . . . gentlemen.'

He spat out the words.

I wanted to ask him if he meant Mrs Gifford. I wanted to know if she found the children outside the Pavilion Theatre where I had seen her and took them to the gaff. I wanted to know who these gentlemen were. I wanted to know where he made the pictures, actually *made* them. I wanted to know if it was just the Nasty Man, or whether there was some other involved.

But I already knew. And now it didn't matter.

'I'm sorry about your animals, Chapman. No one should lose what's so precious to them.'

I saw his eyes flicker to the picture of Em and his lips tighten. He folded the thick paper around the little bundle of pictures and re-tied the string.

'Have *you* got the pictures what George Kevill left?'

I shook my head.

'And the letter what he wrote?'

No.

'He hid them somewhere, when he knew the Nasty Man was onto him. Couldn't be trusted, you see. George said that he would write it all down – for he was something of a scholar – and made sure that the Queen and parliament knew what was going on. I know he kept back some pictures. To show what they were up to. Bishops and dukes and do-gooders and—'

He coughed hard and spat into his hand.

We might have been frozen there like living waxworks if Mr Abrahams had not come down the stairs and found us. It was the first time I have ever heard him speak angrily.

'Alfred,' he cried, 'what are you about, man? Nothing at all! You *stumer!* Off with you now! Work! And you, Bob Chapman, sprawled upon the floor? Do I pay you to greet our visitors like a suck-pot?'

Pikemartin disappeared into the waxwork room, and I heard his heavy footsteps clattering up the back stairs. Mr Abrahams turned upon me again. He was disappointed, he said, though he understood how a man might succumb to drink if his nerves were sorely tried as mine had been. But it was not the answer to my difficulties, and he was sorry to see me in such a state within the walls of this place, the Aquarium, where I was held in such esteem. I was embarrassed and, whilst he watched me with a sorrowful face, I clumsily swept the hall and then fetched the mop and bucket also. I had penance to perform.

Mrs Gifford scurried past me on an errand. Pikemartin did not reappear all day, and when Conn came down to fetch the other bottle of Old Tom, I knew where he had taken refuge. So it was left to me to turn down the lights of that eerie place, starting at the top, and try not to listen to the sound of Pikemartin crying or to see shadows where there were none. I had just reached the waxwork room when there was a sudden loud knock upon the front door, followed by a battery

271

of thuds that made my heart, as they say, leap into my throat.

Will and Trim stood upon the step like a pair of bookends, beaming and breathing hard.

'Get your coat, Chapman!' cried Trim. 'Quickly! Brutus and Nero are found!'

Will took my arm and propelled me along the street, talking all the time.

'Don't get his hopes up, Trim, but Bob, we've heard a rumour that there are some dogs fitting your fine fellows' description in a low place not far from here.'

'If it's a case of professional dog-napping,' put in Trim, 'I think you'll be able to press charges. Talk to my lawyer, Carpenter. He'll take the case for you.'

They were so excited, one good friend on either arm, propelling me this way and that along the dark, wintry streets, talking nineteen to the dozen about their discovery and how delighted they were that those good creatures were found, that I caught their infection immediately and allowed them to lift my spirits until I was almost delirious.

'There,' cried Will, 'he smiles for the first time in weeks, Trim!'

Yes, if I could have shouted and sung with joy I would have risked arrest and shinned up a lamppost and made a complete fool of myself! And I was so utterly taken with the delight of my two friends' news and my own light-headedness, that I hardly noticed the direction we had taken until we began to tramp through the mud and around the fencing of a railway cutting on which, when Trim took my arm and pointed, I saw a bill for the Royal Crown Theatre.

'Here you are, Bob! Your name and, what's more important, that of your talented dogs, taken in vain! Someone has stolen your dogs, your name *and* your show!'

'I've heard of such things happening,' agreed Will. 'Some terror masqueraded once as me in a gaff – called himself Bill Lovegrope or something like! The audacity!'

My heart sank and I could have wept, there and then, in the street. My friends couldn't understand why I pointed to my name on the flapping bill and those of Brutus and Nero, and shook my head. They were old bills, from weeks ago, and not showing a date (they never did – another showman's trick). How could my friends have known?

But Trim was unwilling to give up the possibility. 'Yes, I know it seems a coincidence,' he urged, propelling me down the street, 'but believe me, I write coincidences every day, and they *do* happen. We will go to this gaff and catch them in the middle of their act, you'll see.'

How the bills had survived being torn down or pasted over, I had no idea, but here they were still on the wall where I had last seen them. The massy letters shouted me loud to all-comers, though I had never seen a sign of my namesake or his dogs in the flesh, as it were, at the gaff. But even though my spirits had been dashed to pieces, I felt a sudden stab of optimism. Perhaps the bills had been left on purpose. Perhaps Chapman (the counterfeit) was simply engaged for a future date and at this very moment Brutus and Nero were performing their tricks on that wretched gaff stage for some tuppenny-halfpenny impostor. It could be! We turned the corner into Fish-lane.

Apart from the drunk on the steps of the Wretched Fly begging 'a penny for a glass', it was dark. No pie man calling, no cries of 'potatoes hot', only the distant sounds of a row and perhaps fisticuffs, a baby crying, a woman shouting. There was no harmonium on the pavement, no showman's drum, no gaudily dressed youths pressing passers-by to 'Step inside!' The gaff was silent and still.

I had not been there since the night Brutus and Nero 'seized' the Nasty Man and, although I had read that the magistrate had arrested the company and closed the show down, I was still surprised that its doors and windows were shut, and not only shut, but boarded. Usually these gaffs spring open again within days of being closed down, with a new proprietor and a new name, but really nothing changed, including the company. Which is what I had been expecting.

'Where's the theatre, Chapman?' said Trim looking about him. 'I thought it would have been bursting at the seams.'

The gaudy giant posters had been taken down (to be used again elsewhere), but there were remnants of other handbills pasted to the blind windows and plastered all over the door, announcing the Royal Crown Theatre and Chapman's Canines, as well as the waxwork exhibition and all its bloody horrors.

'This very much looks as if we've raised your hopes, only to dash them utterly,' said Will, trying the door. 'I'm so sorry, old friend.'

But I could not turn and walk away, and against the easy tears rose a desperate hope that, in spite of all appearances, my friends were still right and Brutus and Nero were here, in the gaff or the yard. Not to act in a play, but perhaps brought to fight, for hadn't the Growler asked me if they were fighting dogs? I put my shoulder to the door and, with Will's help, it gave, was probably not even locked, and we staggered into the dark hallway and then, feeling our way along the passage, to the exhibition room.

It was open to the roof and that roof had more tiles missing than in place, so that the wintry moon lit up the room like a stage. When I was last here it had been full of waxworks and curiosities, and now it was a shell, utterly stripped bare. There were great holes in the floor, where the boards had been ripped up, and from which a foul smell rose. The walls had been reduced to bare bricks and above, where the upstairs front bedroom had been, the ceiling and floor had been taken up. Will looked about him in wonder.

'What's happened here then, Bob? Have they stripped out everything they could sell, do you think?'

I nodded yes. Every foot of lead, every scrap of timber, everything that might have a value was taken: one man's rubbish was another man's meal.

'I think we should leave,' Trim said, anxiously. 'This is not a place I want to be found in, alive or dead, and it seems to me very likely that the latter might present itself. What is that dreadful stink?'

'There's not a soul here, Trim. Not in the building. We'll leave as soon as we've made sure that Brutus and Nero are not imprisoned outside,' said Will. 'We can't have Chapman wondering whether his dogs were within twenty paces of him and he didn't look for them.'

My hopes rose again. Yes, they could be tied up in the yard, or in the outbuildings next door or – and I balked at the thought – in the stable. We edged out into the passage, and then into the yard where the stable stood, lit by the moon, and beyond it, the cavernous regions of the cutting and the tunnel. Even knowing they were so close turned my mouth dry. But Will and Trim had no such knowledge and no qualms and, tiptoeing about the yard, soon established that there was no one here. And no dogs either.

Will rattled the gate into Pilgrim's yard and opened it easily. I wanted to tell them, 'Nothing here, just a mad man, unless he's run away,' but my friends had already gone in. They poked about the yard and disturbed the nesting rats, and Will whispered that he would just peep through the window 'to see if Bluebeard's at home'. But he had no need, for Pilgrim's back door stood open, the very door that he always locked and barred so carefully. And this struck me as so very strange that I held Will's arm to stop him.

'What's up?' he whispered. 'Do you know this place?'

I nodded. Oh yes. If only I had a voice, what tales I could tell!

'And the man who lives here? Are we in trouble?'

I didn't think so, but all the same it was odd to find the door standing ajar. The familiar stink of must and damp seeped out as I went first, groping into the little scullery and then into the passage where it was pitch dark. I ran my hands along the wainscoting and through spiders' webs, disturbing the other creatures that lived in the old place, behind the decades of paper, the years of books. Underfoot was wet and boggy, a lumpy, uneven skin of worn druggets, piled one upon the other, and warping floorboards. I tripped, my foot caught beneath the rotten matting, and stumbled into the shop. It was very cold, and Will slapped his shoulders and sides and stamped his feet; the book towers shuddered and swayed.

'Does a man *live* here? Ye gods! *How* could a man live here? It's hell-fire cold, Bob, and smells as if there's a sewer running through it!'

'Who is he?' said Trim, who had opened a blind at the front and was scrabbling around trying to light a candle or two. 'Shall we call him?'

Will hallooed loudly, but there was no reply, no sound at all. My friend wasn't here, I was sure, and neither was anyone else. In Pilgrim's bower, the wall of books laid in good English bond was beginning to show signs of wear. The alcove which had fitted so snugly about his head and shoulders had collapsed, and the neat piles of Histories and Treatises which had formed his seat were covered in the fallen volumes. Nevertheless, I cleared a path and, with Trim's assistance, lit some of the stubs of candles which sat in their own puddles of grease around the bower, and for the first time surveyed the landscape of Pilgrim's shop. The room was much smaller from that low seat, but the flickering candles made the upper reaches even darker and blacker. Pilgrim's cup sat on its shelf – the book, much stained by rings and spills, was *Camellia sinensis: the tea-plant, its history and cultivation* – and I realized that this, which I called his bower because I could think of nothing more suitable, was also his workplace. From his seat, Pilgrim could reach his cup, his candle and matches, his spare shoes, ledger and pen, inkpot and so on, all perched on promontories and crevasses fashioned from the stacked volumes. A larger book, two even, held his slippers; on a single, fat tome (a dictionary) was his milk can, and in the spaces left by removing a volume here and there, were inserted his envelopes, embossed paper, string, and bundles of quills, stamps and penwipers. I smiled at the ingeniousness of my odd friend, and brought down the book on which a flat candle stub floated – *The Life-cycle of the Lampyridae* – to examine the arrangement more closely. I pulled out large-size calling-cards (showing a picture of a much younger Pilgrim frowning seriously at a book), letters shrouded in dust and skeins of spiders' webs, writing paper so damp that it was flowered with mildew, seals which crumbled in my fingers, and a dry ink pot. Nothing here had been used for some time.

Then something caught my eye, just at my shoulder. Something moving. I raised the candle and there, pressing its black body between two upright volumes, was a huge spider. It was grossly fat and its long legs, covered in thick hair, pedalled against the spines of the books in an effort to squeeze into the thin crevice. In the stillness of the shop, I could hear the faint rasp of its feet on the leather as it tried to gain purchase on the rough binding. The way it scrabbled and turned itself about, pushing and flailing its legs, was so repulsive that I grabbed the nearest book to throw at the awful creature. I missed by a furlong, but it was startled and lost its grip and fell with a soft 'plop' somewhere near my feet. The thought of that gross black body and wriggling legs clutching at my boot-laces and clinging to my trouser-bottoms sent me into a panic and I leaped up, and caught my elbow in the turret of books. A wobble and a little shower of leather and dust fell upon me, which I quickly threw in all directions, lest that fat, black creature had a colony of companions.

The candles flickered in the draught and one tumbled to the floor, but was not extinguished, and as I quickly picked it up, being very careful not to grasp the spider by accident, I saw, lying amongst the volumes, a fat packet, carefully tied with string, and sealed. It fell open in my hand.

Inside were photographic likenesses, dozens of them, as real as if the figures were standing before me. They were what showmen once called 'Frenchies', supposedly because the French produce the dirtiest images of naked women that can be bought on the fairground or street-corner. And though I have seen 'Frenchies' – what man hasn't who has been to Barnet Fair? – I have never seen ones quite as vile as these. They were not the usual pictures of a woman undressing whilst a grinning constable watches her through an open window. Nor of a naked, sleeping nymph ogled by a passing swain.

No. These were of quite a different order.

Here were men in the robes and uniforms of judges and bishops and admirals. The judges wore their wigs, the bishop his holy hat, lords in their ermine cloaks and garter robes, a musician, I guessed, in his pique wig, a military man in a dark uniform and cocked hat. Neither were they play-actors. No, I could put a name to this lord and this reverend gentleman, to that temperance man and minor royal, all using young women and children in the crudest and most violent manner. Here was my Lord X, who only last week had been seen with the Queen on his arm, as he bent to his task of flogging the bare arse of a fair-faced young woman. And here His Grace the Bishop of Y, dandling upon his knee a naked little girl. The very same bishop who had recently christened a royal babe and opened a foundling hospital. And a much-decorated general, not long back from the wars, enjoying a curly-haired boy. Here was the Duke of Z belabouring a maid whilst another encouraged him with a whip across his back. Picture after picture showed do-gooder and banker, knight of the realm and clergyman, in their ceremonial and garb, and the poor objects of their lust captured in images so sharp and real that to look upon them was like parting the curtains and peering through a window. My hands shook and I dropped one which hit my foot and turned over. It showed a booted and buttoned general in the act of violating a child, whose look of fear and pain was in awful contrast to the grim intensity of her abuser. They were arranged upon an elegant chaise (I recognized its twisty legs!), and there was drapery in the background, torn and creased, and the bare wood of a wall.

But there was another, separate packet, smaller, carefully tied. Inside it, a letter and five photographs, evil pictures of a child and a man I have never seen before.

I sank to my knees, unable to stop myself, and Will and Trim came to my rescue. They were cheerful, if cold, and had been marvelling at the chaos and repulsed at the blooms of fungus which were sprouting around and behind the shelves.

Trim laughed, catching my arm. 'Careful, Bob,' he said, 'you'll be buried under an avalanche of – I say – what's the matter? What is it?'

They stood over me, rubbing their cold hands and holding their candles up to look with interest, and then with horror, at what I had found. I unfolded the letter and it handed to Will. He read it slowly,

Pictures taken by me, George Kevill, on this day, Saturday, 11th October 18 –, at Kevill's Photographic Emporium, Fishlane. Child is Alice Corcoran, aged 10. Man is –

'I know him,' cried Trim, shaking the picture. 'He is always at the races and at the ringside! He lent me money, only the other month. He was generous – with the amount and with terms. I never thought—'

'Hush! There's more,' said Will. 'Listen to this.'

All pictures signed on the back and dated by me, George Kevill. Three children murdered by this man – Patience Rhodes, Mary

O'Malley, Polly Evans. Other children taken and killed by accident or purposely. Their bodies—

He stopped and looked at each of us, horrified. 'It says, "by arrangement, but never by permission, with John Bunyan Pilgrim, buried in the cellar of his bookshop, Fish-lane".'

He went on, but I didn't hear him. George Kevill gave Pilgrim the pictures and the letter which would send this wicked man – perhaps this was the uncle that Barney had spoken of – to the gallows. But my friend hid them among his books, knowing that they were dangerous, like fireworks in a haystack. Why did he not get rid of them? Send them to the police, magistrates, the prime minister? Or simply destroy them?

Will and I had the same idea at the same time.

In the cellar.

We should look.

CHAPTER 17

PILGRIM – THE NASTY MAN – DESCENT INTO DARKNESS

There was a door, unlocked, and steep steps descending into darkness: I counted twenty to keep myself from running away in fear and panic. The foulness which had struck us when we first pushed open the door and which hung about Pilgrim's shop was much stronger now, borne on gusts of cold air. Will wrapped his scarf over his face. We reached the bottom where our flickering candles showed a long, low cellar (Will, who is quite six feet tall, had to duck his head, and I could touch the roof easily) stretching in both directions – under Pilgrim's shop, but also next door, under the gaff and theatre, for the holes in the floor above were dimly visible where the moonlight shone through them. It was a cellar which, at one time, long ago, must have served a single large house, and now still ran, uninterrupted, beneath two.

'This accounts for the dreadful stink, then,' whispered Trim. 'Nasty and damp. It's a wonder your friend didn't get the cholera.'

'And rats, too,' said Will who, I know, has a

284

horror of the creatures. 'There must be hundreds of them down here.'

We were unwilling to stray far from the safety of the steps, taking in the scene before us and adjusting to the near darkness. It was Trim who discovered half a dozen lanterns within a few paces of the bottom step, carefully placed and with fresh candles. We didn't stop to wonder why they should be there, but lit them all and, holding them up, ventured forward. The low roof was a blanket of dust and spiders' webs and ugly clusters of fungus. Underfoot, instead of brick and stone, was earth, much compressed and flattened over the centuries. The sensation of uneven ground beneath our feet and creeping insects above was very unpleasant. We turned our faces towards the beams of light dropping down from the holes in the gaff floor, shuffling forward a step at a time, and clinging to each other and the wall, each of us terrified of being left alone in that awful darkness.

But a sudden movement nearby froze us in our tracks and Will clutched my arm, and whispered, horrified, 'Oh my dear Lord, Bob, it's rats, and I can't bear 'em, you know.' I fervently hoped he was wrong and indeed, as we peered into the gloom, saw – we all did – that there was someone – or something – crouched against the far wall.

'Chapman,' said Trim, very quietly, 'does your pal Pilgrim favour sitting in the dark?'

The figure moved and leaned into the light. Indeed, it was Pilgrim, but much changed since

I last saw him. His face was thin and his hair, no longer confined by hat or turban, flew out in a shock of whiteness. He was trembling and mouthing and his bare arms were a bloody mess of cuts and scratches.

'Who's that?' he cried, and the fear in his voice was palpable. 'I'm not mad. I won't go to the madhouse!'

('He's found them, Pilgrim. Soft head. Fool. Idiot.')

'Have you found them? Have you?'

('He has. Look.')

'Ooh! Ooh! There is a storm in my head!'

He began to cry and moan and pull his hair.

Will watched him for a moment and then turned to me. 'Bob, you know, your friend should be cared for, treated kindly. He shouldn't be squatting on the ground in the dark like a dog.'

And as if he had heard him, Pilgrim gave a terrible howl of rage and pain.

'I don't know, Lovegrove,' said Trim. 'He looks dangerous to me. We should fetch a constable. More than one. And let them take him to Bedlam or somewhere.'

'Not dangerous,' Will replied, quietly, never taking his eyes from the agonized Pilgrim, 'but frightened because something in his head tells him terrible things.' He frowned. 'And he should not go Bedlam. Or any of those places. Poor, poor fellow.'

Will was right, of course. Pilgrim was mad, had

286

been mad for many years, and now it was as though whatever demons he had managed to keep subdued had broken free. He rocked back and forth, talking and howling, sometimes to himself (and to that invisible other who sat by his shoulder), and sometimes to us. One moment he was gibbering nonsense, the next quoting speeches from Shakespeare and other poets, 'Blind among enemies, O worse than chains,' he cried, sobbing in pain and passion. But for all his madness, I could not imagine that he would harm anyone, and when he began to cry, like a child, I was overcome with pity for my old friend. I wanted to find him clean clothes, tend his wounds, wipe his face. Perhaps *I* could look after him. Even take him with me to Strong's Gardens where I know Titus Strong, that good Christian man, would welcome him.

'Bob Chapman? My friend?'

I held up the lantern so that he could see it was me. His face broke into a smile, and then, as quickly, a shadow passed across it.

'Don't come any closer! Stay there!'

('Ah, don't listen to him! He doesn't know. Come over, my friend. Let me shake you by the hand!')

He reached out to me and I stepped forward to take his hand, just as a great crash came from above. The ceiling seemed to bulge and buckle, and showers of dust flew down between the cracks. If shock and surprise hadn't stopped me, if I had taken just three more steps to grasp Pilgrim's out-stretched hand, I would have fallen down a great black hole in the cellar's earth floor. As it was, Will caught my arm just in time with a cry of 'God's teeth!' and dragged me back, the floor collapsing beneath my feet. As the loose soil slipped away and the ground shuddered, we advanced cautiously and held up our lanterns. They revealed a gulf, perhaps five or six feet wide, plunging down, goodness knows how far, into the earth and from which a foul stench rose with each gust of cold air. The sides appeared sheer, and even as we watched, clods of the earth floor were breaking off and crumbling away into the blackness. Pilgrim howled and pulled his hair and tottered from side to side, opening imaginary doors, fighting off unseen assailants and wrestling with his frantic other self.

'He's trapped!' cried Will, and we looked desper-ately around. 'There must be a way for him to get around that pit.'

As he spoke, there was another tremor and more of the cellar floor collapsed.

'Stay back, Bob Chapman,' cried Pilgrim, 'or the earth will eat you!'

('Like the kiddies. We nursed them, didn't we, and one day they were gone. Stolen.')

'I put the children down here and now they've gone. I'll be whipped soundly this time.'

('Little Freddy Forskyn / Tight in his lamb-skin / Cook him up a good lamb pie! / Give everyone a *slice* of Freddy / Good and rare and toby-red.)

I recognized that vile and terrible rhyme. Pilgrim knew the Nasty Man. He imitated him to a T.

The lanterns flickered in the draught from the chasm and the rumbling overhead continued.

'I think we should get out,' whispered Trim.

'We can't leave the poor creature here.'

'But the whole building is about to collapse!'

Pilgrim looked up and beamed, his face suddenly restored. He clapped his hands like a child.

'He's right, of course. The house is falling down. It's the workings, you see. The deep tunnel. The engineers didn't take account of the clay and the lost river. I think there might be two. I've consulted *Banks' Subterranean Rivers and Conduits: Part I, London and its Environs*, which states quite clearly that a tributary of the Fleet (if there could be such a thing!) was recorded long ago by Flavius (a pseudonym) as running near here. It seems fantastic, but it was a river in which could be found many fish. Including trout. Hence, Fish-lane.'

Now I knew why that cold, thick stink was familiar, and why the house was rocking and the ground was opening up. Why there was dust falling like snow all the time and great blooms of fungus were pushing up into the damp corners. Why Pilgrim had plastered his floor with old druggets and thick wodges of paper.

There was a tunnel underneath us.

Even Barney had warned me about it. Didn't he say that another tunnel was being dug below, deeper, taking another direction? That tunnel was under Fish-lane and Pilgrim's shop and the gaff, undermining every building, the street itself, as it burrowed through the old soil, and found the old river.

Pilgrim chattered on, blissfully unaware, his face transformed by goodwill and honest intent. It was difficult to imagine that he might have taken any part in the Nasty Man's terrible business.

'Mr Pilgrim,' interrupted Will, gently, 'here is your good friend Bob Chapman, and we are *his* friends. This is Fortinbras Trimmer and I am Will Lovegrove. But stay very still, will you, Mr Pilgrim, whilst we find a way of bringing you out of here? I'm afraid the floor is not at all safe and we fear that if you don't take great care you might – well, you might hurt yourself.'

'Obliged to you, sir, for your concern,' said Pilgrim, and he gave an old-fashioned bow, and looked expectantly from one to the other of us.

'Will, we must hurry if we're to rescue him.'

'I agree, but look at the floor!'

He pointed to the pit, which was now grown to a black chasm, wider in some parts than others, and disintegrating into the darkness by the moment.

'The whole building is falling, but the cellar will go first. Look where the ground's giving way!'

Will edged along the wall, his lantern held aloft, into the part of the cellar directly under the gaff. We followed him and held up our lanterns to add light to a landscape of pits and depressions, collapsing into the chasm with little more than a shudder, and in the corner, where the ground had already given way in part, there were only islands of earth. And then, as the ground shifted again, we saw that they were not islands of earth, but bodies, wrapped in sheets, like pale grubs. We shrank back as the ground shook again and they began to slide away into the black earth. Our moment of realization was accompanied by another terrific crash overhead as though an army, at least, was marching through the gaff and Pilgrim's shop, demolishing walls and doors, destroying all before them.

'He's back,' whispered Pilgrim. 'He's looking for the letter.'

The one that was in the pocket inside my coat, where it was burning my skin.

'Kevill gave it to me. If he was taken, I should give it to the magistrate.'

('He danced the Newgate hornpipe! Jaunty!')

'But I didn't. I should have. Suffer the children. Ah, but I was too scared. This one threatened me hard.'

('Clap-mouth! Think of the coin!')

'And the Nasty Man showed me the madhouse and the chains and whips.'

He looked up calmly.

'I hope he doesn't destroy my *Pilgrim's Progress*. I believe it is a rare copy. Chapman?'

('Sew up his mouth.')

'Chapman was a friend to me when I was whipped because of you. I should have listened to him.'

('Keep him quiet! Keep them all quiet!')

His face contorted with the effort and he dug his nails into his arm until the blood ran.

'Bob, I buried the children here. As per the arrangement.' He was eager to explain. 'But one got away. I saw her dead. Now it's the madhouse.'

('We looked through the hole in the wall.')

'I went back to the shop, to the cellar, to prepare. Look, look, I made a hole!'

He pointed with trembling finger at the vast black chasm before him.

'But when I went to collect her, she had gone.'

('Stolen. Thief.')

Pikemartin, I thought. The first child that had died since Kevill had gone, and his replacement knew nothing of the 'arrangement' with Pilgrim. He had wrapped her in the only thing that came to hand. A piece of carpet. He had hidden her under the floorboards and then taken her to the only place where he thought she would not be found. The tunnel.

'My God,' said Will quietly in my ear. 'What horrors have been happening in this place?'

Trim was anxious. 'We can't wait! Let's find a ladder or a floorboard and get him out quickly, and save ourselves.'

We left some of the lanterns so Pilgrim shouldn't be in the dark, and my two friends hurried up the

292

stairs whilst I followed, turning every step to look anxiously after Pilgrim, who was calm now. He smiled and waved to me, as if I was trotting to the shop for a can of milk, and called after me words of encouragement.

'Be careful, Bob! Watch the steps – they're rotten! Don't bring Brutus and Nero down here, will you? Far too dangerous and difficult for dogs. Even such remarkably intelligent ones as yours!' He laughed and clapped his hands.

In the thick darkness of the passage, Will and Trim agreed that floorboards from one of the rooms upstairs would be the quickest and easiest remedy.

'We can bridge the void, I think,' said Will, 'but let's not waste a moment.'

Great bulges were evident in every wall and, in the shop, shelves and bookcases collapsed even as their contents slid onto the floor, bringing with them clouds of dust and cobwebs. Suddenly, the window panes – bullseyes, uncommon these days – burst in explosions of glass and I stepped back and covered my face to avoid the shards.

I didn't hear the Nasty Man until he was at my shoulder.

Until the heel of his hand met the apple of my throat, and his right hand grasped my opposing wrist. It was efficiently done. I was pinned and helpless. And I was immediately almost insensible. The smallest pressure and I would be dead.

'Where is it?'

Quietly spoken, but no niceties now. I could feel the thud of his heart and his quick breath.

'George Kevill left a packet. You have it. Give it me, and I'll let you go. Otherwise, I'll choke you here.'

The world went black for a moment and then there was a rushing in my ears and head as he released his grip.

'Come, I followed you here. I know you have it.' He pulled on my wrist, wrenching my head back again and throwing me off balance. 'And I have your dogs.'

I knew he must be lying. Every word that he spoke should have burned his mouth and turned his tongue to ashes.

'They're not far away. In the next street. I'll take you to them. But I want the packet first. Quickly.'

How could I believe him, knowing what I knew? He had backed me out of the shop and we were standing in the passage. I could hear Will and Trim above pulling up floorboards.

He sent waves crashing into my ears again. 'They're sad creatures without you, Bob Chapman. I left them tied up in a yard. They're outside in this cold, cold weather.'

I gulped and choked, struggling as he wrenched at my wrist.

'A gentleman from Putney wanted them for his daughters, but I got a better price on the Highway. A man I know has a pit.'

Dog-fighting! Even though I knew he was lying,

I couldn't take the risk, and I nodded feebly and clutched his hand and would have fallen if he hadn't kept a tight hold upon me.

'Do take care, my dear!' he said, brightly. 'Now, is this it? Inside your coat?'

He was so quick that I had no opportunity to stop him and, with a laugh, he pushed me away.

'Practice, my dear. One takes an apprenticeship and with effort and experience, behold, the nasty man crowns his profession!'

He turned the pictures over quickly.

'Kevill,' he muttered as he folded the packet up and put it in his pocket. 'A pygmy. A mouse in the ring. Gallows-bait.'

A noise and a sudden flood of light in the passage made us both turn. The back door was open, and in it stood Barney, stopper in his hand. The Nasty Man took a step backwards.

'I said I'd serve you out and I will. For my Pa.'

'Your Pa was soft. A bubble. Put your stopper away, boy. Remember what happened last time.' The Nasty Man had recovered his composure quickly, but he was still nervous. 'Don't let the coppers see you with it. Six months' hard for that weapon.'

He spoke mildly, but never took his eyes off the boy, who was advancing slowly along the passage, the gun poised in his hand.

'You fitted up my Pa. He never killed anyone. Not a ladybird, not anyone.'

'That's true, Barney. But he was becoming a

putty cove. You know what I mean. He thought about the business too much. He wrote a letter, kept pictures which didn't belong to him. And my – partner – was nervous.'

'Is that the uncle Pa borrowed money off?'

'It is.'

'And the dirty cove in the pictures.'

'Again.'

'Then I shall serve him out as well.'

The Nasty Man backed away a little further. He had half an eye upon the shop and the front door – or the window – to get away. But there was another rumble, another shudder, running through the house, and the walls wobbled as though they were made of paper. Even the staircase was shifting as Will and Trim clattered down it, carrying two long floorboards. They stopped short of the passage, seeing Barney still advancing, the stopper dropping a little in his hand, and the Nasty Man talking and edging away. 'You don't need to serve me or him out, Barney,' he was saying. 'You could inherit your father's business. I think he would have wanted that, don't you, cocky?'

Barney hesitated and the Nasty Man turned to run. But he stumbled, his foot caught beneath the worn drugget. He wrestled to free it, and falling off balance, clutched at the cellar door. The more he struggled, the more certainly he was trapped by the frayed mat and the one underneath it, the mouldy layers of paper, the splintering wood. Then he slipped. His vast weight dragged him over and he crashed like a grotesque ballet dancer, all arms and legs, through the rotten wood of the door. I heard his head thud against the wall, his arm crack, the heels of his boots drag upon the cellar stairs, and he struck the trembling earth with a thud.

Pilgrim moaned and cried out.

There was a mighty shudder. We watched as the Nasty Man grasped at the air and shifting earth and slid away into the darkness.

CHAPTER 18

COLLAPSE AND FALL

B arney led me through the creaking wreckage of the shop and into the street. Behind us, Lovegrove and Trim had thrown the floorboards across the chasm and helped Pilgrim to safety. Not a moment too soon, it seemed, for the instant they emerged from the shop it shivered and, like one of Mr Lombard's scenes, disappeared. The gaff, too, seemed to hover before a ripple ran across the snow-dusted roof and the front wall trembled and then all fell like a house of cards. In the interval, as the dust cleared, snow-storms of paper fluttered in the wintry breeze and were scooped up into the sky, and fell upon neighbouring housetops and into the street. The houses either side were mutilated by the collapse, walls ripped away and the inhabitants left shocked and crying at the windows. In one, the kitchen range still clung to the wall when all around it had fallen. The fire was glowing and a kettle boiling water for the teapot which had been put to warm. Upstairs, the children whimpered in their bedroom and their mother screamed, all standing as though they were upon a stage, for the front of the house was fallen into the street.

As weeks passed (I leap momentarily into the future), and nothing was done to assist those poor souls who had lost houses, livelihoods and loved ones, rumbles of resentment and anger arose against the railway company for taking so little care. There were reports and inquiries, visits by members of parliament and sympathetic church-men, and much shaking of heads. Equally, those people who, supposedly, support the poor and take their part, anarchists and the like, promised to rally the masses and march upon the offices of the railway company and demand that 'something be done'. Of course, nothing happened. The homeless disappeared, along with the members of parliament, churchmen and radicals (or whatever they called themselves). But the railways, of course, blundered on, chewing the city into pieces and spitting it out.

Now, standing in the street, covered in dust and shivering with fear and cold, we were jostled by the usual crowds that gather, some people wanting to look at the debris of the collapsed buildings, some wanting to see if 'anyone's caught it', and some simply wanting to stare at us, and ask 'What goes?' A man brought a horse blanket for Pilgrim and a bandage for Barney's knee, and another, a woman as poor as they, but seeing them looking pale and out of sorts, took them into her home for the night. This contagion of benevolence continued for a whole day, with cups of tea and nips of gin being doled out by rich and poor alike, and then as the dust cleared, the adventurous and curious went closer to inspect the ruins, and to see if there was anything to be had. But it was too dangerous even for these hardened pinchers, and when the police arrived, they melted away. Order was restored, looting ceased and the sergeant sent in his men to see whether there were any 'stiff uns' among the rubble.

Will nudged me and said, quietly, 'Now's your chance, Bob, to put this terrible business in someone else's hands. It shouldn't be your trouble, old fellow. Would you like me to open proceedings?'

He looked tired, and there was a cut across his forehead where a falling brick had caught him a glancing blow, but Will Lovegrove, ever the faithful friend, took my arm and together we went to the sergeant, who directed us to the station house. There, Will told all he knew, gathered from me, and I produced the packet which contained George Kevill's letter, and which the sergeant, Bliss by name, read very carefully. Then he looked at the pictures and blinked hard and covered them with a police-blotter.

Will did not realize, and I could not tell him, that I had fooled the Nasty Man.

It had been too dark for him to see that the pictures he held in his hand, which he had thought belonged to George Kevill, wrapped up in the letter that should have been sent to magistrates and members of parliament, were nothing more than Pilgrim's elegant calling cards, inside a sheet of his mouldy writing paper.

It was the first time in all my life I had ever done anything clever or brave.

And no one would ever know.

We left the station house as the sun rose on a cold, bright morning.

'Now then, Bob,' said Will, 'how about we step it out to Garraway's and eat a chop and drink coffee and warm our toes by the fire for a while? Until the hour is more respectable.'

It was a clever plan. We ate a chop and fell asleep immediately, with our heads upon the table, before the wheezing waiter could arrive with the coffee, and he, good man, left us to snore until the street grew busy and his parlour also. Scarcely three hours' sleep, yet when I woke, I felt as refreshed as if I had slept for a day and a night on a feather bed. And cheered also to see Barney Kevill, scrubbed and neat, swinging his legs on the chair and eating a cold potato. He rubbed his eye and looked at me.

'I come because I heard what the Nasty Man said to you about your dogs. How they was tied up somewhere. I thought you would want to go and scout about and see – what's what.'

Will bit his lip – he is an emotional sort – and clapped Barney upon the shoulder.

301

'An excellent idea, Barney Kevill,' he said. His voice was hoarse and trembled a little. Then he coughed and cleared his throat, and Will was himself again. 'Then will you bring Bob to my lodgings?' He wrote down the address. 'You should put up with me for a while, my friend. My landlady is more amenable than handsome, but as long as you don't see her in her hair rags, you're quite safe!'

How could I refuse him! He is the best of men and the kindest of friends.

Barney and I searched the yards and courts around Fishlane. We inspected the sheds and stables, and tracked, once again, the course of the railway cutting. I steeled my terror and, sure, it faded when I scoured the ground for signs of Brutus and Nero. We covered many miles that morning, but as the church clocks struck midday, I put a hand upon my young companion's shoulder. Barney frowned at me and then nodded. 'Well, we didn't find them today, but we will, won't we? We'll keep on looking and one day – oh joy! – we'll open a gate and there they'll be, a-waitin' an' a-waggin' their tails . . .'

He broke off, unable to continue, and turned away to wipe his eyes on his sleeve.

I was glad to be mute at that moment, for had I a voice, I would have cried my agony so loud that the angels in heaven would have stopped their ears.

CHAPTER 19

THE AQUARIUM, CHRISTMAS EVE – PRINCESS TINY AND BLACK BOOTS

O ne of Trim's penny novels could not contain the drama of the days that followed our narrow escape, for it didn't end in the fall of two houses in Fish-lane. One, due to be demolished, fell in upon itself with forty cazzelties and their families sleeping inside. The quantity of brick and stone made it impossible to reach all but a few of them, and their groans and cries for help were, as the newspapers put it, 'very affecting'. More chasms opened up in the street, one after the other, as the church bells struck eleven. Religious folk said it was the end of the world. Fish-lane emptied within a week and soon it was one of those streets, so familiar these days, which are the haunts of the desperate homeless those who, in the depths of winter, will sleep anywhere as long as it has a roof.

Finally, a fire broke out in the ruins of Pilgrim's shop, spread to the next-door gaff, and everything was reduced to ashes. There was no effort to put it out and no attempt to rescue anything. If it had consumed the entire street, I think no one would have cared. We sat long after hours in the Aquarium or in our corner in the Cheese, discussing it. Will was firmly of the opinion that the fire was deliberately started.

'I've spoken to the landlord of the Wretched Fly, and he swears that a gang of roughs were around the place the evening it went up,' he said. 'It would be just like the Nasty Man to make sure no one found the – evidence.'

He couldn't say the words – the bodies of the children, murdered, buried in the earth beneath Pilgrim's shop. We had told Sergeant Bliss that he might find them there, and said we were anxious that parents should no longer wonder over their children's disappearance. Perhaps a search could be made in the cellar. But the ruins of the shop, even before the fire, were treacherous, and we knew that he would not risk the lives of his men to bring out the dead children. Even so, we hoped the evil men responsible would be brought to justice, and watched the newspapers for any news of arrests and court appearances. But after our interview, Sergeant Bliss was silent. He had other, more immediate concerns. A young woman had been murdered in a pub yard in Whitechapel and there were fears her killer might be on a spree. Besides, as Will said, tapping his nose, perhaps there were those who would rather keep the matter quiet. Gentlemen who had known Fish-lane and were anxious to relocate.

So we watched and waited, as they say, but even

as the weeks passed, not one of us felt easy. The Nasty Man cast a long shadow.

It was the night before Christmas Eve. We were invited, Will Lovegrove, Trimmer and I, to the Aquarium to 'cheer in the joyful season'. After our recent adventures and evenings spent in gloomy contemplation, the prospect of paying our best seasonal respects to the Princess and Herr Swann and Moses Dann if he was, as Will said, 'up and shaking his bones', was not at all unpleasant. We were gently tipsy (having already enjoyed the hospitality of the Two Tuns and the Yorkshire Grey) as we slipped and slid along the icy streets, to the accompaniment of *The Mistletoe Bough* in a jovial version sung by Will with frequent interruptions when he stopped to greet a handsome young woman with his 'Merry Christmas!' and, if he could, kiss her cheek. Narrowly avoiding any mishaps, we fell through the great door of the Aquarium and into the hall, where Mr Abrahams had insisted upon displaying a Christmas tree (despite his adherence to Israel), decked out with sugar ornaments and candles in fancy holders. I drew the bolts quickly: the constant draught from the opening of the street door blew out the candles and it had been my task all day to relight them!

We stopped to admire it, and even Trimmer could not resist stealing a pink-striped sugar-cane from one of the upper branches and crunched upon it as we hurried up the grand staircase to the first-floor salon. The company was, as it were, assembled: the Princess on her throne, Herr Swann on one side, Barney Kevill on the other, and Moses Dann wrapped in an oriental blanket against the cold. And our new novelties, Professor Long and his two daughters, who gave exhibitions of strength, La Milano, a lady from the *poses plastiques* profession who could imitate a Greek statue and stand motionless for hours, and Colonel Buxton, the great military swordsman. Even Mrs Gifford was there, hard-eyed and narrow-lipped. Conn, with a glass in his hand (Nightman was already at his work), was joined by Alf Pikemartin, who stumbled through the door some minutes after us. Mr Abrahams presided at a table set with punch, glasses, cake and sweets and served everyone himself. And Em, fair and radiant, with eyes only for Will, and he likewise, I think, straight away taking her arm and walking her up and down the salon as though they were in Hyde Park on a Sunday afternoon. The celebrations had already begun, with Herr Swann at the piano hammering out one of the new polkas and La Milano teaching Colonel Buxton the steps, and everyone clapping and laughing and in good spirits.

Any stranger opening the door would marvel, I am sure, at the extraordinary setting. Everywhere was a blaze of light, even the alcoves which were usually gloomy. There were candelabra on every surface and lanterns on every window sill. Of course, the curiosities seemed less wonderful in the glare: the Egyptian mummy case was cracked and flaking, even the newly acquired skeleton of a huge bird, suspended by ropes and wires from the ceiling, was less awful. And my friends, all illuminated by the same merciless lights, were revealed, as it were, in their true colours. Many were dark-eyed and weary, and their merriment was strained through their haggard faces and pained movements. The little Princess, in particular, was sallow and frail, and though she seemed cheerful, I observed her frowning and looking anxious and distracted, and nervously pulling at her muff. Perhaps I, too, appeared worried to anyone who cared to notice. Though I did my utmost to fight off melancholy and laughed and drank and was of 'good cheer', my heart felt hollow and all this merriment seemed out of place. I thought of Pilgrim and the Nasty Man, and watched Pikemartin's hand shake as he drank and stared at Em hanging upon Will's arm. I saw the line of Mrs Gifford's mouth draw itself into a thread and watched her pick at her gloves, and even Mr Abrahams' smile seemed forced and his joviality an effort.

I was not in the mood for merriment, and decided I should leave. I went swiftly and unnoticed down the length of the salon, past the trays of butterflies pinned to a board, the dead kittens playing hide-and-seek among the dead flowers. Out on the landing, shutting the door behind me, the silence of the Aquarium wrapped me up. It is never really silent, of course. Noises from the menagerie drift down the stairwell, and shouts from the street echo up from the hall. Even the stairs creak and groan. I have been up and down them so many times, dragging my shadow behind me, that I know which is the creaking step, which the uneven, the step with a hole in it, the protruding nail and the splintered rail, the stair which groans and cries, just by the shelf on which sits the little house made entirely of shells. I know every inch of the staircase, from the shining wainscoting on the walls to the smooth newel posts and carved spindles.

The staircase is grandest on the first two floors. They were, Mr Abrahams once told me, the public rooms, those the owners of the warehouse used to impress potential customers, but what it sold or stored I never discovered. These grand salons might have once housed beautiful carpets or furniture from the East, or china or sculptures. Certainly, on the first landing is a marvellous mirror, quite ten feet high, set in an old gold frame carved with bunches of grapes and other fruits. And, coming upon oneself, in the dim light of a winter's afternoon or, glancing into the mirror and half-seeing a figure reflected upon the stairs – well, I long ago learned to hasten my steps. And going up to the second floor, I also scuttle past the strange portrait of a melancholy lady which, now and again, weeps real tears. The legend underneath it, written, I suppose, by Mr Abrahams, reads 'Portrait of a weeping woman, c. 1423,

German. She mourns the death of her only child, a daughter disappeared and thought to have been kidnapped by gypsies. On Saints days, a trail of salty tears oozes from the picture and collects in the cup which the lady holds in her hands'.

I stopped and looked up into the dizzying gloom of the stairwell. I wondered how easy it would be to leap into oblivion from there. Would I perch upon the banister and close my eyes and wait for the cold embrace of the marble floor? Or would I find one of Mr Calcraft's ropes and sling it around the newel post and put the noose, tied with his knot, about my neck? I have thought about it before. Many times.

Shivering and pulling my coat about me, I opened the door into the salon. It was dimly lit by the low gas lights and the new addition of the Eternal Flame, which danced and flickered in the draught. My little stage, my screen, the boxes, balls and eggs, even my milk can, were gone, packed in a tea chest one morning with Mr Abrahams looking on, and carried by Pikemartin to be stored in the room off the second-floor landing – 'Until you should want it again, Bob,' Mr Abrahams had said, patting my arm. That time would never come. One day, years hence, I imagine someone finding it and looking at the painted board and wondering who Brutus and Nero were, and their master Mr Bob Chapman, and why the china eggs and packets of letters were stored so carefully in a tea chest and, having wondered, shrugging their shoulders and sending it all to the bonfire. But I wanted to look, perhaps for the last time, at the old place, my old stand, though, for I was thinking more and more about Titus Strong and whether he would take me on without horse and cart, and simply as a labourer in his fields. And perhaps Pilgrim, too.

My corner had been swept and dusted and in place of my few things stood a case of stuffed owls, and a very large wooden cabinet, black and inlaid with mother-of-pearl and painted with strange signs and symbols – the Magical Cabinet of Dr Dee. Pinned to the wall where my picture of the Queen had been was one of Mr Abrahams' neatly written signs which read 'Temporary Exhibition'. And that reminded me – I could not remember putting my picture of Her Majesty in the tea chest with the other things from the stand, so I ducked behind the case of owls to see if it had been dropped or left. There it was, wedged between the Magical Cabinet and the wall. It was a tight squeeze, but I was determined to have it and was crawling behind the owls – a large glass-fronted case showing the cream of the taxidermist's art – when I heard a footfall on the creaking step and the door to the salon opened and someone came in. Thinking it was probably Trim or Will come to find me – they were planning a late supper at the Cheese – I smiled to myself, planning how I might jump out and surprise them!

But I wanted first to get the picture and, though

I strained and stretched, it was just out of my reach. And I could see something else there as well: one of Nero's china eggs, gathering dust and spiders. I would have them both. I put my shoulder to it, and tried to move the cabinet, but it was solid and very heavy, though it would shift with another pair of hands. I was about to summon my friends when I stopped; I realized that the footsteps slowly pacing around the salon were those of someone looking at the exhibits and pausing in front of the cabinets. A customer, in fact, unfamiliar with the Aquarium. Not one of us. I peered around the cabinet. Whoever it was, kept to the other side of the room, in the shadow, though I could see his feet under the table with its little display of ceremonial swords and daggers and the new centre-piece of the Eternal Flame. Black leather boots, a cane with a silver tip, a long, black Benjamin, beautifully tailored and wet around the bottom, but not sodden, where it had dragged in the snow. Not the Benjamin of someone who had walked the streets, even a short distance. More the Benjamin of someone who had arrived in a carriage and just stepped out.

But if it was a visitor, I reasoned, they must have come in through the back door, for I had thrown the bolt behind me. I held my breath. There was danger in the air and I was unable to escape unheard or unseen.

Then there were more footsteps, light and quick – and unmistakable. Under the table appeared a pair of miniature pink shoes tied with pink ribbons.

'I can't stay here long,' said the Princess in a strange dry voice. 'My friends will miss me.'

'I'm hoping our business won't take long,' said the other. A deep voice, refined. Not at all familiar.

'It's very simple,' she said. 'I want my money. The Nasty Man said – well, that I should apply to you.'

There was a silence. The toe of the black boot tapped on the floor.

'George Kevill must have left a tidy amount and I want my share.'

Again there was silence, until the Princess sighed with irritation.

'There must be. Ever since we started the business. I bought the machines and George made the photographs.'

'Of course. An investment, then. A partnership.'

'Yes,' said the Princess.

Where was her foreign way of speaking? Her Italian words?

'And you trusted Kevill completely, no doubt?'

'George Kevill was a good man. We had an agreement. We would share.'

'Of course you would. Georgie makes pictures of sweet kiddies, playing find the mouse and—'

'No,' she said, quickly. 'He made cabinet photographs for gentlemen and portraits in the studio. He worked the fairs with his travelling machine and in his studio in the off-season. I paid the rent.'

Black boots laughed.

'Such a surprise, this, Princess. I had no idea. Cabinet photographs, you say. For respectable gentlemen. A genteel sitting, I expect, among the ferns?'

'Yes, of course. They weren't cheap. Good quality and artistic, we agreed that from the beginning. Sometimes they came here to the Aquarium to collect them.'

'Yes, I know. And these respectable gentlemen. They paid Georgie did they?'

'Yes, you know that was the agreement. The coin first. George said that you can't trust anyone. Not even gentlemen.'

'Oh, indeed. How true, Princess.'

I think Black boots was laughing.

'Sometimes I saw the gentlemen myself. When Pikemartin or Gifford were busy. They were very kind and attentive. They often gave me a small consideration – for my time, for the audience.'

Black boots turned and walked about the salon. There was dangerous laughter again in his voice.

'You saw the gentlemen? And the pictures? George's artistic work?'

'No. They were in packets, labelled, sealed. You know that George brought them here to save the gentlemen having to go all that distance to the studio to collect them.'

'Of course, of course. You weren't curious? Didn't have a peek?'

'No. Why should I? Cabinet photographs. And some trade.'

'Trade, of course,' Black boots said.

'No matter. I simply want my share of the money now that George has – gone – and the Nasty Man – Gifford says he has gone too. Left. The rest of the coin can go to Barney. He is his father's son, but I am his business partner.'

'Certainly. But I have an interest too.'

'Oh? Well, you can keep the machinery. Or sell it.'

'Gone in the fire, Princess. Hadn't you heard?'

I was crouched upon the floor, with my legs screaming for relief, and unable to move or make a noise. But I had to listen.

'There is no fortune.'

'I think you're wrong. I'm not a fool. George was making a good profit. He told me so.'

'But he didn't tell you that he spent the money as fast as he made it?'

'No. He was saving it.'

'He made a lot of coin, Princess. He was trapping your respectable and wealthy clients, and he was cheeking you. And me.'

'You're wrong.' She whispered so quietly I could hardly hear her.

'We've both been deceived, my dear. You must be terribly shocked.'

'I don't believe you. I think – I think you want it all for yourself.'

'Only what I was due, and that, I'm afraid, took most of the coin we could find. There is no fortune, Princess. Naughty Georgie punted excessively at

314

the races and got skinned at the tables. He enjoyed ratting and dog fights. He lost everything and borrowed more. From me.'

I saw her little pink shoes. The ribbons had come undone.

'Then he tried to skin me.'

'George and I,' she said, and her thin voice wavered, '– we had an agreement. He knew I wanted to see my home again. In Italy.'

'Oh dear!' said Black boots. 'How disappointed you must be.'

'You see, I am dying,' she said, weakly. 'In this cold, in this city. It kills me. I need the sunshine and warmth. George promised me we would have enough money for me to go home. I think you have cheated me!' the Princess cried, suddenly. '*You* tell lies!' She stamped her foot. 'You have stolen my money!'

He advanced upon her – he took two strides to put himself in front of her. The tips of his black boots touched her tiny pink shoes. Then he squatted down, and the skirts of his Benjamin spread about him.

'Listen to me and hear the truth. George Kevill was a cheat. He cheated you. He took your money and pretended to keep it. And you pretend, too. Italy is no more your home than you are a princess. You are Aily O'Dwyer. Your father was Tommy O'Dwyer from the Green Isle. Your mother was an ignorant gypsy woman from nowhere.'

'Not true,' breathed the Princess.

'Your father sold you to a showman in Dublin when you were a baby. He wanted rid of you. He might have left you on the steps of the church. Or thrown you into a bog. But he found he could make a few pennies, so he sold you to a showman, and that showman sold you to another when he could get a good price. You were sold again and again. A German showman bought you, and an Italian. You had a good ear, Princess. You acquired snatches of their language.'

'Not true, not true,' said the Princess, faintly. 'My father loved me.'

'You were sold to George Kevill and because he didn't ill-treat you, you had some regard for him. He was kind, for a showman, and brought you to London and found you a shop at the Aquarium. How much did your sainted Abrahams pay for you? Enough to keep Kevill's punting tastes satisfied for a week? But he fell on hard times again and he came to you and you helped him. He told you that a good living could be made out of photographs.'

The Eternal Flame spluttered.

'You're wrong,' she said.

I think she was crying.

'Enough!' said Black boots, standing again. 'Old ground, my dear. Now, if our business is concluded, I have another enterprise in hand.'

'Ha,' said the Princess bitterly, 'more pictures.'

'Not at all. I am contemplating a philanthropic venture to assist young women who are unlucky to find themselves in pup. I have taken a house on Holywell-street for the duration. Your Mrs Gifford has offered her services as a lady's companion. Has even discovered a likely subject for my – charity.'

I shifted so that I could get a better view and glimpsed his face.

I stared as hard as I could, so the image of his face was impressed on my eyes like a photograph.

This was the man I had seen in the pictures, the ones in Pilgrim's bower. Five photographs wrapped up in George Kevill's letter.

Black boots was preparing to leave. I couldn't see, but I think he was pulling on his gloves and picking up his stick. He murmured, 'Princess,' in farewell and walked easily down the salon. He only turned when she cried out, and I stood up, rocking the cabinet of owls, to see her tiny figure, her face crumpled in rage, her teeth bared, and a thin knife in her hand, flying at him like a wild cat. She held the knife above her head and brought it down smartly into his leg, just above the knee. He roared in pain and with one swipe of his hand, knocked her to the ground. He was still clutching his leg and staggering when I sent the cabinet crashing to the floor and leaped upon the table and grabbed the largest sword.

It should have worked. In Trim's dramas, on the Pavilion stage, the dumb man, weak and oppressed, would have righted wrongs in fire and blood. The sword would have flown to my hand and, as if it

317

were my nature, I would know how to use it. But I could not move it, for each sword and dagger was secured by chain and bolt to the table, and my effort succeeded only in stirring the dust underneath them and rattling the Eternal Flame in its iron pot!

When he had recovered from his surprise and, still clutching his leg on which a pool of scarlet blood was spreading, Black boots laughed.

'Who is this, Princess? Dr Dee? Has he been holed up in that dark cupboard for three hundred years?! No wonder he's speechless!'

He struck the back of my legs with his stick and I slipped off the table and landed heavily upon the floor. When I looked up, he was standing over me. I backed away, looking about for something with which to defend myself. Will's hero, Redland Strongarm, would not have backed away. He would have drawn his sword and fought until he ran the villain through! Then he would cry 'Justice!' or 'Victory!' and clasp Susan Goodchild to his breast and the audience would cheer!

But it is a put-together world, as Will said, and not ever what it seems to be. There are no heroes on the stage, only ones made of costume and burnt-cork and fine words. They are what we would like them to be. I was no Redland Strongarm. Black boots was taller and stronger, and I was no match for him. I cast about once again and vainly wrenched at a display of decorative swords. One came loose just as he lunged at me. I staggered out of his reach and he, clumsily, caught with his arm the lamp containing the Eternal Flame. It toppled and fell to the floor with a great crash, spilling oil everywhere. The flame flickered and danced in the draught and then sprang back to life and, as though it suddenly had purpose, spread across the sea of oil in a wave of blue and gold. Black boots retreated, limped to the door and stood on the threshold to watch as the Princess, on her feet and still grasping the knife, stumbled towards him. The hem of her dress trailed though the burning oil and the fine material caught the flames. When she realized, the Princess tried to put it out, shaking it to and fro, but all the time fanning the flames and making them stronger. In moments, not only her dress but her hair was alight and she panicked, running wildly about the room and crying out as the wicked yellow flame wrapped about her. Her screams were terrible as she tore at her hair and the flaming dress and when I finally snatched her up and covered her in my coat, hugging her to me to douse the flames, I knew she was beyond my aid.

Black boots raced down the stairs. I heard the groaning steps, the loose step, I even heard him trip upon the nail. I heard his boots clatter upon the marble floor, the bolts being drawn, the door slam. All around me, the oil was burning and so, with the Princess in my arms, I walked through the fire and brought her to the stairs. The flames caught the table and Oriental rug. Before very long, the whole Aquarium would be on fire.

Cradled to my chest, I thought she was dead for it was some minutes before she opened her eyes and many more before she spoke. 'I have a favour to ask of you, Bob Chapman.'

Her skin, dry as parchment, was shrivelled and blistered, her fine hair burned away. She flinched and frowned at the pain.

'Death I don't fear,' she breathed, with difficulty, 'for even now the Holy Mother opens her arms to me and beckons me to her side. But, Bob, when I am gone, please have the priest bury me quickly. And don't tell anyone where I am laid.'

She coughed.

'There are people who will offer you much money for my body. They will say it is for medicine, so that doctors may learn about such as me. They lie. They will boil my body till my flesh falls away. Then put my bones into a box and show me in a barn for a penny!'

Her voice was cracked and dry, her face a terrible mass of burned flesh.

'I will never sleep, never rest. I will be dragged from fair to fair, stared at even when I am dead. Promise me, Bob. I beg you.'

There were tears in her eyes. She was dying, and I knew she was right to be afraid. I have seen the skeletons of giants and dwarfs and fairies at the great fairs and I know that some were got by wrongful means. When Patrick Kelly, the Irish Giant, knew he was dying, he bought promises from everyone that they would see him buried, quietly and with respect, in one piece. But he was sold to a showman before he was cold, and it is said that his flesh was being stripped from his bones before the last breath left his body. So I silently promised the Princess that I would see her gently and carefully buried, and cradled her closer as she sank into sleep.

I sat on the second-floor stairs, watching the pool of flame as it spread around the salon, and it was not a moment too soon that Will arrived, followed by Trim, Pikemartin and Conn, and they, seeing the state of things, asked no questions but rushed to the water buckets – six on each landing, Mr Abrahams insisted – and quickly doused the fire. Herr Swann was called and he, with an expression of such dreadful agony that it broke my heart to see him, took the poor body of the Princess from me, still wrapped in my coat, and held her in his arms until she died.

My hands were burned and blistered. My arms also, and my chest.

But pain was a friend and companion these days and I hardly noticed as Em gently bandaged them, saying, with tears in her eyes, what a brave fellow I was.

The little Princess was buried a week later, early in the morning, in a distant graveyard by a Latin priest. Herr Swann and I were the only mourners. There was no headstone and nothing to show where she lay.

EPILOGUE

Not an empty seat remains in the Pavilion Theatre for the Boxing Day performance of *Elenore the Female Pirate; or the Gold of the Mountain King, A Christmas Extravaganza*, and there are disappointed patrons queuing in the snowy street hoping that Mr Carrier's able gallery packers (who can fit twenty people on a row made for ten if they have to!) will work their magic and squeeze them in. Like fleas on a beggar's back, they shove and push in the furnace heat at the top of the theatre to find an inch of board on which to sit, and there are calls of 'Oi! Watch yer elbow!' and 'Mind my trotters!', but all in good humour and causing much excited laughter. Oranges are passed from hand to hand and the compulsory jar of ginger beer, nuts also (cracked with expertise by the boots of lumpers) and sweet biscuits to follow.

When the orchestra assembles, there is a cheer. When Mr Bilker arrives, baton in hand and his hair shining with macassar oil, there is a roar. The overture is attended to and appreciated, and rows of excited girls sway to its popular tunes. All eyes are fixed upon the trembling curtain, and whenever a foot can be seen beneath it or a shape fills out one of the folds, there is a cheer and a cry of, 'Oh lor, who can that be? Is it he or is it she?' and the more it is chorused, the more hilarious it becomes. The children can hardly sit in their seats or on their mother's knee for excitement. What wonders has Mr Carrier in store behind the curtain!

It twitches again and the orchestra plays a final, a very final, chord. Dutiful applause from the crowded house, and everyone, from the gallery to the stalls, leans forward. Mr Bilker's baton is raised, the first act prelude begins, and the curtain swings open to a great and resounding cheer, which is followed immediately by a wholesale intake of breath, as if the entire theatre were breathing as one. Then, as the amber light of a hundred gas-jets reveals the quayside at Portsmouth (rendered to the life by Mr Lombard), a great sigh is heard and some 'Hurrahs' from the naval population in the audience. The Christmas extravaganza – not a pantomime, but as good as – has begun.

There are fairies and pirates in the Pavilion Theatre. They live upon an exotic island, twice as handsome and three times as comfortable as Robinson Crusoe's. The sand is white, the sea as blue as the sky, and the sun has real golden rays. When it rises and sets, the many-coloured flowers on the island open and close and run about. They are little children wearing petals around their heads and on their arms, who wave and bend precisely as Mons. Villechamps has instructed them. In the tall trees, in which Mr Lombard's men have constructed convenient platforms, sit child-birds with long plumes of red and green feathers, and on the many rocks perch brilliantly spotted child-insects which twitch and preen. In the sea, child-fish fly, child-sea horses gallop and mermaids (not at all childlike!) sing, and a ship, all rigged, drifts onto the stage (in act three), as though it were just sailing by. There is wind in its sails and waves lapping around its bows, and pirates to scurry here and there on the deck and up and down the rigging. There are comical pirates who stand upon each other's shoulders and sing a funny song, and a fat and bumbling Admiral who is taken captive by them and is tied to a barrel. Best of all, there is a beautiful female pirate, Elenore, who is not at all afraid to wear tight britches and stand with her legs apart and hands upon her hips. She stalks and parades about the stage, and stamps her feet and tosses her head, and every man in the theatre is very much taken by her and quite a few are in love with her. Miss Jacques is a different creature when she puts on her long boots and straps a sword to her hips and becomes Elenore. She is not at all complaining, and has a string of admirers, including, we are told, the son of a duke. Will Lovegrove is very relieved. Now their embraces last only a minute and Miss Jacques has her eye constantly trained upon the side of the stage looking for her aristocratic admirer. And Will, as Redland Strongarm, the good, handsome pirate, roars and sings and duels with a heroic flourish, and has eyes only for the sweet girl who waits for him and takes his arm when we are done. Em Pikemartin and he were married on Christmas Eve, secretly and quietly, with only her father and Conn as witnesses. After the Princess had died, they saw me comfortable and my burns treated, and on the morrow, fresh from their wedding vows, came for me to enjoy, with them, a wedding breakfast at their lodgings. They say they will take Barney to live with them as their own, and send him to school.

There is nothing left of my heart to break now.

Time passes.

I am employed at both the Aquarium and the Pavilion. I sweep the floors and shift scenery. I have tried to begin Mr Abraham's inventory with the abacus from Egypt and the phile of aconite found in the dressing case of Lucrezia Borgia, but it is a slow business and my writing is very poor.

When I have finished my work, I continue to walk the streets in search of my dogs.

Titus Strong has sent word to me that I am welcome to go and help in the gardens. He has taken Pilgrim already. Mrs Strong is searching for their daughter Lucy herself, and is often away. I think my old friend is lonely.

I will go one day. Perhaps in the spring.

But for now I must keep searching.

There is nothing more.

GLOSSARY

Benjamin: a long overcoat. A greatcoat was often called an upper Benjamin

Draw claret: to punch someone (often their nose) and draw blood. A boxing term.

Flip-flap: somersault

Gaff, penny gaff, penny show, penny theatre: one of the lowest kinds of theatrical and exhibition entertainments, generally found in cities. They were sited in abandoned shops, railway arches and cellars. There are instances of the interiors of dwelling houses being ripped out and the buildings turned over to the performance of abbreviated versions of popular plays and variety entertainments. They were very popular with young boys and men. During the 1830s, London in particular saw a rash of these unlicensed theatres and they were regularly raided by police who regarded them as the 'nurseries' of thieves

Highway, the: Ratcliffe Highway, a mile-long road in the East End of London which, by the nineteenth century, had become infamous for its resorts of crime, prostitution, rating and dog-fighting

Hook it, macaroni!: Get off (the stage), leave.

327.

Macaroni was a term often applied to Italians, or people who were of a Mediterranean appearance

Last Confession: sold by street-vendors at public executions, these purported to be the life story and crimes told by the guilty offender

Lumper: a man who loads and unloads ships

Make a fist of Bordeaux!: *see* Draw claret!

Methody: Methodist, disapproving of the theatre

Newgate jig: a hanging

Talking fish: a sea lion, frequently found in penny exhibitions

Three-legged mare: the gallows

Sheeney: a Jew

Stretched: to be hung